TO DIE FOR

TO DIE FOR

COLIN WARD

Published by *In As Many Words*

www.inasmanywords.com

ISBN 978-1-9998089-1-4

Cover & book design by Colin Ward

Photography provided with permission from:
Fluid Arts (front)
Daniel Sturley (front)
Gary S. Crutchley (paperback only)

Although every precaution has been taken in the preparation
of this book, the publisher and author assume no
responsibility for errors or omissions. Neither is any liability
assumed for damages resulting from the use of information
contained herein.

All characters and events in this publication, other than
those clearly in the public domain, are fictitious and any
resemblance to real persons, living or dead, is purely
coincidental.

First printed August 2017

For all those voices silenced by hatred,
in the hope that one day they might be heard again
by love.

It's raining, it's pouring,
the old man is snoring.
He went to bed and bumped his head,
and couldn't get up in the morning.

Prologue

His heart pounded as he ran faster than his legs could keep up with, momentum and gravity doing most of the work. The beast that was trying to escape through his chest also clawed at the insides of his head. His mouth was sandpaper dry and his nose scorched by the cold air.

The darkness was broken only by slivers of light that were barely enough to make out the branches and trunks that snatched, scraped, and sliced his arms as he battled through. His footfall only just managed to keep within the limits of a thin track. No choice but to follow it.

But then it vanished.

He felt a sudden sensation of turning, twisting weightlessness, followed by a crushing blow to his side. His breath vanished in a single mighty gasp. Something in the darkness, a hidden trap, had brought him crashing down, but he had to get up and keep going. He had to keep running.

He'd stopped breathing for long enough to hear that the voices all around were still chasing. A beam of light cut through the darkness like a lightsabre, dancing for a moment, and then vanishing as fast as it had appeared.

Scrambling, falling from one foot to the next, over and over, stabbed by the rough surface, he continued his escape through the woods and down a slope. The adrenaline was rushing and pain had yet to set in, so he kept going.

The noise of his heavy, rasping breathing and the pounding drum of his heart were masking the chasing voices again.

He had to keep going.

The pitch-black fingers and arms of trees began to spread out and reach higher into the sky. Thicker bushes clawed away at the skin of his arms. Adjusting to the changes in light, his eyes began to make out more shapes: short, fat buildings like houses; a road, perhaps; fences and lampposts. There was no time to stop, and barely enough time to turn and look for pursuers.

It took one final push to break through the edge of the woodland. The last bush scratched viciously at all the exposed skin on his arms and legs, etching lines of heat through his body, as if the woods were trying to drag him back.

Within an instant, the icy wind hit his face. The chase was still close behind, and although his instinct had been to run, his body now cried out to stop for just a few moments.

Scanning the open ground as quickly as possible, he could just about make out metal shards, wooden panels, and wire fencing. It looked like the kind of ground that in daylight promised great adventure, but at that moment gave him a chance to hide.

Battling through a small, low twist in the fence, he crawled across and found refuge behind a pair of rusted steel barrels. He followed a split-second thought to move a few pieces of wood, hiding himself from view, before the voices caught up.

And then he just sat.

Listened.

The voices seemed some distance away: they'd taken a different winding path through the trees. He managed to take a few deep breaths. Slow and forced. His muscles began to tighten...

...and the pain set in.

He tried not to cry out, knowing that he couldn't afford to be discovered. So, he bit down on the pain and clenched his fists.

That's when he felt the oozing wetness trapped between his fingers.

As he looked down in the faint, cold moonlight, he saw the dark crimson blood covering his ten-year-old hands.

Chapter 1

DI Mike Stone had not managed to muster up a good mood on the way back to the Steelhouse Lane station. He had no intention of wasting much time on questioning the one man they'd managed to round up out of the three who had been involved in a violent shop robbery earlier. Nothing over the police radio had sounded very positive about catching either of the other two suspects – whoever they were – so it looked like the beginning of a long night of shrugged shoulders and 'no comments' typical of the average low-life Birmingham criminal.

At least this one's thick enough to possibly slip up.

Stone made his way through to the custody suite at the rear of the station and nodded a 'hello' to the custody sergeant, who stood judge-like behind the high counter.

The sergeant recognised Stone's long leather coat instantly. It hung heavily over the stocky inspector: aged and well-worn, with layers of wrinkles that spoke more of its quality than cheapness, and spoke even more of its constant use. It was as if the mahogany brown coat carried as much of a reputation as its wearer.

Who was equally well-worn.

'What brings you here, Mike?' the sergeant sniggered. 'Your demotion finally come good?'

'Shut it, sergeant,' Stone replied, holding out an expectant hand.

'What you here for, then?'

'Holding DS Sharp's hand on this Wigfield robbery.'

The sergeant was genuinely surprised. It wasn't often that the esteemed Stone of the Force CID, Specialist Aston team, would be sent to deal with a mere robbery case.

'You been a naughty boy, Mike? Or are you just here to piss in my bathtub?' The sergeant passed him the file without any qualms and leaned over onto his counter as if to get close enough to share a whispered gossip.

Sergeant Steve 'The Bear' Graves was a bony figure with inordinately hairy forearms that seem to jut out of his starch-stiff short-sleeve shirt. He was in his mid-forties – a real 'career-copper', not easily fazed by the more intimidating inspectors like Mike Stone. He had a certainty about his nature, a confidence that Stone respected.

And he was good at his job: which Stone respected above all else.

'I've no bloody idea why I'm here,' Stone replied, flicking through the file, scanning the notes with as much interest as a teenager checking for homework. 'Barry-fucking-Wigfield.'

'The one and only.'

'What's his game, then? Robbery's not his usual trade.'

'Sir?'

'He's too thick to make a decent job of it.'

'Maybe he's gone up in the world,' the sergeant quipped with layers of sarcasm.

Stone took a few moments to look over the notes and paused on one phrase. His head tilted to the side as if he was listening to a voice whispering over his shoulder.

'The thing is, Steve,' he began, almost speaking to himself, 'Barry Wigfield is a low-life scumbag. He steals handbags from grannies, mobiles from kids, gets involved in the odd scuffle – shit, the worst he's ever been nicked for was car theft.'

'They've all gotta start somewhere.' The sergeant's Brummie accent began to thicken, and he scratched at his thinning dark grey hair, not sure he cared too much about Barry Wigfield's criminal record, but intrigued at the idea that something was ticking in the DI's head.

'Start, yes,' Stone continued. 'But stepping up a gear to an armed robbery – and a vicious one at that – usually has something, or some*one* else behind it.'

'How's the old man? The shopkeep: he gonna live?'

'Well, he's not going to die. As for *living* after this attack: that's a whole other question.'

Stone had been given a short briefing by the chief superintendent on his way over to the city centre station, which had included quite a detailed description of the attack and some photos from the SOCO team that showed the job had been more than a mere robbery. Three men in balaclavas doing over a shop in broad daylight, and the one they'd caught had taken his time over scaring the hell out of the 58-year-old Asian shopkeeper. The attack didn't even carry any of the trademark race-hate crime factors, either.

Stone handed the file back to the sergeant and made his way to the interview room to catch up on progress. Something niggled at him. He didn't often work robbery cases any more. As one of the DIs for the specialist Force CID team at Aston, he mainly led serious cases such as murder, rape, or organised crimes and large drugs cases. But a simple shop robbery on a Friday afternoon was not normally on his radar.

Unless there was more to it that hadn't yet been mentioned.

* * *

'Come on, Barry,' whined Sharp, 'this is going to be a lot easier on all of us if you actually answer some of our questions.'

'No comment.' The scrawny-looking man had no hair, sunken eyes, and a complexion that made a zombie look well-pampered. He was a well-known petty criminal who'd been on the wrong side of the police since before his conception. Not the sharpest tool in the box, he tended to fall from crime to crime, trip over opportunities, and be about as artful at life as the cheap tattoos on his arms.

Stone stood in the corner of the square interview room with his hands in his pockets. It was more a statement of lethargy than defiance. Stone would never be a nine-to-five office job man, but this Friday was dragging.

Sharp, on the other hand, was a cocky little upstart who didn't deserve to be a sergeant. He didn't really deserve to be a copper, in Stone's eyes. He sat opposite Barry Wigfield, leaning back in his chair with his arms folded and his legs straight, crossed over only at the ankles. It was if he was trying to 'plank' the chair at an angle.

'You were caught running from the scene,' Sharp continued.

'No comment,' Barry sneered, digging his elbow into the arm of his solicitor.

Mr Arnold Schaeffer was a duty solicitor who seemed to pride himself on getting in the way of anything the police were trying to achieve. He was fat and overpaid, and everyone assumed the two were connected. His grey-beige suit crumpled under the awkwardness of his size and did nothing to hide the sweat patches under his arms or around the fat of his neck. He was, in every way, a grotesque man.

'You were covered in the victim's blood, for Christ's sake!' Sharp was getting closer to shouting.

Schaeffer perked up. 'There is no need to begin intimidating my client, detective.'

Sharp glared at him. 'Your *client* has no problem with intimidation, thank you. You should see the look of Mr Patel.'

'My client has already made it clear that he attempted to help Mr Patel in what appeared to have been a distressing incident.'

'Yeah.' Barry joined in, raising his hands and shrugging his shoulders in that way only obnoxious teenagers can.

Even though he was in his thirties. 'I was tryin' to help him, sergeant.'

'Okay, fine. Let's say you helped him. Let's say you *helped* him whilst wearing a balaclava. And after helping him, you ran out of the shop and were seen –'

'Allegedly seen, please,' the fat solicitor interjected.

Sharp grunted in response. 'Allegedly seen handing something into a car which drove off.'

'No. Freakin'. Comment,' Barry replied, pointing his chin with each word in a way that made him move like a broken puppet.

'What was it you gave to the driver, Barry?' Sharp put a hand up to silence the solicitor. 'It must have been important. Or valuable. You didn't get much cash from the shop – allegedly – so I'm thinking it was something else. Barry?'

A silence hung in the air like a foul stench. Barry enjoyed the moment, milking it for all he could as he looked at Schaeffer with his gap-toothed grin. Without warning, he produced a mucus-filled snort of a laugh before placing a bony, nicotine-stained finger to his dried, peeling lips.

Sharp turned to look at Stone, who continued to stand in the corner looking like he wanted to be anywhere else. 'DI Stone?'

'Do you smoke, Barry?' Stone asked, somewhat politely.

'Y'what?' Barry managed to screw his face into something rather resembling a pug-dog.

'Do. You. Smoke?' Stone repeated. 'Cigarettes?'

'Detective, I hardly see how my client's personal…'

10

Stone cut him off. 'Barry?'

'Yeh. So? Not a crime, is it?' Barry looked at the other two men at the table for clues to what Stone was getting at.

'And how is your eyesight? Still good, yes?' Stone maintained his calm, almost friendly tone, but he was by no means playing 'good cop'.

'Twenny-twenny, mate. That's how I can see you bacon smokin' so well.'

Sharp gave Stone one of those *Where the hell are you going with this?* looks. A lot of people did that to Stone for most of the time in interview rooms.

Stone switched on his puzzled look. 'Well, that's a bit confusing, Barry. I mean, if your eyesight is that good, why did you need to get so close to the cigarette display if not to read the prices?'

'My client has already told you that he...'

Stone cut Schaeffer off again. 'It's just that there were two footprints – that's one left, and one right, next to each other, in front of the cigarettes.'

'Not mine,' Barry blurted as he sat back, defiantly folding his arms.

'Okay. We'll get our lab to look into that later, comparing your trainers – which had blood on them – to the footprints we lifted.' Stone paused. 'But let's not worry about that for now, right?' Stone walked to the other end of the room, standing in the back corner behind Barry. He ran his finger from his chin down the front of his neck, unconsciously pausing on the scar in the middle of his throat, just above his collar-bones. 'The thing is, Barry, I have a little bit of a problem, to be entirely honest.'

'You shittin' me?' Barry sniggered.

'It's called circumstantial evidence, you see.' Sharp tried to glare at Stone, but faltered as he remembered rank. 'You see,' Stone continued, 'there's no point me trying to prove you were at the scene of the crime, because you readily admitted that. Since you already told us that you tried to help Mr Patel – highly commendable, I might add – there's little point in me making much of the fact that you had his blood on your clothes.'

Barry turned to Schaeffer. 'This guy's doing a better job than you, mate.'

'Sir, a word outside?' Sharp stood up, but was immediately forced down again by a steely glare from the inspector, as if Stone had been standing by him with his hands on his shoulders. Sharp's forehead had begun to dampen with a mild, cloying sweat of anger, which was denied an outlet by rank and experience.

Don't you fucking dare, you little prick.

The air thickened with warning of dissent. Stone's eyes remained fixed on Sharp's. There was no alpha-male battle going on. Just some well-aimed pond-pissing.

'So, Barry, I need your help,' Stone continued. 'You and I both know that without a weapon, or other physical evidence, we're going nowhere with this.'

'Don't I know it,' said Barry, hardly able to hide his smugness as he slapped Schaeffer on the arm and nodded at him as if to share a wink and a joke.

'So, what I am going to do is get some of my science-y, CSI blokes to come in here and do a couple of tests. And I think one of them could end up killing our case against you completely. You know, if we don't find what we are looking for.'

Schaeffer shuffled in his seat and motioned to object. Sharp just watched. Listened.

'So, what do you say?' Stone asked, moving to lean on the table right in front of the bony man. 'Willing to give it a shot?'

'What tests?' Barry tried to hide his nerves under an unsteady laugh.

'Tests for blood, Barry.'

The three other men all looked equally perplexed.

Stone continued. 'You see, I am betting that we can find blood under your fingernails.'

'I already told you…'

'Yes, I know, Barry – you went to poor Mr Patel's aid. And that's also why we'll find blood on your face, isn't it? As he coughed up blood on the one man trying to help him.'

Barry smiled, sat back again and folded his arms. 'Now I know you're lying.'

'Not at all, Barry, not at all. Even when we do find tiny little blood spots all over your face, our dear Mr Schaeffer here will no doubt point out that it's merely circumstantial evidence because you said you were being a model citizen trying to save the life of an injured man. All I need you to do is consent to us having a look.'

'This is highly irregular, Detective,' piped up the frustrated solicitor. 'And I must advise my client against any such consent.'

'Nah, I'll do it,' Barry confidently insisted. 'Let them do their stupid test. Then they'll see how wrong they are.'

Schaeffer shot a glance at Stone. It was one of recognition. He knew what the detective was doing.

'Barry, I think we should talk about this alone,' the solicitor pleaded.

'Nah, it's fine, let them do their stupid test.'

'Do go and call the gentlemen in, Sergeant,' Stone asked Sharp in his best patronising manner.

Stone took a seat as he watched the solicitor desperately try to silence his client, whilst Sharp stood up, not quite sure what he was supposed to do.

'He's lying! I know he ain't got no CSI out there,' said Barry, cocky in his certainty. 'You're lying, you stinkin' pig. I know you ain't sending no CSI in here to search my face!'

'Sergeant.' Stone repeated the command whilst fixing his gaze on the bony man. This was a poker game and both held their final hand. All in.

Go on, you little shit. Bite.

'Yeh, Sergeant,' Barry mocked, 'you call your CSI, 'cause you ain't finding no blood on my face. No way!'

'Oh, I think we will. I am sure of it,' Stone said.

Barry launched to his feet. 'No way. You're fucking bluffing me. You ain't got no CSI out there and you won't find no blood on my face.'

'Then do the test, Barry. Prove me wrong.'

'Not if I was wearing a balaclava, you fucking won't.'

There was a stunned pause. Schaeffer put his head in his hands. The penny finally dropped for Sharp, who fought to hold back a smile.

'Tell me,' Stone said, leaning back in his chair, 'why were you wearing a balaclava in the shop, Barry? If you were just there to help him.'

14

Barry Wigfield looked at all the men, almost pleadingly as it began to dawn on him what he'd just said.

'No, no,' he said, 'what I mean…what I'm saying is…'

'So, we know you were there, Barry. And we know you weren't a customer.' Stone leant in very close. 'Why *were* you in that shop, Barry? Tell me.'

There was nowhere to turn, even though the bony man tried.

Stone pressed further.

'What did you give to the man in the car, Barry? We know you took something from the shop…'

'No!'

'Come on, Barry. This is all above you. Attempted murder in a little shop for a tiny bit of cash? You don't fool me, Barry. *What* was it for? Really?'

DS Sharp tried to play a hand. 'Drugs?' he proffered.

Schaeffer cut in, sweating and glowing red, fumbling with his pen to scrawl notes. 'Stop this immediately, gentlemen.'

'Is that why you did it, Barry? Drugs?' Stone barked.

'No!' he stammered.

'Then what? *Why?*' Stone pressed.

'It was just one bottle. And I don't know who. And fuck knows why.'

'A bottle? Of what?'

'That fizzy wine. The posh stuff. Moh-et.'

There was a moment of silence as everyone in the room besides Barry Wigfield pondered the irony of a low-life criminal robbing a shop in Nechells – one of Birmingham's well-known crime hotspots – and only taking a single bottle of expensive Champagne.

'All yours, Sergeant Sharp,' said Stone, as he left the room, deep in thought.

A single bottle of Moët. What the f…?

Chapter 2

It was the end of a very long week, and the only thing Mike Stone needed was a drink. Or two.

Or more.

After dropping off his car at his flat, he made his way to his preferred drinking hole in the centre of the city, stopping off in a small newsagent opposite St Philip's Cathedral – or 'Pigeon Park' as the locals called it, for the most obvious of reasons.

After a quick scan over the front pages of the papers – for amusement rather than information – Stone poked unenthusiastically at the few wrinkled sandwiches and lukewarm sausage rolls in the fridge unit that seemed warmer than the rest of the shop. He noticed the disapproving sneer of the shopkeeper, so he settled for a bar of chocolate. Hardly a nourishing meal, but he'd always had a taste for chocolate.

Stone made his way past St Philip's and down one of the side streets leading down to the pedestrianised New Street. It was still relatively early in the evening, so the drinking crowds had yet to fill the pubs. When he got to the Trocadero, it didn't seem too busy from the outside.

The Trocadero was a Victorian-fronted building that appeared tiny from the outside but wound back, Tardis-like, into several nooks and crannies. Stone could never work out if the pub was genuinely old or if its features were all a modern pastiche. But he didn't really care, either. The drinks were good, the prices were fair, the food was palatable, and the atmosphere just right. It wasn't the typical dark, police-filled pub one would expect a detective to go to, but several coppers used it. The management and the punters shared an unspoken recognition of this.

Stone had bought his usual starter for the night. A pint of lager, half a lemonade, a bag of dry-roasted peanuts, and a bag of 'blue' crisps.

He made his way to a back room, a tight corner with a little fireplace and a collection of tables and chairs that seemed to match in their own mismatched way. Music was always playing in the Trocadero, but the back room had no speakers, nor one of those flat-screen TVs that serve to ruin a good atmosphere with football and rugby. It was a private little tucked-away room that, on occasion, with a quiet word in the landlord's ear, Stone had managed to reserve for his own personal use, to the point where other punters would be politely asked to move to another part of the bar.

Sometimes just *accidentally* dropping a few choice hints into an overheard conversation could achieve the same effect.

Thank fuck that week is over.

He let out a deep sigh as if to mark the end of the day as he tucked himself into his corner, which allowed him to observe if he chose. It was position he often took in a room: standing in a corner, 'working the outer circle', meant that no one could come up from behind him. And nothing could be missed.

He downed the lemonade quickly, as if to underline the end of the week, and devoured the crisps just as rapidly.

It was a kind of routine of his rather than anything close to a responsible drinking method. He'd never been one for downing alcoholic drinks, so when he settled in for a few rounds, he'd always start off with a fast lemonade and crisps, marking the time as his.

It was a ritual that many noticed him doing, but few understood. Not that he cared.

He was off duty tonight. And properly off duty. He wouldn't be taking any calls, and planned on doing the same for the whole weekend.

Planned.

'All right, sir?' came a voice from behind him that made him smile. DS Sandra Bolton dropped into the seat opposite.

It wasn't a question, nor was it clever rhetoric.

Stone gave the customary response of a nod up to the ceiling.

It wasn't an answer, nor was it a meaningful reply.

19

'Have some of my nuts,' Stone offered, with all the innuendo intended. Bolton took the cue and grabbed a few. She didn't especially like nuts, and never bought them herself, but this was a little ritual of theirs.

Sandra 'Jedi' Bolton was a tall, attractive woman with long, dark hair tied back into a functional ponytail. She had strong features and a medium build. Attractive, but not sexy; good-looking, but not pretty. Stone had always thought her attractiveness came from her intelligence and the way she was comfortable around men without feeling the need to be either a doll or a feminist.

He was attracted to her, indeed. But he hadn't…

And hadn't tried…

And wouldn't…

But he had decided that if the situation was thrust upon him, he wouldn't protest too much. Although he did fear what state she'd leave *his* nuts in, considering the way he'd seen her 'apprehend' violent suspects on many occasions.

'Where've you been all afternoon?' asked Bolton.

'Carter had me wiping DS Shit-face's arse on a robbery case.'

'Robbery?'

'She felt there was more to it: maybe some high-level drugs, I dunno.' He shrugged, but paused a second for a niggle deep in his mind.

'So, there was something about it?' Bolton smiled, able to read him very well.

'A bottle of Moët.'

'What are we celebrating?'

Stoned rolled his eyes at her. 'No, Sands. That's all they took – from the shop Nechells. A single bottle of bloody Moët.'

She could barely hold back the smirk. 'Must have been a middle class…'

'Barry Wigfield…'

'Oh.' Bolton took a moment. 'So, are Moët-related crimes now our remit?'

Stone let out a dismissive sigh that seemed to speak volumes of something deeper lurking in his mind.

Bolton was pretty much the only copper who could see right through Mike Stone when she needed to. That was how she'd got the nickname 'Jedi' – from always being able to finish Stone's sentences, and having an uncanny ability to see his little foibles as signs of thought, not vacancy. At times it even seemed as if she could intuitively know what he was thinking.

But as Stone was always quick to affirm: *seemed* is not the same as *could*.

'Do you ever wonder whether we have reached the depths of human depravity?' asked Stone.

'Wow!' She was uncharacteristically stunned.

'I just think it's what we're always waiting for.' Stone caressed the scar on his throat again, brushing up against the evening stubble.

'Waiting for, or looking for, Mike?'

'Take that rape on Monday.'

'Nasty.'

'Nasty? He tore her up so bad, Sands. I've even wondered whether it would have been better if she hadn't...'

'Don't you bloody dare!'

Bolton knew she was talking to *Mike*, and not *Stone*, when he called her Sands. Not Sandy – she hated that. She'd always maintained it made her sound like a blonde from a cheesy American musical.

'I mean, would you…' Stone began.

'Oh, no, no, Mike. Screw that. No way I'm letting my mind even go there,' Bolton replied, hands raised almost in defence of the untouchable thought. 'You know damn well that rape has nothing to do with gender: it's all about power.'

'I know that.'

'So, don't go asking me what I would… want… just because I'm a woman.'

'I wasn't asking you as a woman. I wouldn't dare.' A wink.

There was a much-needed moment of silence. Not uncomfortable or awkward. Just needed.

'I've finished off your nuts, and they were so very salty…' she smiled.

Dirty cow.

Stone picked up their empty glasses and opened his mouth to speak.

'Beck's. Green. And hurry up – I need the loo.'

The bar was getting busier and Mike wasn't in the mood to spend his time squashing between punters. Part of him always weighed up the pros and cons of getting his warrant card out and making it look like he had urgent police business to attend to in order to gain the upper hand. But he knew all too well that would never work in the real world. One of the girls behind the bar caught his eye and gave a sideways nod towards the end of the bar. Stone recognised her as one of the regular staff and hoped he wasn't going to get the usual 'You're a cop, I don't suppose you could…' which would lead to him having to lie about having left his warrant card at home, so sorry, miss, he didn't suppose he could.

'The usual, love?' she asked as she began collecting for another punter's order.

Stone nodded for his pint, added a Beck's and a bag of green crisps. He handed her ten pounds, and the thought crossed his mind that she might be coming on to him. He was single, so he could do whatever he – or she – wanted, with no strings attached.

Or with some strings attached, if that was her thing.

No cuffs, though. That would be an inappropriate misuse of police-issue equipment. Not to mention very hard to explain if she cuffed him to the bed and stole the key, and he had to get freed by a colleague – probably Sharp – when they eventually thought to look for him after he failed to turn up to work.

Christ, I need a holiday.

Bolton got up to make her way to the toilets as soon as she caught sight of Stone making his way back to the table. Their relationship had been subject to a lot of gossip over the past year since Bolton had joined the Force CID team at the Aston station. There was no formal 'partner' system, but most officers seemed to frequently work with regulars when assigned to cases. Carter neither approved nor disapproved, leaving it to the DIs to make such staffing decisions. 'So, are you going to tell me what's on your mind, or are we just going to get completely rat-arsed?' Bolton said matter-of-factly as she returned to the nook.

'I'm not planning on staying too late,' he said.

'Fine. So, what's wrong?' she pressed. 'You remembered to send Jack a birthday card, didn't you?'

Jack was Stone's son. And a topic that was very rarely open for discussion.

Mike didn't answer the question, but he did take a slightly larger mouthful from his pint. His son's birthday had been the previous weekend, and Stone had been too busy to take his card round in person. He'd put it in the work outgoing post as he'd rushed out on a call.

He'd received no phone call from his ex, Claire, or from his son all week. It had been four years since he'd separated from his wife, and they had remained on good terms. He had also continued to make an effort to see his son.

At first.

But the visits had grown less frequent when Claire remarried, and Jack, at ten, wasn't really of the age where they could keep in contact without going through proper channels first.

Bolton didn't push any more, and changed the subject.

After a few more drinks, both of them loosened up and relaxed a little. It wasn't a hard-drinking night at all, but they stretched it out. Or rather, *she* stretched it out. Work in the Force CID was long and hard, and emotionally demanding. It was unforgiving on social lives and personal lives, especially for those who seemed to be driven by something that came from their core. But Bolton had wondered for a while if something was steering the DI she respected a little off course.

She never raised it, though, not wanting to jeopardise the occasional chance to go out for several drinks with a man she knew she could trust. She knew these evenings also allowed Mike Stone respite from a world he was fighting to save.

Or living to fight.

They stayed in the Trocadero until last orders. As they left, Mike had gone to say a more genuine and emphatic 'thank you' than usual, a little influenced by the alcohol. But Bolton had just raised her hand, not in dismissal, but more in understanding, as she got into the taxi.

* * *

Mike Stone always walked when he needed to think, and the cold air helped to sober him up. His mind had wandered back to his son: a place filled equally with joy and frustration. He was tempted to call but usually managed to find a way to avoid it, especially since it all too often meant he had to speak to that new husband of hers. It had repeatedly seemed as though the bastard was screening all her calls, as it didn't matter whether Stone called on the home phone or on his ex-wife's mobile, *he* always answered.

Mike had tried his hardest to resent the new man on the scene, but his mind was always fast enough to point the glaring finger right back at him as a reminder that his replacement plugged a gaping hole he had left.

He always enjoyed a walk along the canals, and since his apartment overlooked one, it made sense to take a route that required the least thought. He'd made his way up New Street towards Victoria Square, turning in the opposite direction to his apartment and heading in the direction of the new Library and Rep Theatre. It was a deliberately long walk he liked to take. He made a point of avoiding Broad Street – the clubbing capital of Birmingham on a Friday and Saturday night, always packed out with loud-mouthed morons and scantily clad females.

Females. Not *women*; certainly not *ladies*. The thought that any of them were *girls* made him physically shiver.

Jail-bait.

In truth, Stone did not want to meet the women shortly before they became his next butchered victim pinned to his incident-room board. It only angered him because he knew he could probably walk down Broad Street and pick out all the most likely potential victims. Then he could round up potential perpetrators all night long and still barely scratch the surface of the depravity he loathed.

The depravity he needed, though. Bolton was right. After all, without his job, who was he, really?

A man who missed his son.

It was a serious road accident, resulting in a fortnight's stay in hospital, that had marked the start of the slippery slope for his marriage. He'd needed emergency surgery to clear his damaged airway. The scar on his throat was a constant and lasting reminder.

The scar that reminded him of the accident his wife and son had also been in.

Losing his wife had hurt. But losing the daily family life with his son had cast a much darker shadow over his world. The only answer he found was to work.

He hated the melodrama, but he knew all too well that his job really was what he needed to live for.

As his mind wandered, he made his way on autopilot behind the Library, the Rep Theatre on his left, the small City Centre Garden on his right. He got to the canal at the junction with the famous National Indoor Arena.

Mike Stone had always felt an affinity with walking the canals. They always seemed to be so quiet, peaceful. Dipped just below the hectic world above, the canals slowed down the tides, breaking waves, and sometime-tsunamis of life. Life was softened into a murmur of soft ripples. Sometimes absolute stillness.

There was no romance in them, and they didn't claim any beauty. Indeed, they were often weighty, industrial places, filled with putrid water. Mike found the crunching sound the small gravel made under his feet strangely reassuring. Like there was a connection even he didn't understand.

Mike made his way carefully along the tow-path, aware that although he might not have been paralytic, he wasn't exactly in full control of his balance, and the very low bridge did take some careful ducking. He often mused about the fact that the Health and Safety army had thus far failed to ruin the canals with their doctrine.

When he got close to his apartment, he stopped and just stared at the water wobbling gently. There had been many times when he'd stayed out almost the whole night. And he was tempted to – if it wasn't for the heavy feeling in his head that told him it was time to drink that pint of water and fall asleep on the sofa in front of mundane late-night Friday TV.

Chapter 3

The shrill sound of a ringtone rattled Stone awake.

Carter? Fuck sake.

'Mike?'

Rubbing his eyes with a pinch, 'Detective Inspector *off-duty* Stone here, at ten to eight, on a Saturday he'd kept himself off rota…'

'I need you at a house over in Erdington. Now.'

You have got to be kidding me.

'And I don't suppose there's any point me repeating that I am not actually…'

'No, there isn't.' There was something about her tone. Stone couldn't quite pin it down.

'Right, okay…' He let a moment hang, as if to ask why it had to be him.

'Mike.' An unusual pause and a softening, almost a cracking, crept into Carter's voice. 'It's a nasty one.'

'You're already there?'

'Yes.'

It was the flicker of confusion that sent a chilling and sobering wash over his mind. Why did she need a DI – especially an off-duty one – if she, the chief super, was already there?

'Gimme the basics.'

'Look, you just need to see it, Mike, okay? I'm sorry to call you this weekend, but just get your bloody arse here, okay?' The line went dead.

She wasn't normally so blunt, and although Stone knew better than to read too much into anything like that, his mind started kicking into gear.

More depravity?

The previous night's ramblings with Bolton took on a sudden irony.

It took Stone just fifteen minutes to rush a quick shower, throw on the usual attire, and make it out the door. As he made his way down to the private car park under his apartment block, he sent Bolton a text. There was no conversation to be had, just instructions to be relayed and apologies to be offered.

The humble pie could wait for later.

He got into his car, switched the engine on, and waited for a moment as he squeezed his eyes tight shut, trying to frown away the beginning of a headache. He pinched the bridge of his nose as he tilted his head to the side, as if listening to a voice over his shoulder.

Why this weekend?

* * *

The North Birmingham area of Erdington had always felt a little disconnected from the city in Stone's view, as if the artery that was the M6 cut it off from the rest of Birmingham, almost like the way the M25 put a belt around London. The area was flat and wholly uneventful, with areas of suburbia that rang at a slightly different tone from the rest of the city. Stone put it down to the region having historically been a part of Warwickshire, with its own council constituency. Politics and boundaries aside, it just 'felt' different to him. If the city where he'd born and bred was to be considered a microcosm of England, he was definitely going 'up North'.

Stone turned into the Erdington street and waited for two of the bored-looking uniform officers to lift the blue-and-white police tape so he could drive through. He immediately started scanning the area and spotted the telling, morose marching of Chief Superintendent Carter. Something about her body language said this was indeed a 'nasty one'.

He pulled up to the kerb on the opposite side of the road to the house that seemed to have a steady traffic of people coming in and out. Stone liked to call the Scenes of Crime team officers Smurfs, with their disposable blue suits, white face masks and shoe covers reminding him of the similarly coloured characters from decades-old children's TV.

Stone got out of his car and began the usual process, donning the overalls, shoe covers and gloves. He understood their necessity, but loathed the sweaty feeling they always left him with.

The house was a standard three-bedroom semi-detached that boasted nothing, but was ashamed of even less. As soon as he got through the front door, Stone started his scanning immediately.

His mind ticked over like it was logging everything. He tended not to use a notepad whilst at a scene of crime, instead preferring to let the images file themselves into folders and cabinets in his brain.

A set of keys on the side table – definitely a man's set. Too many keys, and too few useless keyrings to be a woman's set. There was a base unit for a cordless phone that oddly sat facing the front door. Of course, it could have been moved at any time, but Stone made a mental note of anything that seemed out of place.

As he turned to walk into the living room, he noticed the musky smell of the previous night and the blanket roughly spread half on the sofa and half dragged across the floor. The remains of a greasy takeaway sat in an open polystyrene box, along with a couple of lager cans crumpled precisely in the middle as if to mark their emptiness. It was clear that someone had slept on the sofa last night, but the questions were *who,* and *why?*

Pictures on a fireplace showed a man, a woman, and a young girl, probably about ten years old. Jack's age. More of the man and woman together; the man on his own; the woman on her own. Far fewer of the girl.

Where are all the baby photos?

Stone moved on to the small, open-plan kitchen-diner. It had the low-gloss feel of a well-aged kitchen, but the

LED fixture lights in the ceiling begged to be seen as modern. He quickly scanned around the room, noted the dining table set for two, dirty plates still in place, and an open bottle of wine sitting in the centre.

There was something about the bottle's position that seemed odd to Stone. It was stood exactly in the centre, label pointing his way.

Like I am meant to see this.

Stone turned and headed down the hallway, eager to get to find out what was so urgent he had to be brought in from off duty. Part of him didn't mind too much. Another part of him was pissed off; it was like being taken for granted.

He noted more photos dotted around the wall as he made his way back towards the front door, which was opposite the stairs.

Standing at the bottom of the stairs, Stone saw the metal floor plates that SOCO teams laid out to protect the scene from contamination by police footprints. He slowly made his way up the stairs, noticing the occasional light creaking coming from three or four of them.

Why did no one hear the stairs?

He turned the corner near the top of the stairs and then took the last three up onto the landing. A new mixture of smells hit him. There was a lingering chemical and floral air that must have come from a bathroom, stirred up with another musky smell.

Depravity.

'This way, Inspector.' The crisp, home-counties accent chirped from a room to Stone's left, so he turned and continued to follow the route of metal plates. One of the

SOCO team saw him coming and waited at the door as if they were in a child's playground, shimmying around the climbing frame and giving way to the older boy whose seniority was wordlessly observed.

The master bedroom was filled with an almost indeterminable number of slowly moving crime scene Smurfs. They spread around the room at all levels, with an array of brushes, lights and tweezers. It looked like a strange music video from the 90's.

Stone caught the eye of one of them who confidently made his way over, dictaphone in hand.

'What have we got then, Reg?' Stone said to the approaching suit.

Dr Reg Walters replied in all his home-counties glory. 'Rather a chilling wake-up call, one might say,' he said, without humour. He continued as Stone slowly moved around to look. 'The deceased: female; thirty-four years of age. Severe lacerations to genitals and lower abdomen.'

'Any idea what the weapon was?' Stone asked.

'Impossible to say at the moment. I'll need to take a closer look.'

Stone looked at him. Reg Walters was as picture-perfect an Englishman as he could possibly be. He had the accent carved out of years of private education, coupled with blond hair, smooth skin, and practised posture that would satisfy the Royal Ballet. That aside, he was the best pathologist Stone had ever worked with. 'I'm not asking for a committed answer, Reg. Just an idea. Knife? Size? Type of blade?'

'Sorry, Mike. But you should know better. What I can say, however, is that it is very likely there was more than one weapon used, due to the differences in some of the injuries. I'll know more when I can get a closer look.'

'Christ!' The voice came from Bolton, standing at the door to the room.

'You took your time,' Stone said.

'Sorry, I was in the shower when…'

'Was she moved, Reg?'

'Yes,' he replied. 'But I only say that because given the amount of pain she must have felt, she looks too calmly posed…'

Bolton cut in. 'Do we have time of death yet?'

'That's part of the problem,' replied Walters. 'Liver temperature has been affected by an unusually high ambient temperature. And there's another problem.' Reg indicated around the bed as if inviting the two detectives to play some kind of game. Stone and Bolton looked at each other, and then perused the scene before them.

The woman was lying on her back in the centre of the bed, legs up and separated, and hands holding onto the top of the headboard. Her head was propped up on a pillow so that her face could be seen clearly.

'She's definitely been posed,' Bolton said quietly, nodding in agreement.

'Mid-act, it would seem,' Stone replied, but without a crass overtone.

'It's as if the killer wanted us to see what she looked like when she was having intercourse,' Reg added. The tall man gently shook his head as if he was doubting what he was looking at. Not his opinion, just his eyes.

'This is a sexual attack, then?' Bolton didn't hide the disgust in her voice.

'No, this isn't about rape. This is about something else,' Stone replied.

'Rape isn't about sex, sir.' Bolton dared to correct him. To remind him.

Stone moved around the bed. He got as close as he could to the body, causing one of the SOCOs with a camera to move out of his way. He moved his hands close to her body, almost as if he was performing some kind of ritual, sensing something, keeping his hand an inch or so from the skin.

'Reg. Is she the right colour?' he asked.

Reg was expecting the question. 'She's too pale.'

'But the body does go pale after the blood pools at the lowest point, if she'd been here long enough,' Bolton tried to affirm.

'Then where's the blood pooling? She's no darker at the lower points,' Stone replied.

'And given the apparent number of lacerations,' Reg continued, 'there's simply not enough blood here.'

Everyone looked at each other and then back at the body on the bed. Nothing was said, but there was a shared confusion about the lack of blood.

Finally, Bolton threw a theory in. 'So... she was killed elsewhere then brought here?'

'Doubt that, ma'am,' perked up one of the Scenes of Crime staff, who was immediately met with semi-surprised glares from the two detectives, and a look of slight chastisement from Reg Walters. She continued, nervously: 'I mean, there has so far been absolutely not a spot of physical evidence in the house to support the idea that she was...' She trailed off.

Stone and Bolton looked at each other; looked back at the SOCO; and back at the body, apparently accepting a very good point.

'Look, Mike, I need to get this body out of here and down to the mortuary,' Reg said. 'I've had them take significant numbers of photographs, but given the lack of blood – or visible evidence of blood – I need to get this body open as soon as possible.'

'T.O.D. ballpark?' Stone asked the pathologist.

'Look, Mike, it's hard to say with any real accuracy at this stage. However, given the onset of rigor, the lack of decomp smell, and the current stability of the soft tissue like the eyeballs, I'm okay with saying I would be surprised if it was any more than twelve hours.'

'Thanks, Reg.' Stone said. 'That's close enough for now.'

'No problem. The body is fine to be moved now. I'll get a few guys downstairs to sort that out. And then the scene is all yours.' Reg turned and began his march across the metal stepping stones.

'Sir, come and look at this.' Bolton guided him round to the other side of the bed and pointed out some small marks on the beige carpet.

'Blood?' Stone asked.

'No, it's the wrong colour,' Bolton replied. 'That is what happens when you start walking around on expensive carpet before your toenails have dried.'

'Why would you make that mistake if you'd spent that much on the carpet, Sands?'

As usual, her answer was the next question she knew was lingering in his mind. 'More accurately, what made her forget *this* time?'

Stone was already beginning to build a narrative of the events in the room. Had she been startled to her feet by something… or someone… she had seen or heard? She'd be unlikely to get up for her husband if he'd entered the room. Unless the way he'd come in was unusual.

Or had it been it someone she wasn't expecting to see?

'Make sure there's a photo of that, and get someone to bag a sample from the carpet,' he said as he went to leave the room.

'Where are you going?'

'I'm going to find out where the doting husband is.'

Stone made his way out of the room and back down the stairs. He went back into the living room at the front of the house and had a quick look around.

His mental notepad flipped open again. This was a family home. Comfortable, but not extravagant. Tidy, clean, but evidently lived-in. The sofa had definitely been slept on, and a pair of shoes sat out of place just inside the door. Stone walked over to the coffee table and picked up the remote control, switching the TV on. He wasn't surprised to see it was tuned to one of the channels that would constantly loop round old comedies all night long. Perfect for late-night drunken viewing.

How could he have been down here whilst she was…?

Stone left the living room and made his way back into the kitchen, this time heading for the back door. It was a classic wood-panelled design, with nine small panes of glass at the top. The pane closest to the lock was broken, and the key was in the lock. Glass had collected on the floor just inside the door and the frame had already been dusted for prints. It was littered with them, as you'd expect in a house. He'd learnt from his earliest days as a trainee that it wasn't a matter of finding prints in a house, but of finding the right ones – or the wrong ones, depending on how you looked at it. And finding none usually meant some degree of wiping down had occurred.

The rest of the kitchen was the same as the living room – not messy or dirty, but clearly lived in. And lived in last night. A couple of saucepans on the hob. Two places at the small dining table – not three. A bottle of wine and two glasses. Again, the bottle caught his eye.

It's too central. Too… posed.

'Inspector,' Carter barked over his shoulder. 'Thoughts?'

'Where's the daughter?' Stone replied, without looking up from the table.

'With grandparents. She was away with them for the weekend. They picked her up from school, according to the husband.'

Stone called over one of the SOCOs with a camera. 'Have you got shots of the table yet?' The SOCO shook their head. 'Do it, please, and make sure you get close-ups of the glasses, and bag them up for Forensics. With the bottle.' He turned to Carter. 'Did you find anything interesting upstairs?'

'Isn't that what I'm supposed to ask you, Mike? Look, I want you as SIO on this one. I'm up to my neck at the moment. Pass your other cases on to DCs, but keep your eye on them. I want you focused on *this*. I'm heading back now. I'll get the incident room set up.' Carter kept dictating to Stone as they walked back down to the front door. 'You and DS Bolton get back as soon as possible for a briefing. Reg says he'll get straight on to the post-mortem, but it could be at least four to six hours before he is ready to give any preliminary reports. I have a meeting with the Chief Constable today, and I'd like to be able to give them *something* positive.'

Stone had that slightly vacant look, only intelligible to those who knew him well, that meant he was mulling something over. He stopped by the living room door. 'Ma'am, what does this room look like to you?'

'A bloody tip.' She smiled. 'A bit like your flat, I'd imagine.'

'Exactly. This is man-debris. Either from a night in, or from a man getting home late after a night out.'

'Your point?'

'Upstairs was…'

'A woman getting ready to go out, but never got the chance.'

Bolton finished the sentence for him as she got to the bottom of the stairs. 'Also, a woman who wasn't pregnant.' Bolton held up a plastic bag containing a pregnancy test.

'And you think that's relevant to this investigation?' Carter asked.

'Everything is relevant until we rule it out,' Stone mumbled. 'Where's the husband?'

'He's the one who called it in, first thing this morning. We've already taken him to the station. And remember, until we have enough physical evidence, he's helping with enquiries, not under arrest.'

That was the official line, but each of them knew that when it came to a murder, the first people you look at are always those closest.

Stone's head turned slightly, as if he was hearing something over his left shoulder.

'So, we have a daughter staying away; a father on a night in, or back from a night out; and a mother getting ready to go out on a night of her own. One night, one family: three separate lives.'

'There's a lot wrong with this,' Bolton replied.

They all made their way out of the house and began moving back to their cars. Stone stopped on the road between his car and Bolton's. She came over.

'Sir?'

He turned almost full circle, taking in his surroundings. *Why here? Why this area? This street – this family?*

Bolton waited. Listening to the sounds of the city around. The noise from the motorway was clear, and the sound of a passing train at the nearby Gravely Hill station shuddered the damp air. Despite all the activity surrounding the crime scene and the growing crowd of onlookers, the house seemed unnervingly still.

Stone finally replied: 'I want you to question the husband. Get Harry in with you.'

'Where are you going, sir?'

'I'm going to see if I can give Reg a nudge along with this one.'

'You don't want to be first to question the husband?' Bolton wasn't normally one to publicly question Stone, but she knew better than to overstep her place in the pecking order in major crimes. 'You know Carter won't be happy with that, sir.'

'And you should know better than to use the words *Carter* and *happy* in the same sentence.' Stone started walking towards his car. 'You get the husband on side. Get his story and emphasise he is helping us as a witness at the moment. I don't want him arrested until we have something to arrest him for.'

More importantly, Stone was well aware that people tended to be more co-operative when they thought they were being helpful.

Especially when they were guilty.

Chapter 4

Driving back into the city centre after having been at his own Aston station to launch the case, Stone kept running over every tiny detail he'd written in his mental notebook. What bothered him the most was the fact that he couldn't find what he called the 'story' of the killing. He'd spent the past few hours listening to the hustle and bustle of the incident room being set up, running over the scene in his mind.

He couldn't see the route the murderer had taken through the house. There were no signs of a struggle or a fight. From a cursory look around, there were no immediate signs that they were dealing with a burglary.

And the killer had taken his time. Too much time.

Which meant this murder had to be personal. If not to the woman, it was to the killer.

Stone's mind had already started shooting round the possibilities that the husband had sent the daughter away for the weekend to get her out of the way.

Husband?

He had already jumped to the conclusion that the man in the photos was the husband he hadn't met. But he'd also made a conscious decision to call him the husband of the victim, and not the father of the girl.

Fathers dote on their daughters.

As Stone passed the red-brick court buildings in Birmingham and headed down Newton Street to the coroner's court, he began to get a strange sensation that something was going to be quite different about this case. He didn't know why, and he'd already given up on rational thought. The 'Spider-sense' was prickling away, and he could feel himself standing at the bottom of a tall building, poising his fingers on the brickwork, wondering how high he was going to need to climb.

Stone made his way down the narrow private access road to the back of the court and parked his car next to Reg Walters' silver Audi.

Perfect car for the posh git.

Assuming that Reg would need a little more time to get ready, he took out his phone and sent a text to the pathologist to let him know he was in town and wanted to oversee this post-mortem. His phone rang almost immediately.

'You don't hang around, do you, Mike?' Reg said.

'The guv'nor said I should get down here as soon as possible. So, I'm just doing as I've been told, like a good little detective.'

'Bollocks!' Reg might have been posh, and swearing always sounded amusing in his clipped accent, but there was a laugh that came with it. 'You just want your dirty little fingers ready for the interview room.'

He was right.

'I wanted to watch an artist at work,' Stone batted back.

'I tell you what, Mike. I'll get my assistants to prep the body and I'll meet you out front in five minutes.'

Stone hung up and waited out at the front of the coroner's court. An overcast morning had turned into an oppressive gloom, as if Mother Nature herself was performing some kind of ritual. The shiver that shot up Stone's back said as much of the chilling nature of the Erdington crime scene as it did of the whistling wind that was sneaking down his collar.

Minutes later, Reg appeared in his usual attire: a silver three-piece suit that made his extremely well-kept blond hair look even brighter. Stone always thought he dressed more like a flash young lawyer than a middle-aged pathologist.

'Fancy a *luncheon* meeting?' Stone mocked, not really expecting the offer to be accepted, but more amused at the quip about Reg's heritage.

'Before a procedure? Probably not a good idea with this one, Mike.' Reg got a packet of cigarettes out and offered one to the detective.

Stone didn't smoke. Any more.

But he did today.

'I don't know how you do your job *and* smoke there, Reg.'

'I don't, old chap,' Reg replied, mocking his own accent. 'Not looking forward to this one, though, so: fuck it.'

'Do you ever *look forward* to cutting a body open?'

'You know me, detective. I like my job, and goodness knows I have a great respect for the fascinations it hides and reveals. But…'

'Not looking forward to the secrets in this one?'

'Off the record?' Reg said – as much an instruction as it was a request. Stone didn't reply. 'I take it you saw the bruising on the lower abdomen?'

'Yup. All concentrated around the stomach.'

'Lower than the stomach, Mike. Come on. GCSE biology. The uterus.'

'We found a negative pregnancy test at the scene.'

'Well.' The pathologist sighed out the smoke. 'That is one saving grace. I assume you also saw the cuts on the skin, too?'

'Yes. Any idea what he stabbed her with?'

'They aren't stab wounds, Mike. But before we venture into this one, I think a drop of Dutch courage is needed,' Reg whispered, as if it was one of most daring things he could admit to a police officer. Or anyone, for that matter.

'I really can't condone you being under the influence whilst at work, not as an officer of the law,' Stone mockingly replied.

'In that case, can I invite one of my dearest friends for a shot or two of purely medicinal mild sedative prescribed by a doctor to calm nerves?'

Both men smiled as they began the short walk to the pathologist's other favourite '*laboratory*'.

* * *

The post-mortem began with standard procedures and the usual slicing, cutting and crunching. The crunching was the part Stone didn't enjoy. Organs were removed and weighed, and all notes were made verbally, recorded via a Bluetooth headset linked to the computer at the side of the lab. Reg Walters dressed like a Victorian lawyer at work, and a lord at home, but he held no fear of using technology in his workplace. Nor did he shy away from splattering his green plastic apron with blood and bits of carcass with the unnerving nonchalance of a true scientist.

He waved Stone over to take a closer look as he began to work on the lower section of the woman's body. Stone knew they still wouldn't discuss what was being found, but the pathologist seemed to be narrating to him as much as he was to his Bluetooth.

'Multiple lacerations to the lower abdomen, coupled with severe bruising, focuses mainly around the uterus. Indication of the presence of foreign materials inside the uterus.' His fingers gently poked and prodded at the skin. He invited Stone to feel for himself.

Stone declined.

'On opening the uterus,' the pathologist continued, 'we find a range of pieces of glass collected inside. This glass appears to have broken whilst inside the uterus, and internal bleeding suggests that these injuries were sustained ante mortem.'

Stone mouthed 'ante mortem?' – not because he didn't understand the term to mean 'before death', but more to question the logic.

Reg continued. 'Detective Inspector, please feel free to ask your questions: you are allowed to be on these recordings. But to answer your question, I would suggest they are ante mortem because none of the cuts sustained from the glass appear to have made significant enough an injury to threaten life. The injuries would not be comparable to a peri-mortem stab wound to the heart, for example.' Reg looked at Stone and realised he might have taken one step too far into Latin. 'During, or as part of the process of death.'

Stone nodded in acknowledgement, but, not having an academic background, he never could understand the point of using Latin. He assumed it was all just a way of looking down on people who never bothered with a need to underline everything they said with an academic's tongue. He took a moment to look away, collecting his thoughts, and struggling to witness this particular case.

The pathologist continued, almost coldly.

'Further lacerations to the cervix, the vaginal canal, and the external tissues around the genitals would suggest that glass pieces or objects were inserted forcibly, but whole, and then broken by applying pressure externally, most likely with some kind of blunt force trauma. A tool strong enough to break the glass, but blunt enough not to leave any distinctive markings.'

'Any signs of…' Stone paused, not sure how to ask the question on tape, as if it made him suddenly self-conscious.

'Sexual assault? Well, there are no immediate signs of semen, but I will take swabs for DNA and run tests for spermicidal fluids, et al. Usual kit.'

'Cause of death?' Stone asked.

'These injuries, although severe, and likely to have been extremely painful, were not the cause of death.' Reg indicated the woman's arms, and turned them over so Stone could see the insides of the elbows. 'On closer inspection, I found very small puncture wounds just inside the elbow joints, right into the veins on each arm. Slight bruising and the small amount of bleeding show that these were almost certainly needle wounds.'

'Needles?' Stone asked. 'You mean she was injected with something?'

'No.' Walters brought the overhead light down, closer to the body. 'Judging by these markings, which look like they were caused by some kind of sticky tape, I would say that the needle was an IV line stuck to her arm.'

Stone was grasping at straws. 'He had her on a drip?'

'I don't think so. He wasn't adding: he was draining. The victim's blood was drained from the arms whilst her heart was still beating.'

Stone looked straight at the pathologist. 'Cause of death?'

'At this time, I can only record the official cause of death as cardiac arrest, likely to have been due to a severe drop in blood pressure.'

'Because he drained her blood?'

'I can state that the body has clearly lost a lot of blood, and I can make a causal link to cardiac arrest. I can also surmise that loss of blood was likely to have happened via an IV. But I'm a scientist, and proof is a big word for me. I'll leave the theories to you and the CPS and some clever barristers.'

Stone turned and walked away from the body. He seemed to be going over everything he'd seen and heard, noting it and moving it, filing it and searching it. His head angled to the side again, but this time there wasn't a voice to help him.

The pathologist paused the recording on the computer with a touch of a button on the headset. They were off the record now, and more like two men than two job titles. 'Mike, your sick bastard rammed glass objects into her uterus, hit them to break them from the outside, and drained her blood until she died.'

Stone could do nothing but gently shake his head and remember, with some cruel irony, his comments the night before.

'Depravity,' he said softly to himself.

'I wouldn't argue with that choice of word right now,' Reg replied. He continued, pointing at another mark on the woman's skin. 'Take a look at this. It's another tiny puncture wound around where I would extract urine from the bladder.'

'You mean... he did the pregnancy test?'

Reg nodded. 'I would guess so, but I wouldn't go on record with that just yet.'

Stone took his gloves off and threw them into a yellow medical waste bin. 'How did he do this? Did he sedate her? He must have done.'

Reg shrugs his shoulders. 'I'm still waiting for the toxicology report to come back. But let me tell you this. She would have experienced pain significant enough to warrant some serious painkillers, almost anaesthetic in nature, to have her stay still enough for her blood to be

50

drained. How he did this, I don't know. All I can give you in my report is the timing of the different injuries as a best guess.'

'Time of death? Any closer?' Stone pressed.

'Medically speaking, with all the factors included: ambient temperature, loss of blood…' Reg snapped off his latex gloves as he led Stone through the heavy double doors into the corridor. He ran a hand through his long hair, freeing it from its medical cap. It had darkened under the sweat. His frown showed the reluctance in his answer. 'I would say between eight pm and midnight last night.'

'Thanks.' Stone knew how important it was not to get that detail wrong.

'But I will be recording that as an estimation open to revision. You'll need to find more evidence to support it than the condition of the body. I'm not putting my balls on the block in a court on that one.'

'Don't worry about that, Reg. It won't be *your* balls on the block in court.'

Chapter 5

The Boy

The ice-cold air was freezing his fingers. The only thought now was to wash them, to make them clean. To wash away what he'd had to do. He looked around desperately for a source of water – even a puddle would have done. But it hadn't rained for days.

He'd run so fast for so long that he couldn't tell where he was exactly. He had a rough idea that he wasn't too lost. '*Getting lost is just a chance to play hide and seek with the world,*' his dad had always told him.

That's when he heard the voices and shouts again. Getting closer. He had to move. Desperately scrabbling to his feet, but feeling every part of his body claw back in pain, he looked around, trying to get his bearings. Four tall, dark buildings filled the skyline and gave him a clue.

He didn't know the name of the road he was on, but he did know that he was close to somewhere he could really hide.

He took as deep a breath as he could and ran towards the buildings. Swinging round the roads, twisting and turning between the unfinished buildings and materials on the site, his feet hit sand, stones, gravel, and wooden boards, but all the time he knew he had to make the buildings get bigger in his view.

The voices were approaching as he broke out into the open onto the long, swerving road, and his internal map suddenly clicked into play. With newfound confidence, he pushed his legs through the burn as he swerved round Masshouse Lane, leaning into the bend like a rider taking a turn.

The four buildings grew to become giants of the skies. Giant, dark, stony monsters that had always terrified him. This time, they might be the only thing that could save him.

When he reached a bridge, he almost shouted out with joy at having remembered his way. It was a small success, but he couldn't stop. The chase was still in full swing.

He ran over the bridge, trying to remember how to get down below and out of sight. Turning onto the path put the first of the giant buildings right in front of him, as the voices came thick and fast, closing in from behind. There was no choice. He had to break through the brambles and bushes to get off the path. But it was an immediate, steep drop, and he tumbled further, scraping and bashing his arms and legs, wishing he had worn jeans and not shorts. The fall was short as he grabbed hold of a tree with both hands and launched himself down onto the towpath below with all his force, rolling over and over.

But the force had been too great and he rolled too fast. The ground vanished from beneath him.

His world suddenly became black and cold.

Chapter 6

'Listen up, listen up,' Stone barked at the rolling noise of the incident room as he came out of the office where he had based himself that morning.

The rest of the open-plan incident room was split into tables arranged with four cubicles that pointed officers towards each other. Each had a phone and computer poised ready for action. There were two main desks closer to the DI's office. One of these had become Bolton's territory. It was generally recognised that Bolton was Stone's first calling point. Besides the usual office gossip, there wasn't really any bad feeling attached to their professional set-up. Most detectives in the station would quietly admit to knowing that she was indeed an excellent sergeant who could not be far from promotion.

The other desk close by was DS Pete Barry's patch. He was a completely different kind of sergeant, focused primarily behind his desk with the key role of bringing cases together before sending them to the CPS.

Both sergeants needed to be within easy shouting distance of the DI. They also both happened to be the desks closest to the tea and coffee facilities

'Do you want to give the info on the husband, sir?' asked Bolton, referring to the preliminary information she'd got whilst he was at the post-mortem with Reg Walters.

'No, I'll get you to do that as and when,' he replied. She was used to him delegating such tasks, as he often liked to hear details over and over anyway.

Stone stood at the front of the room before the long expanse of whiteboard, which was already populated with pictures, names, lists, and times. Soon they'd be accompanied by maps, diagrams, detailed medical pictures, even arrows and thought bubbles. Effectively, it would be the working wall for the case – a shared mind-map. Despite the plethora of computer software that could organise all the information, Stone still preferred the hard copy as a way of keeping in full view the whole picture of the complex crimes they investigated.

Many detectives fantasised about staring at the boards and having an epiphany that broke a case.

Few actually had one.

'Mrs Grace Peters.' Stone always began with the victim's name. 'Grace Peters. A name you are going to remember. Everyone is going to remember it. And when the press get their grubby little hands on it, the name will become the stuff of nightmares.' It was quickly becoming clear that this case was going to be anything but 'any normal case'.

Stone scanned around the room, checking that everyone was listening. He was also scoping out his team. A major case could command upwards of thirty or forty staff when in full swing, and something told Stone that this incident room would be filling up more and more each day.

He continued. 'Grace Peters was murdered last night, probably at some time between 8pm and midnight.'

'Probably, sir?' asked an indistinct voice.

'Yes: probably. I've just got back from the post-mortem and will explain more about time of death issues in due course.' A few looks were already passing round the room. 'This was a brutal, violent murder. It was sexual in nature, but we don't yet know if sexual assault was the motive.'

'I don't understand,' said DC Sarah King.

'You rarely do, love,' joked another DC, Martin Greer. The joke was not shared by anyone else in the room.

Stone looked at King and gave her the *'bust his balls for that later'* look. 'No, you're right to question that one, Sarah,' he continued. 'Legally speaking, there was serious sexual assault committed as part of the offence, but at this present time we can't establish if intercourse took place. Consensual or otherwise. We are waiting on forensics. Suffice to say, it was extremely violent.'

Call it bloody torture.

A chill seemed to instantly drop the temperature in the room.

'Some basics. The family is comprised of three people – Grace Peters; the husband, Aaron Peters; and a ten-year-old daughter. The girl was spending the weekend with her grandparents in Stratford. The family have been informed, and I will be assigning Family Liaison at the end of this meeting.'

DC Harindar Khan raised his hand. He was a fresh young detective flying high very quickly. He'd only been a DC on a local team for a year before he was picked up by the more specialist Force CID, spotted as a bit of high-flying talent. Khan had been exactly the kind of DC that stood shoulders above the likes of Sharp, and it was from that team that Stone had plucked him.

Besides his policing talent, Stone liked Khan. He could rely on him.

He trusted him.

'What about the husband?' the young detective asked, instantly looking uncertain about his own question as he slowly retracted his arm. It made him look like an embarrassed school kid.

Bolton knew that was her cue. 'Mr Aaron Peters was the one to call it in this morning,' she began, 'after having found the body. He was on a night out with friends last night, and said his wife planned to go out with her friends.'

'Separate nights out? Sounds like bliss,' Greer piped up again.

Bolton continued. 'He says he got back to the house at about two am and went straight into the living room. He admits he was very drunk and even though he did manage to get two beers from the kitchen, he failed to notice whether the window in the door was broken or not.'

'Didn't he go upstairs at all, even to use the bathroom or toilet?' King asked. She was an experienced detective but still had the thirst at the start of a new case that made her sound like a rookie on their first ever murder.

'Peters says he just crashed on the sofa with a kebab he bought from the local takeaway on the way home. He only went upstairs when he woke in the morning and noticed his wife wasn't up and about making his breakfast.'

Sniggers from around the room mixed with groans. Chauvinism hadn't completely died.

'That's hardly an alibi, is it?' Greer snorted.

'At the moment, he is officially helping us with enquiries, so we're not pressing too hard, too soon,' Stone jumped in, beginning to get a little annoyed. It irked him that too many detectives failed to understand the concept of not playing one's hand too early.

'Come off it, sir…'

'What you are going to do, Greer, is make your way down to the takeaway with a photo of the husband and see if they remember him. You are also going to see if they, or anyone else, can provide CCTV to back up his story of getting back at two. Okay?'

It was enough to shut him up.

Bolton continued to give a few more details before Stone took back the attention of the room. 'We also now know that Mr Peters is the second husband, and is step-father to the daughter. We are beginning to get forensics back, but it's unlikely that fingerprints and DNA are going to be quick case-breakers on this one.' He let that reminder sink in, knowing that DNA was often the catch-all for many detectives. 'DS Barry will be the inside sergeant. Everything goes to him without delay.' He gathered a few of the team around him and began reeling off a list of instructions as everyone else returned to their hustle and bustle.

'Pete, make a note of these, will you?' He waited for Pete to give him a nod, which he knew meant that he'd set up a new spreadsheet.

DS Pete Barry was a real old-school detective, but he was unique in the sense that he loved the desk job. He liked doing organisational work far more than going out on the job, and the prospects of promotion didn't interest him at all. He was grey before his time, and his frequently grimacing face, coupled with a cuttingly dry sense of humour, made him a little 'scary'. Much amusement was had when a temporary senior officer took SIO position for an investigation and tried to assign him as Family Liaison Officer.

It didn't go well.

DS Barry was far better at working with information *about* people than *with* people themselves. He looked older than his years, and always had his reading glasses poised on the edge of his nose. The DS was also a lot more skilled with computers and technology than people often realised, especially since he still did most of his typing with his two index fingers.

Stone delivered his to-do lists the same way every time. Without pleasantries. 'I want all the names of husband's mates, and check out the alibi he will probably need – along with any taxi company he used. Greer will be going into the takeaway with his photo. They probably won't remember him, but check for CCTV and seize it for us.

62

On a night out, he possibly paid for some things in cash, but see if he used his cards anywhere.'

He paused for a moment, turning his head slightly to listen to that voice over his shoulder.

'So, are we going back to the husband, sir?' Bolton asked, plucking him from his reverie. 'He's waiting downstairs, still under the impression that he's helping with our enquiries.'

'He *is* helping.'

'Yes, but is he a suspect?'

'Let's not play all our cards too soon, Sands.' He changed the line of thought. 'Sands: if you were going on a night out with friends and you didn't show up...'

Bolton joined the thoughts together. 'I don't remember anyone mentioning picking up her mobile.'

At that moment, Carter marched into the room in less than a good mood. Her thickset eyebrows had taken on a cartoon-like curl that signalled her mood as clearly as a neon sign. 'My office – now,' she snapped at Stone, and left before he could even reply.

* * *

Chief Superintendent Carter's office was a large L-shaped space with a small, casual seating area by the door. The low, square-backed office chairs would have looked at home in a school staff room. Stone called it the 'fluffy social worker' corner. Carter's desk was in the corner of the room, set at a commanding diagonal line that connected the 'fluff' with the modern: a glass-topped, chrome-legged table with five black leather seats.

'So, the first bloody thing you do, Mike – sit down – is let the prime suspect sit on his arse like a special guest for a whole day.' It wasn't a question, but it demanded an answer as her eyebrows and distinct extra blink said, 'Go on, explain yourself.'

'Aaron Peters is not the prime suspect.'

Carter gesticulated in frustrated exasperation, letting her arms drop and slap against her thighs as she slowly shook her head in search of what to say. 'When the hell was *that* decided? Before or after you ordered tea and cakes for a friendly sodding chat?'

'There's nothing solid pointing at him, but a lot pointing away from him.'

'Have you got anything pointing anywhere? At anyone?'

'Not even my remote control pointing at my TV on my weekend off. I'm missing endless cooking shows for this.'

Come on, old bat: find that sense of humour.

Sensing that her bluntness was patronising, Carter relented with a sigh. 'I just had a hell of a meeting with seniors and they are insisting that we hit the ground running with this.'

'Insisting?' Stone scoffed. 'What's wrong? Are we not getting enough *likes* on FaceTwit?'

He finally got the smile he was looking for. It wasn't that Stone treated his job like a joke, but he always resisted the constant badgering about statistics and targets. His opinion was simple. Criminals didn't meet to discuss data and use it to commit a crime, so using data to force the police into decisions was a foolish way to approach policing in any sense of the word.

'I'm not going to start calling someone a suspect just to play the media game, ma'am,' Stone said, sternly reminding her.

'I know you're doing your bit,' Carter continued. 'And I know you're a bloody good detective. But at the end of the day...'

'Statistics?' Stone stood up. He had already been feeling twitchy before he came into the office, and he knew full well where she was going. 'Have you had a chance to read the pathology report yet?'

'I scanned it, but not in detail yet. Why?'

'Well, you take a look at what this woman went through, and *then* tell me that statistics are all that matter.'

Carter was stunned by the outburst. 'Right, okay.' She paused for a moment and leant forward on her desk. Her arms were thick, stern, heavy-looking. Her complexion was almost as rough as her voice. 'Is there something I should know, Mike?'

Stone subconsciously played with his stubble and ran his fingers over the scar. 'There's something odd about this case, that's all. I can't put my finger on it. But Aaron Peters did not do this.'

'Mike, you know I trust your instinct, but please don't tell me it's in his eyes.'

'No. That's my point. It's *not* in his eyes. Fear, terror and shock are in his eyes, and he only saw the body for a moment. No, those eyes could not have lasted the time it took to carry this out.'

'So, what is it? The real killer has a special message we are all missing?' She didn't mean to be condescending, but she was a chief superintendent for a reason. Decisive, direct, and as blunt as a house brick when she needed to be. 'I suggest you get downstairs and interview him, push his buttons – whatever. If, after that, you still don't see him doing this, fine.'

Stone took his cue and walked over to the door. He stopped just before opening it. 'It's like this is only the beginning,' Stone said over his shoulder.

'Of what?'

He left without saying what he thought.

The beginning of depravity on a whole new level.

Chapter 7

The man looked terrible, Stone thought to himself. But then, many a skilled liar had been dragged through a Stone and Bolton interview. Oscar-winning performances seldom worked.

'Your daughter was with her grandparents last night? That would be *your* parents, would it?'

'No, Grace's parents. You know that.'

'Of course, sorry.' Stone didn't look at him. And he wasn't sorry.

'And she's not really my daughter – well, she is – but she's my stepdaughter, and…'

'There is no need to explain, Mr Peters, that is fine too.' Stone deliberately patronised the man to see if he could get a reaction.

Not a dickie-bird.

'Is her dad on the scene at all?' Stone asked, continuing to push buttons where he could.

Peters snorted. 'That loser? He's never had anything to do with his own daughter: he doesn't care. In fact, Sophie doesn't want anything to do with him.'

'I am sure that fits in with you, doesn't it?'

'He did it all himself, before I was on the scene,' Peters continued. 'By the time I got to know Grace…well, Sophie had no desire to see her so-called father.'

Stone turned to Bolton as if to check for himself what she thought. She was making notes on the man in front of them – mentally. The atmosphere in the small interview room was tense, and Aaron Peters was clearly beginning to feel the strain as his left leg started bouncing involuntarily. He looked uncomfortable, so Stone decided it was about time he began to lay it on a bit thicker.

'Take me through it from the beginning,' Stone asked.

'I phoned when I woke up…'

'Of last night, sir.'

'We were both going out.'

'Together?'

'No, with our own friends.'

'Separately?'

'Yes. Is that a crime?' The man looked at Bolton as if for some kind of help.

Stone held a steely, poker-face glare.

'We weren't having problems, if that is what you are trying to suggest,' said Peters, beginning to show his frustration. His breathing was getting stronger, and a very gentle sheen of sweat was forming on his forehead.

Stone always believed it was his job to set the pace and tone of an interview, no matter how hard anyone else tried. 'What did you do before you went out?'

'We ate dinner. What else do people do before they go out?'

'Watch TV, get ready…'

'Well, yes.' Peters began to fumble his answers. 'We did that, too.'

'Have sex.' Stone looked up. He wanted to see the reaction.

'What?'

'What did you have for dinner?' He skipped the question for a moment.

'Does it matter?' The man began to get more agitated. 'Some bastard raped and murdered my wife, and he's out there, and I'm in here – *you* are in here – and you want to know what I ate last night.'

Silence.

Bolton took her cue and sat down at the table, making sure to flash her generous cleavage. A test to see how he responded to temptation.

'Kebab, wasn't it?' Stone didn't change his tone to respond to his growing anger. He just sped up the questions.

'Yes. No. Pasta.' The barrage of questions was having the desired effect. 'We had pasta together. I had a kebab on the way home.'

'So, you walked home? You told the sergeant here you got a taxi.' Stone deliberately made his tone accusatory.

'I did. To the kebab shop. Then I walked home from there.'

'Did you have sex last night, Mr Peters?' Bolton jumped in.

'I'm not fucking cheating on my wife.' He stood up. He was fired up for defence.

'Sit down, Mr Peters.' Stone didn't respond to the angry outburst. 'I meant, did you have sex with your wife last night? Before you went out.'

Aaron Peters was now beginning to look tired and confused; tears were streaming down his stubble-covered, greyed face. He looked desperately between the two detectives, hoping to find some kind of salvation.

'Yes, we had sex. We had dinner. Then some sex, and then I went out, leaving her to get ready for her night out. What have I done wrong? Why are you being like this – I don't understand. My wife has been murdered and you're interrogating me like…'

Stone cut him off, not wanting him to mention arrests or solicitors just yet: 'These questions might seem personal and they might seem cold, Mr Peters. It is our job to find out who did it. You can either help us now, or we can do it later and treat you as a suspect.'

'Isn't that how you are treating me now?'

'Answer me this, Mr Peters.' Stone leant forward on the table and looked straight in his eyes. He rubbed the scar on his neck with his thumb. 'What wine did you have with your dinner last night? The wine you shared with your wife.'

Peters was perplexed by the question and looked at Bolton. She in turn only just about resisted the temptation to ask the DI exactly what his point was.

The man shrugged his shoulders. 'I don't know. Something red. She bought it. I don't drink much wine.'

'How many beers did you have last night?'

'Too many,' said Peters as tears streamed down his face and his head began to hang closer to hands that seemed too weak to catch it. 'Maybe if I hadn't... if I'd gone upstairs... what if I'd...?'

That's a bloody good question, my friend.

'Gone upstairs when you got back? Why didn't you?'

'We went out separately. We do this once in a while, with our own mates. Then we spend Saturday night together – a film, maybe – then Sophie comes back Sunday morning.'

'What time did you get home?'

'Two, two-thirty-ish. I don't know. I drank a *lot*. It would have taken me about fifteen minutes to get home from...' His voice really began to crack. 'What if that's when it happened? What if I missed him by minutes because I stopped off to get a fucking kebab?' His eyes widened in a kind of self-hating rage.

'And you never noticed any broken glass or cold draught, any noises from upstairs?'

He just shrugged his shoulders. Then he broke down. Stone gazed intently at the man crumbling in front of him as he stood up. He waited for a moment before saying, with a measured jollity that jarred with the atmosphere of the room: 'Thank you, Mr Peters. That'll be all for now.'

Peters was caught out. It wasn't clear whether confusion, elation or even anger dominated his broken voice. 'You mean I can go?' He eyes darted between the two detectives as he wearily fumbled to his feet, not sure whether this was some kind of ruse or test.

'You've never been under arrest, Mr Peters. You've been free to leave at any time, just as the sergeant here explained to you. We'll get the officers at the front to help sort out reuniting you with your *step*daughter.'

The two detectives watched as the broken man slowly stood and walked towards the door to the interview room. He moved slowly and awkwardly, as if like an old man with a bad back. It was true, Stone thought, that a crippled mind cripples the body.

'You *have* volunteered your prints and DNA, haven't you, Mr Peters?' Stone said. Pushing a final button.

'No!' said Peters, looking like a rabbit in headlights. 'I thought I wasn't under arrest.'

'Merely routine.'

The man gave Stone one last suspicious look as he was led away.

Stone turned to Bolton.

'What do you think, Sands?'

She thought for a moment. 'He's a self-centred chauvinistic prick who can't resist a glance at my tits, despite what has happened. But he's not a murderer.'

Stone smiled.

She continued. 'For starters, he's not lying, and he hasn't put any effort into making the ludicrous situation seem any better, so far. He just walked himself into looking and sounding like a complete prat.'

'We'll book him for that, then,' Stone smiled as they left the interview room.

'What was all that about the wine, sir?'

'The wine bottle in the kitchen had been put back down in the centre of the table, with the label pointing towards where he sat for his dinner.'

'How do you know where he sat?'

'Two dirty plates – the one with a smaller sauce-stain would have been hers.'

Bolton shot Stone a raised eyebrow. 'Little food for the little lady? I expect better from *you*, Sir.'

Stone felt a twang of embarrassment. 'If you'd noticed the wider spread of sauce on the other side of the table – I'd safely say that was man-slurp.'

'Fair enough,' Bolton replied with a smirk.

'So why would anyone place the bottle of wine down right between them and their dinner partner unless they were more enamoured with the wine than the wife?'

'So, you think the perp picked up the bottle?'

'Which means he was able to break in, take his time, and then go and kill her.' Stone replied.

'How do you know he sat down, sir?'

'I don't know yet, but I just do.'

Bolton took a moment to think about it, and mentally reviewed the scene. 'Assuming the times match up for when he got in…'

Stone finished: '…He would have got back too late to have killed her.'

'And judging by the way he looked –' Bolton carried the thought through '– he hasn't changed or showered. Which means there should be blood all over him.'

'Go and make sure that is checked. I don't want some smart-arse defence barrister picking holes in nothing.'

Stone started going up the stairs, heading back to the incident room.

'How do you *know* it wasn't Peters, sir?'

Stone took a deep breath. 'Because he said she was raped.'

Bolton said nothing but asked the question with her eyes and a mild shake of the head.

He turned away as he answered: 'Which means he has no idea that what she *really* went through was far, far worse.'

Chapter 8

Khan knocked on Stone's car window after having hovered for a few moments with a day's work in his hands. He looked like something between a loyal dog and a brown-nosing schoolboy who'd finished his essay well ahead of the deadline.

'Hello, Harry,' Stone said, winding down the window.

'Sir.' He hovered for a moment, with papers flickering in the wind, before realising that was his cue to get into the car. A small man, lightly built, with thin-framed glasses on a face that had an unnervingly smooth complexion. He looked young enough to need to show ID to get into a nightclub, let alone to hold a DC badge.

But he was a bloody good DC, in Stone's opinion.

'Go on, then,' Stone said, 'tell me what you've got. Oh, and constable: I really hope it is as exciting as you are making it look.'

'Yes, sir. Right.' Harry took a breath. 'I've done some research on the ex – Malcom Glenn – and it seems that there is a long-standing custody battle between him and Mrs Peters.' He waited for a nod from Stone.

Or some kind of dog biscuit, Stone thought.

Khan continued. 'Mrs Peters appears to have been preventing *any* contact between him and his daughter.'

Stone was now interested. 'Any records? Violence, abuse, restraining orders?'

'There was a short note about a domestic issue, covered by uniform. The mother had claimed assault, but changed her tune and dropped the complaint. I also found out that there have been issues with the girl's schooling and reports made to Social Services.'

'Anything else?'

'Yes, sir. A little bit more unconventional, though,' he said, with a slight air of nervousness. 'I checked him out online. Social media, focus groups, Twitter, Facebook, and so on. It didn't take long for me to trace him. All legally, of course: all in the public domain.'

'And…?'

'He's a well-known member of a father's group: FAPAS. Fathers Against Parental Alienation Syndrome,' he said, tapping on the pages Stone needed to look at.

'Fathers for Justice?'

'No, no, sir, it's not the same thing.'

Stone read the details collected by the DC. 'Are there any legal issues, any bad press with this… FAPAS?'

'Oh, no, not at all, sir. They lobby for support, and actually collect some quite compelling legal research and backing on their website.'

'Not a bunch of crazy nut-jobs in superhero suits, then?' Stone asked.

'Far from it. But…' His confidence faltered. 'I think it *could* all point to motive. In Malcolm Glenn's case, at least. We can't ignore it, surely.'

Stone rubbed the scar on his neck for a few moments of silence in the car. Almost like holding a small briefing before starting the engine. 'I don't want any of this brought up when we speak to him. Let's see if he volunteers it himself, first.'

Khan was quite taken aback by the suggestion. 'Do you not think you should take DS Bolton, sir?'

'I don't suppose you thought to get his address?'

'He lives south-side, near Maypole,' replied Khan, gently waving a yellow sticky note up by his Cheshire-cat grin.

Stone started the car with a smile. 'Bloody good work, Harry.'

And he meant it. It was the lifeline of a good lead that he could use to sugar-coat the fact that they'd already pretty much ruled out their only other suspect.

* * *

Stone kept the volume of the music down as he and Khan drove to see the victim's ex-husband. Khan had taken the cue that the inspector wasn't in a chatty mood and rightly let most of the journey go undisturbed by pretending to be flicking through the details he'd copied into his notebook. He was still a little flattered that he'd been taken along to see such an important potential suspect, and put it down to his rather impressive yield of information in just one day.

Which was partly true.

In reality, there was a distinct possibility that if the man they were going to see really did have issues with his ex-wife, taking a female detective to see him might be the wrong move. The potential suspect might have a problem dealing with women in positions of power over him.

Stone wanted to save Bolton for later. Playing his cards close to his chest was a key part of his approach to his work.

And his life.

After wisely leaving the silence undisturbed for as long as he could, Khan tried to fill the car journey down to the south side of Birmingham with a little more conversation than roadworks, traffic and the British favourite, the weather.

'Do you have a strategy you want me to stick to, sir?' he said.

'How do you think we should handle him, Harry?' Stone replied.

'I think we should go in with delivering the news of the death first. Go in all sympathetic, like. See how he responds to it. Then check details with him.'

It sounded like a good tactic, and showed some thought. Stone liked that.

But he also knew that Khan was wrong.

'No, Harry. We first find out what he knows, and what he wants us to know, before we tell him anything.'

'Oh, right.'

'As soon as you show your hand, you are committed and there is no turning back,' Stone continued. 'So, get them to show their hand first. When you question someone who is unprepared for the questions, then you get an honest answer. Whether they realise they have given it to you or not.'

'Or you get someone who tries to give an unprepared lie.'

'Exactly,' Stone replied. 'And *that* is what I want him to do. It's an ugly business, Harry, but we aren't in search of the ugly truth when you start a case like this. First, you have to find the lies, and then work out why they were told to try and stop you getting to the truth.'

The car pulled up into a relatively newly built estate on the south side of Birmingham. Several rows of three-bedroom houses that looked just big enough to house three rabbits were accompanied by a couple of low-rise blocks of flats. Khan pointed out one of the small blocks and Stone pulled up outside. Both men got out of the car and walked slowly up to the entrance door, pushing the buzzer and waiting just a little too long for a reply.

'Hello?' The voice they got was polite, almost welcoming.

Stone went first. 'We're looking for a Mr Malcolm Glenn.'

A pause before the reply over the intercom. 'Who's calling?'

Stone nodded at Khan, who gave the more formal introduction. 'Hello, sir. This is Detective Constable Khan and Detective Inspector Stone from West Midlands Police. Can we come in please?'

Another short pause.

'I'm on the first floor.' The buzzer sounded and the heavy security door clicked open off its large, remote-controlled magnet.

The foyer was clean and tidy, but not particularly inviting, with its cold, tiled floor and city-council paint job. The cheap metal hand rail made the place look more like an old hospital building than a home to several families. Some tenants had attempted a mild brightening with doormats that Stone thought probably contravened a pointless subsection deeply hidden in a tenancy agreement somewhere.

The two men climbed up to the first floor to be greeted by Malcolm Glenn standing in his doorway, drying his hands with a tea towel, and beaming a very welcoming smile. Stone noted the hand wiping, but didn't know why. The smile was somewhere between the maniacal cover of a psychopathic murderer, and the welcome of a naïve ex-husband and father who genuinely had no idea what he was going to hear.

If he's a parent and we're cops, why isn't he shitting himself?

Glenn moved first. 'Good evening, gentlemen, how can I help you? Would you like to come in?'

Stone nodded at Khan to go in first, which he did after shaking the offered hand. Then Stone politely gestured for Glenn to follow Khan, deliberately not shaking his hand.

Stone had always felt that handshakes belonged to a group of signs-of-respect that he liked to reserve for when he actually respected someone. Or when he wanted to make a judgement about someone.

For the time being, he was reserving both.

The two detectives were shown to the living room of the small flat and offered tea, which Stone accepted and glared at Khan to accept, too. Stone wasn't a big tea drinker, but he used it as a prop with the art of an experienced actor. He knew when to take a sip, when to gulp it down, and when to make it clear he didn't like it if he wanted to deliberately piss someone off.

Malcolm Glenn returned to stand at the door as he waited for the kettle to boil.

'So, how can I help you?' he began. 'Nothing I've done, is it?' He tried to make it a joke – not to lighten the atmosphere or cover up nerves, Stone knew, but rather to test the waters. To have a glance at the cards.

'Perhaps you should sit down, Mr Glenn,' Stone said, as morosely as he could muster up. He very much doubted the man would be shedding too many tears over the woman.

'Why? What's wrong? Is someone hurt? Has someone…' Glenn suddenly looked genuinely worried.

'Do you have a daughter, Sophie?' Stone began.

'Oh God, is she is okay?' The panic sparked in his eyes.

Stone paused and looked at Khan, just to add to the theatre of the moment. 'Sophie is fine, Mr Glenn.'

A pause.

Confusion flashed across Malcolm Glenn's face. His eyes pleaded for more information, as if Stone was being somehow cruel to him.

Show me those cards.

'I'm sorry to have to tell you this, sir, but your ex-wife is dead.'

Ex-wife. Not his daughter's mother.

'Grace?' He gasped, shook his head. 'But…oh, God. When? How?' he asked quickly, before adding, 'And where's Sophie?'

'Sophie is with her grandparents: she's fine.' He had no idea how the girl was. 'Would you like Khan to finish making the tea, allow you a chance to take it in?'

'No, no, it's fine, I'll…'

Stone gave Khan a quick, sharp look, and Khan sprang to action instinctively. 'It's okay, I don't mind,' he said, moving quickly out to the kitchen. He was a fast learner, and he knew that Stone didn't want to give this potential prime suspect any time on his own from this point forward until he was either set free, or locked in a cell.

'Mr Glenn, I am very limited as to what I'm allowed to tell you at this time, but I can tell you that your ex-wife's death is being treated as suspicious.' Stone spoke calmly and formally.

'You mean, she was…' He couldn't finish the sentence; tears ran down his face.

If this is an act, it's a bloody good one.

'I'm sorry,' the man continued. 'I know she was only my ex-wife, but still, she's the mother of my daughter, and, marriage break-up or not, it… well… it's still such a shock.'

'I completely understand, sir. There is no need to apologise.'

The voice was whispering over Stone's shoulder. He wondered how many crocodile tears this man would shed for a woman who he believed was turning his daughter against him?

Khan came in with the tea, giving one to Mr Glenn and one to Stone, before going out again to get his own drink.

Stone took a sip of the tea.

I hate this cheap shit. I hate Harry making this cheap shit even more.

'There are a few standard questions that Khan and I need to ask you, just as a matter of routine. Of course.'

The man nodded. 'Yes, it's fine, no problem. I doubt I can help at all, but…' He trailed off.

Yeah, I know: you want to be as helpful as you can.

Stone took his notepad from the pocket of his long coat. He had no intention of actually taking any notes himself, but it served as a cue for Khan to follow suit as he came back into the room. And it was a prop.

'Can you please tell me your whereabouts last night – that is, Friday night – between the hours of, let's say, six pm and six am,' Stone asked, deliberately making it sound as casual a question as possible.

'Well, I finished work at around five,' he began.

'Work?'

'Yeah. I just do handyman work and cleaning. Odd jobs, you know? Nothing special.'

'Right.' Stone looked straight at the man for a few seconds. 'You like things neat and tidy, then?'

Shrugging his shoulders, Glenn let a nervous laugh slip out. 'Who doesn't?'

'Quite.' Stone looked back down at his notepad, flipping back and forth a page to make it look like he was bringing something up. 'And what about after work?'

'Came back home, and I was in all night.'

'What time would you say you got home, roughly?'

'Oh, five-thirty – no later than that.'

'And you didn't go out at all?'

'No.'

Stone paused again. He waited long enough to see the man go to speak, and then cut him off: 'Can anyone confirm this? A friend, a neighbour, perhaps?'

The man shrugged his shoulders. 'I don't know. I didn't really see anyone around last night. It was just a quiet night in. Sorry, detective, I'll try and think harder, but I can't come up with a rock-solid alibi – I was just… *in.*'

'Don't worry about it,' said Stone, almost laughing it off. He looked at Khan with a *your turn* look, and hoped he was ready to ask.

'What did you do all evening? What did you watch on TV?' Khan asked.

'I'm not a huge TV fan, to be honest,' the man replied, still giving his answer to Stone more than to Khan. 'The news. Some crap nineties action film was on at eleven-thirty. I watched some of that, but went to bed halfway through it. Spent most of the evening on the internet, really.'

The man looked at each detective in turn, knowing he wasn't giving them much to go on.

'Don't worry about it,' said Khan. 'We'll just get our tech guys to check. They're good at that kind of stuff.'

Oh, nice shot, Harry.

Stone stood up and started to move towards the door. 'Would you mind if I quickly used your toilet?'

It seemed strangely timed, and inappropriate. But that was Stone's intention. Awkwardness. The man said it was no problem and gave the usual over-detailed directions that nervous people do.

Stone made his way to the toilet and took a quick glance into the kitchen as he walked past. His memory had always been sharp, almost photographic in the way he could quickly scan a room and then walk away to think about what he had seen.

He got to the bathroom and made sure to lock the door behind him. He made a point of lifting the seat and knocking it on the cistern, just in case someone's ears were well tuned enough to listen in.

It wasn't a large bathroom. The bath took up the whole of the back wall, and the toilet and sink faced each other, separated by little more than the width of the door. Stone mused that he could probably get up from the toilet and throw up in the sink without too much effort. Perfect for a morning after a terrible curry the night before.

I definitely need a sodding holiday.

He took a pen out of his pocket and used it to open the cabinet door for a quick perusal of the contents. Tidy, organised. A bottle of cheap aftershave; a bottle of pricey aftershave; a bottle of paracetamol; a box of ibuprofen. Shaving products – all the standard affair.

All neatly placed with labels facing out.

He turned back round to flush the toilet, and then turned the taps on. He didn't mind leaving his prints on the toilet flush handle and the taps, but not the cupboard door. That's when he noticed there was no towel in the bathroom. He wiped his hands quickly on the back of his trousers, left the bathroom and quickly popped back into the kitchen, where he picked up the tea towel to dry his hands.

Another thought struck him. Stored for later.

He went back to the living room, where the two men looked like they were having an awkward chat, waiting for his return.

'Mr Glenn,' Stone said, 'it would really help our investigation if you could come down to the station to submit your statement formally.'

'Now?' asked Glenn, appearing a little worried.

'Why not?'

'You never know, detective, I might be busy.' He smiled weakly. Inappropriately.

'Doing what, exactly?' Stone pressed the man.

'What about Aaron, Grace's husband?' Glenn asked.

'What about him?'

'What about your daughter, sir?' Khan turned the heat up.

'Well, yes, that's what I mean,' the man faltered. 'I couldn't care less about him, really, but I was wondering why my daughter is with her grandparents, and not him.'

'Or with you, surely?' Stone replied, wanting to see if Glenn would offer the information about the custody battle.

He didn't.

Stone and Khan shared a glance. It was just enough for Khan to show he was out of moves and wordlessly ask if they were taking the man in. Stone gave a slight, almost imperceptible shake of his head.

This conversation was over.

'Be at the station first thing tomorrow,' Stone said, handing the man one of his police-issue business cards from his wallet.

'On a Sunday, detective?' he replied, holding the card carefully by the edges as if he didn't wish to dirty it.

Or get a fingerprint on it.

Stone replied: 'A fully twenty-four-seven service, sir. But do make it first thing.'

The three men exchanged pleasantries: nods of the head, hands all shaking. Stone and Khan turned and made their way down the stairs. Stone listened carefully for Malcolm Glenn's door to click shut before allowing any conversation to begin between the two detectives.

'Harry, why didn't you wash your hands when you made the tea?' Stone asked, as if admonishing a child.

Khan was slightly taken aback, fittingly embarrassed and a little confused as to how exactly Stone had known that. 'Maybe I did. You can't know everything, sir!' He thought he'd try humour to get out of it.

'The tea towel was still dry.' Stone let the silence hang so that the young constable had time to pick up the cue.

The penny dropped. 'But sir, if the tea towel was dry when *you* used it, what was Glenn doing with it when we first arrived?'

'Telling his first lie.'

Harry smiled in appreciation as he opened the passenger door. 'I wonder what his next lie will be.'

'One thing's for sure, Harry: those nicely moisturised hands do not do handyman and cleaning work.'

Stone stood at the driver's door for a moment longer and scanned the area, taking in the sights and sounds. His eyes bounced along the panorama with a sense of familiarity, pausing on the four high-rise flats that stood like grey, shadowy giants against the fading evening light.

'Harry, I've got to run a quick errand before we head back to the station. Do you mind?'

Khan's expression was halfway between that of a whimpering puppy and that of a dutiful constable. His inner dilemma was clear. Stone smiled and threw him a bone.

'Tell you what: I'll drop you off by that chippy back there. I'll only be about ten minutes.'

The young constable's eyes lit up as they pulled away.

* * *

Stone turned the engine off and sat alone in the car for a few moments. A light rain had begun to fall as the sky had darkened and he cursed it as though it was an inevitable metaphor for something he had planned to do on this day off. Something that he'd been secretly happy that his unwelcome call to work had ironically saved him from doing.

He got out of his car and pulled the collar of his leather coat right up and around his neck. The rain never bothered him on his face or head – he wasn't an umbrella man at all – but the back of the neck was especially sensitive.

With a deep sigh, he began his short walk across the road and about fifty yards up the path to the small cemetery. He'd driven past the place a number of times over the year, but had yet to pay a visit. Finally, he'd relented to his own conscience.

A black-painted steel fence of the type usually found outlining playgrounds caged the restful world inside. It was met by a kind of mock-gothic stone façade that held a much heavier gate. The mismatch gave away where the funding had been spent, and Mike Stone thought it was a cynically cheap affair, hardly befitting the ceremony of remembrance that people carried out when visiting such a place.

Other people, but not him.

He entered the grounds and followed a small winding path up a slope that seemed uncharacteristic of the rest of the landscaping in the local area. He pondered whether the raised level had been deliberately added to provide for an additional six foot of soil.

This is where the dead come to rest in their final multi-storey parking space.

He took a small piece of paper from his pocket and followed the directions to the one faux marble headstone he had come to see. As he made his way through the grounds, passing a variety of aged and brand-new memorials, his mind slipped back to the conversation he'd had about depravity. The silence of the place seemed to clash with the detective's knowledge that a number of people left 'resting' there would have met their end in far less peaceful ways.

That's when his eye was caught by a brown envelope taped to the top edge of a headstone about twenty feet away. As he approached the headstone, checking its location against his hand-drawn map, it became increasingly clear that this was far more than a coincidence.

As he got to the headstone, he instinctively took a latex glove from the inside pocket of his coat. He knew that the rain would have ruined any trace evidence on the envelope, but also noted that envelope could not have been there for long. Which meant that whoever put it there could not be far away. He gave a cursory look all around as he gently peeled the envelope from the headstone, making sure to keep the sticky tape.

The envelope was unsealed and contained a single photograph. It was a picture of the same location taken a year before, to the date. A small gathering of people stood around the same spot, heads hanging in a sombre respect that seemed more dutiful than sincere.

He turned the photo over to see a short message: 'Where were you, Mike?'

Even the voice over his shoulder was silenced. There were less than a handful of people who knew Mike Stone well enough to know he'd never attended that funeral.

He stood for a moment, staring at the headstone, and winced at the engraving. Something about the word 'beloved' caused more of a shiver than cold rain on the back of the neck.

But it was another, darker thought that began to snowball in Mike Stone's mind. Even though he had no reason, logic or evidence to support the idea, he couldn't help but wonder about the weight of coincidence hanging over the events of the day, right from the surprise case in the morning up to the discovery of this photograph.

And the knowledge that someone was following him.

He took one more swift look around the cemetery as he put the photograph back in the envelope and began walking back to his car. The pit of his stomach told him that he wasn't alone, but he had no intention of sticking around to find out.

Chapter 9

After a long night with virtually no sleep, Stone had rejected the call to his mobile without even looking at the screen as he drove to work. Normally he'd use his phone through his car's Bluetooth system, but having spent the whole night trying to work out who had left that photo meant it was a weary drive to work that morning.

It wasn't until he pulled up in the car park of the Aston station that he looked at the call he'd rejected and felt his mouth go dry.

The ex. And she'd left a message.

'You selfish bastard!' the voice on Stone's voicemail spat. 'No card? No phone call? Don't even think about giving me the bullshit *'busy'* excuse. Jack is heart-broken, and I have to pick up the pieces. As usual.' The line went dead.

Stone shook his head as he hit it repeatedly with the mobile. He'd always remained good friends, and at least civil, with his ex, mainly for the benefit of their son. But he also knew that although the relationship with Claire had broken down, his feelings for her had never really changed.

He genuinely never wanted to hurt Claire.

And especially not Jack.

With a few swipes of the screen he had Claire's number ready to dial, but a thought stopped him. He was well aware that he had put off calling or visiting his son for his birthday for too many days. He'd intended a dreaded call on his son's birthday the previous weekend, but having missed the day itself, the building feelings of dread and guilt kept getting in the way. Claire was right: it was a bullshit excuse to blame work. He'd allowed it to get in the way.

Still, another thought occurred to him as his mind flicked back to the photograph he'd found yesterday. For a split-second he wondered if there was a connection, but he cursed himself, knowing she was not *that* vindictive.

It was at that moment he saw someone approaching the car quickly, with determination. Mike Stone's whole body seemed to sigh into itself as he saw it was Steve Simpson: Claire's newest partner.

What is this? The bloody cavalry?

Stone got out of his car and readied himself for part two of a bollocking as he stood, like a matador, waiting for the raging bull to attack. He was keen not to let it become too much of a scene.

'Steve…' Mike tried to begin.

'No, Mike,' Steve cut in. 'Don't even bother. I'm just here to tell you how much you have pissed off Claire.'

'I literally just got her message.'

'I'm gonna knock your block off, and I don't care who you are, or where we are.'

'This isn't the time or the place, Steve.'

'Well, when is, Mike? When is?' He continued. 'You've got one hell of a boy, and I just don't understand why you don't give a shit about him.'

Few things piqued Mike Stone's anger, but people using his son against him was high on the list. 'Don't you dare come to me all righteous about my own son.'

'Righteous? You selfish prick!'

Steve Simpson wasn't a particularly small man, but Mike Stone's stature was taking the steam out of his attempts at intimidation. He was clean-shaven and very youthful in looks. Perhaps a bit too youthful for Mike's ego.

And Stone had to give it to the guy: he was really going for it.

'Look, Steve,' Stone continued, 'like I said, this is not –
'

'What you gonna do? Arrest me?'

Stone took a determined step closer to the man. 'Steve: get lost. Now.'

Steve reciprocated the move, squaring right up to Mike. You cheeky little bastard.

'No! Jack is a cracking kid. I love him to bits.'

Passion was one thing, but another bloke saying he loved Mike's son was a step too far. His hand shot up and he planted a finger firmly on Steve's chest. His other hand

95

was clenched into a fist. 'This is *not* the time or the place, Steve. What do you think you are doing? We're not on a daytime TV show.'

'Everything all right, sir?' Khan's voice came from behind.

Thank God! Harry, save me!

Stone didn't turn his stare from Steve. 'Back inside, Harry. I've got this. I'll be up in a minute.'

Khan did as he was told and went back in the front entrance of the station, but stayed close enough to keep Stone in sight.

'You are going to calm the hell down,' Stone said. 'You're being extremely short-sighted, having a go at a cop in front of his own station.'

'You make me sick,' Steve replied. 'I bet you've got some rapist or killer in there, and here you are, preferring to spend time with them than deal with your own son.'

It was all Stone could do not to smile at the irony.

But he still couldn't believe what he was hearing. 'If you want to talk, I'll listen. But not like *this*. And not now.'

'When?'

Persistent little shit, aren't you?

'What makes you think that *you* are the one I should talk to?'

'Because I am the one who has to stand by Claire and Jack. Sooner or later, Mike, if you keep behaving like this, I won't be the one to blame for putting me between you and them. I can be the bridge or the fire: not both.'

Don't punch him. Not here.

Not yet.

'Okay, Steve. Let's talk. You piss off for now, and I'll meet you in town at around lunchtime. Right? I'll even take a lunch break just for *you*.' Steve turned and walked away. He couldn't help reading between the lines of that encounter. A lot had clearly not been said. He was fairly sure Claire would not know about Steve's visit, because there was no way she would have approved. And why was he there so early in the morning?

Stone entered the station, drawing a line under the situation with a single deep breath, and shooting Khan a stern *'don't ask'* look.

* * *

Malcolm Glenn was looking decidedly more nervous than he had the night before. People usually do when sitting in a station interview room being asked to go over their alibi again. Stone watched carefully as Khan revisited many of the same questions. It wasn't necessarily to catch the man out – not totally, at least – but more to check his confidence in the answers. And to do it outside Malcolm Glenn's own safety net.

'What was your relationship with Mrs Peters like?' Stone asked.

'What do you mean?' Glenn replied carefully.

'Well, you have a daughter together, but she lives with your ex. Is it joint custody, or…?'

'Oh, I see where you're going with this,' the man continued. 'We are going through a bad patch at the moment.'

'I'd hardly call court action and a full-blown custody battle a *bad patch*, would you?' Stone waited for the reaction.

'Okay, look, there are major problems between us.'

'Which you didn't feel were relevant to mention before?' Khan didn't have to feign his surprise.

'In all honesty, you'd just told me she was dead. I don't know about you, but I am not the kind of person who likes to speak ill of the dead.'

Stone decided to complicate the issue to really test a man who was quickly starting to sound like a suspect. 'So, what have you got against China House?'

'Sorry?' Glenn looked puzzled. So did Khan.

'China House. The delivery takeaway you had last night, which you failed to mention when we asked you – twice – if there was anyone who could confirm your whereabouts.'

'Of course, China House. Yes, I had a takeaway.' Glenn sounded almost relieved. 'I'm sorry, that slipped my mind.'

'Delivered, or picked up?' Khan asked.

'Delivered, at about… eleven-thirty. Ish.'

'So if we go and speak to the takeaway, they will be able to confirm that?' Stone asked.

'Yeah, of course. But I ordered over the internet – one of those takeaway sites.'

Stone saw an opportunity. 'That's okay. We can check that when we seize your computer.' It worked.

'Whoa, hold on a second – why do you need to seize my computer?'

'I'm sorry,' Stone said, again. 'I meant *if* we *need* to seize your computer.'

'Am I under arrest or something?'

Stone sat at the table and leaned forward to Glenn, lowering his voice. 'I'll be straight with you. This is a murder enquiry and we need to make sure we have all the information we can get, especially regarding those closely connected with the victim. Your alibi is a little bit wishy-washy in places.'

'Well, I'm sorry I can't be more specific.'

'And we do like to be thorough – almost as much as our boss likes us to be thorough,' Stone continued. 'And let's face it, you do have one hell of a motive to...'

Stone left the pause to hang. He didn't want to directly accuse Glenn just yet, but he did want to rattle him.

'Now, come on, detective! That's a bit of a leap, isn't it?' Glenn's objection was stern, but without anger.

'We can leave no stone unturned in this kind of investigation,' Stone replied. 'I'm sure you understand.'

'Fine, but still...'

'A bit like I understand why you wouldn't have told us about the organisation you are a member of.'

'What organisation?' Glenn stopped and thought. 'Oh, FAPAS? For God's sake, detective, we're a bunch of fathers wrongly prevented from seeing our children. We're not murderers!'

Stone stood up and slowly circled round behind Malcolm Glenn, leaving Khan at the table to watch.

'How are we supposed to know how far you'd go?' Stone almost whispered into the man's ear.

'Killing people?' He was incredulous in his disbelief.

Stone pushed on. 'How far would you go to see your daughter if everything was stacked against you, Malcolm?'

'If I kill someone, I get locked up. How would that work?'

'You tell me. I mean, what do you people talk about? What do you plan? How do you fight, if not by using some kind of force?'

'We lobby. We use legal expertise. We have solicitors – and I am beginning to wonder if I should call mine right now.'

'You're not under arrest, Malcolm. You can leave any time you like.' Stone gave Khan a look as if to tell him to join in. 'Or are you worried about how that would look?'

Khan had a thought and dared to try a new tone. 'After all, if she's cut your balls off, who's to say you wouldn't want to go as far as you could in order to reattach them?' He threw Stone a glance in search of some kind of recognition that his move was the right one to make.

Stone didn't meet his eyes.

'Is this how you treated Aaron, as well?' Glenn asked.

Stone replied: 'You want to know if we got anything out of him?'

'No, I want to bloody well know if my daughter is living with a psychopathic murderer!'

Stone sat down next to the man. 'Who said anything about a psychopath, Malcolm?' He paused, eyes fixed on the man. 'What makes you say the death of your ex-wife was the result of an attack by a psychopath?'

'I want to know if my daughter is in any danger. I mean, are you holding him?' Glenn's forehead was beginning to develop a tacky, damp look; his skin was flushing; his eyes were darting.

'What do you think he did, Malcolm?' Khan asked. 'Come on, we're just talking here. You aren't under arrest. Be honest with us: what do you think he's done?'

'I don't know what he has done. But I know what he has failed to do. And that is protect my wife… ex-wife. And if he couldn't protect her, then what makes *you* think he can protect my daughter?'

* * *

'Sorry, sir,' Khan said as they stood outside the interview room. 'I'm not sure I was much help in there.'

'You did well.' Stone was being sincere with him, too. 'But there is one thing. At his flat. You led him on the TV alibi. It's too easy to cover up, and it's best to use it to trip him up when he's under a little more pressure and likely to make a mistake. Don't do that again.' Firm but fair.

Khan nodded. Point taken. 'So, what now?'

'Get his prints and DNA, then let him go.'

'But, sir…'

'Harry, listen. If we move too quickly and arrest too early, without enough solid evidence, what are we going to do when we need to charge him or release? No. I want more before we move formally and give him the chance to lawyer up. Something isn't sitting right with all this and I don't want to go screwing it up too early.'

Stone rubbed the scar on his neck. He knew his head was not on the job, not focused, and he didn't like the feeling that he was floundering. He also knew that he had nothing solid to give an already pissed-off chief superintendent.

DC Khan waited for a few moments, and then hazarded his suggestions. 'I think we need to know a lot more about FAPAS: who they are, how it works, how they keep in contact.' He watched as Stone gently nodded. 'I'll also check out the takeaway alibi with the food order, find out what time it was delivered. I think we should also leave a message with his daughter's school and be in there first thing tomorrow morning, find out how home communication goes, if there's anything they think we should know. Anything else?'

'Get on to that after you've sent him on his way.' He started to walk towards the stairs as if he was following the Green Mile to Carter's office. 'Harry, I want a reason to search Glenn's flat. Find me one.'

* * *

'What the bloody hell did you think you were doing, letting him go?' Chief Superintendent Carter almost choked on her coffee.

'Ma'am – we are following up new leads,' said Stone, without conviction. 'And we currently don't have the evidence to arrest him and charge him.'

Stone and Carter sat at the glass meeting table in her office. He noticed that it had been cleaned, polished, buffed and shined to a level that could even be considered procrastination for a cleaner. He hadn't intended to sit down, but Carter had been insistent, perhaps out of expectation of receiving a file-full of custody requests or new documents, timesheets, overtime requests – *anything* that made it seem like some fast progress was being made in the first crucial hours of a murder case.

Carter stared at Stone with steel in her eyes. She was a large woman, but not overweight. Something about her strong build, neck-length dark hair, and slightly oversized eyebrows had flickers of masculinity. But there was at least one of her features that classified her as female without any doubt. Nevertheless, she was a strong woman with a justified reputation. She quite famously put a stop to the usual mutterings about how women in power used their sexuality to get to the top when she overheard an arrogant DC make a joke about it. He and the rest of an incident room had been told: '*I didn't get fucked to get promotion, but I certainly fucked a lot of men like you to get here. And when your arsehole recovers enough that you can start speaking out of it again, I'll be ready to hear your apology.*'

It had been hard not to break into applause at what Stone had felt was a much better way of dealing with the DC's comment than the usual feminist rant and disciplinary action.

Carter was, in his view, exactly the kind of straight-talking copper – woman or not – he'd love to work alongside… and go for a drink with. But that was a different thin blue line that remained as un-blurred as possible.

For now, she was just his boss giving him yet another bollocking.

'Do you even have a clue who the prime suspects are?' Carter asked, not hiding her frustration at all.

'Malcolm Glenn is not off the radar, ma'am,' Stone said, trying to reassure her. 'We still have potential leads to chase up, questions to ask, and forensics to review.'

'So, what the hell are you doing on your arse in my office?'

Getting it firmly kicked.

Chapter 10

The driver of the black cab gave Mike Stone a very funny look when he said he only wanted to go as far as the law courts – barely far enough to break past the minimum charge. Stone told the driver his meeting was connected with a *really* big case… could even be the case-breaker. He knew it slightly excited the driver to think of the prospect of helping the police in such a substantial way. The driver waived the small charge, probably thinking the favour would come good someday. A full media interview and commendation or medal of bravery from Scotland Yard. Stone made a point of thanking the driver on behalf of the police commissioner.

I might as well knight this guy.

Stone met Steve Simpson in the pub on Newton Street, right in the centre of the legal zone of the city. It was close-knit set of gothic-looking buildings that housed the various courts of the city. The pub wasn't a place that ever saw serious trouble, and everyone figured that had something to do with its proximity to the courts.

Stone took off his ID card and put it in his coat pocket before walking inside. The gesture was more to remind himself that he was now off duty for this conversation. This was something Mike Stone, and not DI Stone had to deal with.

Steve Simpson was sitting at a small table just inside the door and it was pretty clear he'd already managed to get through a few pints before Stone's arrival. Besides the empties, he looked like shit.

'Want a pint?' Steve said, lifting up his glass as if to needlessly show what he was referring to. Drunk people often do that: over-explain, over-demonstrate, and over-exaggerate.

Guilty men do that, too. What've you done?

'Just a lemonade,' Mike said, taking his coat off. 'But I'll get the round in.' It was less of a gesture of kindness than an act of self-preservation. He wanted to make sure he only got lemonade, and drunk people weren't known for buying soft drinks.

The pub was L-shaped, with the dark-wood bar running most of its length. Around the corner to the right was a small area with a dartboard and a couple of stools that were clearly the reserve of regulars. Pew-like benches lined the wall opposite the bar, covered with a deep-red cushion that was long overdue a refurbishment. A smattering of small, round, cast-iron tables were arranged well enough to spread the punters around the old parquet floor.

Mike paid for the drinks and gave the land lord a polite nod of recognition. They didn't actually know each other. He turned and made his way back to the table just in time for Steve to put down his empty pint glass. Steve took the pint of lager off Mike, gulping a mouthful before putting it down.

Nothing was said for a couple of awkward minutes.

The rumble of the lunch trade was made up of a strange mixture of well-dressed solicitors and football-top-wearing bellies with matching heads. It was noisy enough that their conversation could be private.

Mike was unnerved by having to sit on a chair that put his back to the bar and most of the room. He much preferred to sit with his back to the wall and have everyone in clear view. But this meeting wouldn't be very long.

'So?' Mike began. 'You want to tell me what is really going on? And none of that shit about how to be a father-figure.'

'I don't get that woman,' Steve began. 'The harder I try, the more difficult she gets. I'm not here for her sake... or mine... but for Jack's.'

'I know exactly what Claire is like. You know that.'

'Honestly, why did you two split?'

'I was a shit husband and I'm a mediocre dad.'

Steve dared to ask: 'And the accident? That did something, didn't it?'

'That is none of your business.'

'Fine. But now, it's like... one minute she wants me more involved; the next minute she's all cold. She was the one who pushed me to move in, you know? Not that I didn't want to, but it was her – it's always her taking the lead. In everything.'

Mike knew all too well how that felt, and what she was like. That still didn't mean he wanted to sit and give relationship advice to the man who was now sharing the same bed that he used to sleep in. He wouldn't admit that he was jealous, and maybe he wasn't, but he certainly missed having that special someone to wake up to every morning. Their faults and all included. He knew relationships took a lot of work, and since his efforts had gone more into his job than his marriage, he could hardly blame *her* for that.

'It's like she doesn't want me around, half the time,' Steve continued.

'I don't know what you want me to say,' Mike began. 'You really want relationship advice from me? Well, here's some. Eat some lunch. Drink some coffee. Buy some mints to suck on. Sober up, and go home with flowers.'

'What? That's it? Where are the promises to see more of your son? When are you going to man up? You walk around all high and mighty in your job, *Detective Inspector Stone*,' Steve said, with a new level of venom, and a little too much volume. 'But when it comes to the basics of just seeing your son, you can't solve that mystery, can you?' The alcohol was clearly centre-stage.

Mike was determined not to rise to the jibes of a drunken man.

Steve continued, his volume slowly rising. 'And now, because *you* can't be bothered, I get it in the neck day in, day out. I don't work enough. I don't do enough for the family. She resents *me* because I can't bring in as much money as you did – even though I am around more than you ever were. How else have I been able to get so close to Jack to know how upset he is about you missing his birthday again?'

Mike was finding it harder to hold his tongue. 'I did not miss Jack's birthday.'

'You didn't even send a card, Mike.'

'Whatever.'

There was an awkward pause. Mike couldn't understand the missing card – probably the shocking postal service.

'Has she told you we're trying for a baby?' Steve said.

What the…

The spark lit. Mike stood up and virtually picked Steve Simpson up off his feet by his collar. He dragged him out the front door of the pub and slammed him into the stone wall outside. A few onlookers moved out of the way and scurried past. Others from across the street stopped to watch momentarily, before shrugging it off as simply not action-packed enough.

'Get your fucking hands off me!' Steve squirmed and spluttered.

Mike knew well enough to put the man down quickly before too many smart phones started recording the scene to post it on social media. But he could still feel the rage, and it took all his restraint not to begin knocking a few new shapes into this pathetic man's face.

'If you can't hack it being around Claire, then you get out. Don't start with the parting cheap shots like *we're trying for a kid of our own*. If I even think you're going to drive a wedge between me and my son…' It took another breath to maintain some control. Mike moved closer so that they were nose to nose. He seemed to tower over Steve. 'Don't you *ever* use my son's name against me again.'

Steve began to laugh. 'I don't think you need any help driving that wedge in, Mike.'

'Go home.' Mike walked back into the pub to collect his coat and caught the eye of the landlord. 'I think he's had one too many, sir. Best not to let him stay and cause your fine establishment any disruption, right?' A smile and nod was all that was needed in return.

Mike stepped outside the pub again and stopped for a moment to look at the pitiful man, doubled over and looking seriously the worse for wear. Mike didn't believe in kicking people when they were down.

Every rule has its exceptions.

* * *

It was when Stone got back to the station and tried to get in the front door that he noticed his ID card had gone from his coat pocket. He gave the duty officer at the front desk a wave and was promptly let in.

'Leave it on your desk again, sir?' said the officer.

Stone just smiled, rolled his eyes in self-deprecation, and waited to be buzzed in through the internal door. He stopped off in the toilet to make a quick call on his mobile to the landlord to ask if his ID had been handed in.

No luck.

When he finally got back to his desk, after having had to wait at a number of ID-scanning doors and deliver the same expression to each, Stone threw his coat over his chair and sat down heavily. The last thing he needed was this personal hassle just as a new murder case had kicked off.

There was a knock at the door. He was relieved that it didn't sound senior.

'All right, sir?' said Bolton as she came in with a rather excitable DC Khan closely following.

Here's the owner and puppy.

'How was Carter?'

He let out a sigh. He gave her a look.

'Well, don't leave it too long,' Bolton replied, wagging a finger and grinning with anticipation.

Stone mouthed something at her.

Fuck off.

'Now, Harry, what have you got? Please, tell me something.'

'Just a quick update, sir.'

Stone now had a small briefing session on his hands, so he shrugged off the last hour and refocused himself on the task in hand.

'Go on then, Harry,' Stone said.

Khan put a few pieces of paper on Stone's desk. 'I've got the name of Glenn's custody solicitor, and even had the chance to speak to her briefly.' He waited for the '*go on*' look. 'Typical client-privilege brick walls went up, but I did manage to get out of her that she doesn't have much face-to-face contact with him. She wouldn't comment on him, even generally, but she did tell me a little about Parent Alienation Syndrome – PAS. Although it is increasingly acknowledged as a factor that affects children,

111

it is not legally or medically recognised as a syndrome or condition in court, yet.'

'Parental Alienation Syndrome?' asked Bolton.

Khan explained: 'When a child is effectively brainwashed by one parent into hating or despising the other parent. This is used significantly more often as a weapon against men than against women. It is also linked to the issue of false allegations of abuse: either the mother or the children, sometimes both, are the allege they are victims, and it pretty much ends the custody debate.'

Stone and Bolton looked at each other. They weren't ignorant of what Khan was telling them, but they could see in each other's eyes that, for all they knew, this case could take a darker turn at any moment.

Khan continued. 'In fact, it's worth noting that in child abuse cases, especially ones where the allegation is false, it is more common that the allegation is made or substantiated by an adult.'

'But is that Parental Alienation how Glenn's daughter feels about him?' Bolton asked.

'And *that* is the next question,' Stone said. 'Sands, I want you to take DC King with you to see the daughter. Remember, she is not a witness and clearly not any kind of suspect. Tread very, very carefully. But I want you to find out as much as you can about her relationship with her dad and stepdad. And before you ask: yes, I am deliberately sending two women. Harry, you're coming with me.'

'Where are we going, sir?' he asked, almost giving away a little excitement that led Stone to cast a quick smile at Bolton.

'Back to the scene, Harry. I want you to see it, and I need to walk it again. Bolton has already been there, so I want a fresh pair of eyes.'

'What are we doing about Malcolm Glenn in the meantime?' Khan asked.

'Leave him to stew on it this evening. Has anyone got anything from DS Barry? DNA at the scene? Prints?'

That was Bolton's cue. 'Forensics have no samples of DNA or prints that are out of place. They still have samples to go through. But I'm wondering something.'

'Go on.'

'How did he get that far through the house and leave absolutely no prints?'

'He wore gloves, surely?' replied Khan.

'What I mean,' she continued, 'is footprints. Not even a useless partial was taken. He walked on two different types of carpet, laminate wood floor, and tiles in the kitchen, and not a single print. We didn't even find any prints outside. Barely a few indentations, but no tread-marks.'

Stone rubbed the scar on his throat and slid a little further down in his chair. It was yet another thing to bother him about this case. Most premeditative criminals think they know forensics thanks to TV programmes like CSI, but for one to leave no evidence at all – even a trace too small to sample accurately – is incredibly rare.

'Is there a way someone can disguise their prints, or cover them up?' Stone asked.

'We have to wear the shoe covers on scene, don't we?' asked Khan, not sure if he was missing the point to an obvious answer.

'What I mean, Harry,' Stone replied, with a touch of frustration, 'is not just picking up or dropping trace samples, but even the outside shape of a foot.' Khan instinctively looked at his feet, wondering how he might do that.

'Something else,' Bolton added. 'The glass in the victim's uterus came back from Forensics.' A sudden thickness filled the air and it felt like the office temperature had dropped ten degrees in an instant. 'It was made up of a clear glass and a dark green tinted glass. Judging by some fragments that were extracted, it looks like it came from a champagne bottle and two glasses.'

She paused, just for a moment: partly to allow the others to collect their thoughts about the evidence; partly to allow a moment of reflection on the brutality.

Bolton continued. 'And from the toxicology reports, and the stomach contents analysis that Reg sent through, it looks highly likely that she consumed most of the bottle of champagne.' She stopped for a moment to get out a small plastic bag, which contain a flattened label stained with blood. 'This label was found inserted whole into the victim rather than being left on the bottle that was inserted… and then smashed from the outside.'

Stone took the label, but kept his eyes on Bolton's. There was a knowing moment between them – a thought shared. She nodded before he looked down at the label.

Moët.

'Now, you know how much I hate coincidences, Sands.'

The voice was murmuring over his shoulder. The bottle stolen in a case Stone was strangely seconded to;

the same type of bottle appearing in a case he shouldn't even be working on; all within the same weekend of such significance for Stone, and that someone else seems to know too much about.

I hate coincidences.

'But why leave the label whole?' Khan asked, missing the subtext of the conversation.

That voice called over Stone's shoulder again.

'He's saying she's worthy. But she was more *worthy* in the death he gave her than she was in her life she had lived.' Images flashed in Stone's mind. The cork; pouring; the chink of glasses; smiling mouths drinking; eyes looking at him.

'A *celebration* of her death?' Khan asked, taking his glasses off to dry the bridge of his nose.

'That's one sick and very personal attack,' Bolton added.

There was a silence in the office as they all pondered the terrifyingly obvious fact they could only wish was not true.

The killer had done this before, or was planning to do it again.

Or both.

Stone didn't know whether what they had so far was telling him more about the victim or killer.

Chapter 11

The Boy

The boy gasped for breath as his face broke through the surface of the water. Freezing, dark, thick water, filling his mouth, his throat and his eyes. Feeling the pull as it tried to drag him under, the boy waved his arms in panic, desperately trying to tread water as he'd learnt at school.

And that was the problem. He'd been taught to swim at school the usual way, starting with shallow water and various floating aids, all in a brightly lit, warm, clear pool. No danger with adults and lifeguards all around. He'd learnt to kick by holding the side; he'd learnt to pull himself along with his arms; and after a while he'd learnt to get his arms and legs to work together. And all the time he'd been surrounded by happy, smiling faces, knowing there was always someone there to reach out for if he needed them.

But he'd never learnt how to deal with panic. How do you cope with the lonely terror, the debilitating cold, and the shattering realisation that no one is coming to help you?

Finally, the boy's toes felt the ground beneath the water, covered unevenly with various rubble. He pushed with his toes, and pushed again, bouncing his face above the water level as he flapped his arms to try to move towards the side of the canal. With his arms and legs burning, his chest tightening, he finally reached the edge.

Desperately gripping the side-wall of the canal, slipping and scraping with his fingertips, he went for what he was sure would be his final push. He managed to bounce up high enough to get his hands onto the surface. Hands, then arms, then one shoulder, one leg, and a swing of the rest of his small, but sodden body. He rolled onto the path, coughing and spluttering acrid, oily water.

A heave lurched from deep within his stomach and his whole body tried to empty itself violently. The boy had never vomited with such brutal force before. Choking and coughing, he felt his throat burn with a mixture of brown, bitter water and bile.

After several bouts of heaving and choking without any vomit, the boy collapsed to the ground and his body began to curl and contort like a thinly cut piece of meat thrown into raging hot oil. He closed his eyes tightly and gave in to the temptation to just lie there.

There was only one thing that could pluck him from this moment of stupor.

Fear.

The sound of the baying enemy crowd perked up his instinct to flee once more, just enough to open his eyes and in darkness find his way. It took him a few moments to realise what he could see. It was indeed a place to hide.

The boy summoned up every scrap of energy he had left. Dragging himself on hands and knees across the crunch of the gravel, he crawled as if through the thickest of tar until he was hidden under the dark ironwork steps that led down from the other side of the canal. Totally disoriented, he lay down once more, wheezing and heaving each breath, curling into the foetal position. The gravel cut into his cheek as he rested his head on the path.

A rumble came from deep inside. His stomach tightened; his chest constricted; and a building sensation crept all the way up the back of his throat. Finally, his mouth was forced open, and out poured the wrenching, sob of a child who realised he might well have got away from his pursuers…

…but he had not escaped his nightmare.

Chapter 12

Stone was determined that his return to the crime scene without the hustle and bustle would give him a chance to look again through different eyes. He wanted to know the story behind the killing.

'Are we coming here with the view that Malcolm Glenn is the key suspect or not?' Khan asked.

'Forget him for now, Harry,' Stone replied. 'I want you to get a *feel* for the scene rather than just *look* at it.'

They got out of the car and waited on the path at the front of the house. Stone took a full turn and looked around the area again. 'What can you see? What can you hear, Harry?'

'Just a normal street, sir. Residential area – family houses. The M6 is close, the traffic is quite heavy. I guess you get used to it if you live here, though. Is that a train?'

'Yes. Closest station is Gravely Hill, and Erdington's not far from here. Let's go inside.' Stone nodded at the officer on duty, glad that it was one he knew so the debacle over his ID card could be left alone for now. Khan didn't dispense with the formality, however, and took great pains to show his ID a little too clearly, much to the amusement of the officers.

Stone took Khan into the house and headed straight down the hallway to the kitchen and back door. They went out into the garden and began at the section in the fence where the killer had climbed over.

'Freshly moved dirt, sir,' Khan said. 'He not only covered his footprint, he also made no attempt to hide this as his entry point.'

'So, he wanted to hide his identity, but not his action or route.' It wasn't clear to Khan whether Stone had said that to him, or was just thinking just out loud. But he noted it down anyway.

The two men then walked up to the back door and looked closely at the method of entry. Khan had a theory. 'Masking tape. Forensics said they found a light adhesive on several fragments of the broken glass. I bet he covered it, or at least crossed it in masking tape before he broke it. Significantly cuts down the noise.'

Stone nodded. 'Then took the time to take the tape away with him.'

They walked into the kitchen and Stone led him to the table. All the cutlery, plates, bottles and glasses had been taken by Forensics, but none of them had revealed anything surprising or out of place so far.

'Why was the table moved, sir?' Khan asked.

Stone was caught out. 'What do you mean?'

Khan took out a small torch and highlighted indentations on the floor that showed the kitchen table – a small, rectangular piece – had been moved. 'Judging by the semi-soft tiles in here, I'd say that move was very recently, as these marks are likely to fade pretty soon.'

My God, this kid is sharp.

'But why, Harry?' he asked.

'Sir, it's like you've said. He wants us to see this. Like the chair here is perfectly centred.'

Stone nodded. 'Let's take a look down the corridor. I think he took his time. Look at these pictures of the family – what do you notice?'

'Where are the pictures of the girl when she was very young?' Khan asked.

'Seems like someone was being cut out of the history of the family. Understandable in a way. If you divorce someone, you don't want their face on the wall, do you?'

'No, sir, but surely you'd still make sure there were pictures of the girl growing up. There's more of the wife and new husband.' Stone nodded in agreement, but Khan hadn't quite finished. 'They're all perfectly straight.' Khan shone his torch up and down the wall to illustrate his point. 'Your initial notes on the house said that it was clean and generally tidy, but clearly lived in, which I agree with. But if you look at all these pictures... they are all *perfectly* straight. All the ones in arm's reach, anyway.'

The two men got to the bottom of the stairs and looked up. A sense of dread filled the air. Stone couldn't quite put his finger on it, but somehow this murder had shaken him more than others. Perhaps it was the conversation earlier and the mention of a serial killer. There wasn't any evidence to suggest that, and he was dearly hoping that they wouldn't find any.

* * *

When they reached the bedroom, they both stood at the foot of the bed. The most obvious thing was still the lack of blood. As they had already discovered from the post-mortem, the victim's blood had been drained. They both looked around the room, knowing that the SOCO team had already scoured it with the finest-tooth comb.

But Stone had always believed that science still could not replace human intuition, and even though physical evidence was paramount in his job, only that keen eye, that human eye, could see when something was wrong.

'Look for the questions, not the answers,' Stone said to himself, just loud enough for Khan to hear.

'What do you mean, sir?'

'I mean we need to look for what is wrong. What's out of place. What doesn't fit the picture.'

'Funny you should say that,' Harry replied. 'I mean, about fitting the picture.' He indicated for Stone to turn around. 'See that?' he said, pointing at the carpet at the foot of a chest of drawers that stood against the wall, directly opposite the bed.

The chest of drawers was just over stomach height. It was a classic old wooden piece, with framed photos on top and a mirror hanging on the wall right above it. The mirror had an ornate frame – a little too dressy for the plain décor of the room, Stone thought.

Mirror, mirror, on the wall.

'This has been moved about two or three centimetres, sir. And it looks like it was moved to put it *exactly* central with the bed.' Stone listened intently to the detective. 'And if you look back here, behind these photos – can you see that?'

'Dust lines. These photos have been rearranged and a void has been left in the middle. Why?'

Khan shook his head slowly. Stone rubbed the scar on his throat as he slowly moved around the room. After a few moments of stillness, he suddenly got on to the bed and began positioning himself. 'This is how the body was left, Harry.'

The young detective was utterly shocked by Stone's boldness, and somewhat uncomfortable with the overtly sexual position his senior officer was now lying in.

'Stand in that void, Harry. In the centre at the bottom of the bed.'

Khan did as he was told.

Stone continued: 'Now crouch down until your head is level with the top of that chest of drawers, and look my way. Look direct at me, between my…well, you know. And look at me. Now what do you see?'

Khan didn't want to say '*your crotch*', but…

'No, look at my face, Harry.'

'I see… you, sir. Posed. Framed. As if…'

'My photo was being taken?' Stone asked.

Khan stood and turned to look at the chest of drawers. 'A camera, sir. He put a camera there, in that void. Probably on a table-top tripod. He was taking her picture.'

Stone was energised by the discovery. 'But why, Harry? *Why?*

A long silence held between the two men as they pondered the thought. But Stone knew exactly what he was facing. He didn't share his thought with the younger detective, as he wanted to mull it over some more, discuss it with Bolton, and weigh up the risks of giving his theory to Carter.

The killer wanted to show them what he'd done, and wanted to keep a picture of it, too. A trophy.

Only one type of killer kept a trophy of a victim.

But they only had one victim.

So far.

Chapter 13

As Stone dropped Khan back at the station that evening, he thought about going in and working a few more hours. Besides, he'd spent his whole 'weekend off' working, anyway.

Who am I kidding? There's bugger all else for me to do.

Instead, he decided that cooking was not on the agenda and he was long overdue the spoils of a takeaway. Which meant he hadn't had one for at least two or three days. He put his usual order of chicken in black bean sauce with boiled rice into his favourite takeaway from his usual place via the mobile app, and timed it for an hour delivery. This gave him plenty of time to get home, but with no need to rush.

It didn't take him long to drive across the city, park in the private car park and take the lift up to his fourth-floor apartment. He entered the open-plan main living room of the apartment, throwing his coat over the back of the black leather sofa, dropping files on the table by the window that overlooked the canal and hanging his suit jacket over the back of a dining chair.

The kitchen area was a modestly sized but generously fitted modern set-up with everything built in and hidden away. That included the fridge, which he opened, only to swear loudly at the lack of lager or wine ready-chilled. He navigated his way round his own culinary debris – which was getting close to three days old and threatening to be the home of new cultures – and found the last remaining bottle of white wine. He put it in the freezer: a trick he had learnt from a fleeting relationship with a girl who wouldn't touch a drink unless it was thoroughly chilled.

Forgivingly, there was one last clean wine glass in the cupboard, and an un-matching knife and fork from the 'clean' drainer, which he took over to the glass coffee table in the middle of the room. With the TV on, set to the news channel, he kicked off his shoes and finished his pre-takeaway preparation by sourcing the cleanest plate he could find. He found one that had only hosted some toast the night before and therefore required just a quick wipe with some kitchen towel.

Mike Stone wasn't typically messy, but without anyone else to worry about, even he would admit he let things slip.

Occasionally.

All through this automatic ritual, his brain was ticking over every detail of the murder scene he'd returned to Khan earlier that evening. Khan had made some salient and intuitive observations. There was no hard evidence at that stage to suggest anything as serious or rare as a serial killer, and no unsolved murder in the city was tapping at his memory. Which meant only one possibility.

This isn't over.

As far as Stone was concerned, the murders he normally investigated showed a very common pattern. They were almost always domestic or, as he liked to call it, 'outdoor domestic' – which meant between allies or rival gangs. The personal link between killer and victim was by far the most common factor in murders, and, despite what TV and films like to portray, a cold or non-existent relationship between the dead and their killer was actually very rare.

Deaths resulting from assaults and robberies were usually unintentional. Even in the bizarre pseudo-logic that many criminals applied to their 'work', most of them knew that a murder was significantly more likely to be resolved by the police because, if truth be told, more time and resources were put into those kinds of cases. In big cities like Birmingham, although there were many assaults and minor crimes to be dealt with by Local Policing Units, murders were not that common. Most years would see as few as fifty or sixty. Serial killers were extremely rare.

Stone did not want the current year to be the exception.

But this case bothered him. The set-up was too detailed. And he couldn't help but wonder if the injuries to the woman were more about childbirth than they were about sexual desire, depravity or degradation. Add into the mix the fact that the victim was embroiled in a custody battle, and it all pointed more towards a psychopathic attack than a personal outburst of rage from a loved one – or previously loved one.

The detective's rallying mind was interrupted by the buzzer. The takeaway had arrived.

Stone let the delivery man in and got some loose change from his pocket. His regular takeaway knew his address, did good food, and always had excellent service. He wasn't sure if this had any connection to the tip of a couple of pounds he gave each time – despite having paid online – or whether it was just a good takeaway. Either way, for the matter of a couple of pounds that the delivery guy got if he simply smiled, Stone thought it was an informal relationship worth keeping.

The door knocked. Stone opened it. The man smiled. He got tipped. Simple.

Stone wondered what it must be like to work in a job where someone gave you a little more money as a pat on the back for a job well done. He couldn't quite imagine any of the victims helped by his successful work tipping him.

Especially not the dead ones.

After grabbing the wine from the freezer and sitting down, Stone managed to switch his working brain off for a little time at least, eating at the coffee table in front of the TV, as usual.

His mobile phone buzzed and beeped a text message, which he decided to ignore for the time being, figuring that if it was anything or anyone important, they would…

It buzzed in another text.

Don't you dare fucking ring.

Stone had always steadfastly refused to engage in 'serious' discussions via text or the dreaded social media, mainly because his own dry wit seldom communicated well in short bursts of text. He sat back with a glass of wine and began a mindless channel hop to find something to eat away the hours he knew he would be awake.

Another text.

Someone was really trying to get in contact. He reluctantly sat up to check the text and as soon as he read them, he regretted doing so.

'hav u seen steve 2day?' the first text said. It was Claire.

Mike Stone hated text shorthand. But he knew that Claire hated predictive text even more and seemed to be stuck somewhere back in the early 2000s.

'i cant get hold of him. can i call u?' The second text seemed a little more odd. Claire never asked if she could call. On the rare occasions that they did talk she told him to call her when he 'could be bothered', or she just called.

'please'

Stone finished off the glass of wine in one go, grabbed his shoes and coat, and made his way out for a walk on the canal-side. He needed a walk anyway, and decided that if he was outside it would definitely stop him from shouting down the phone, which he figured was a distinct possibility, given the nature of his conversation with Steve earlier that day. He also assumed that Steve had relayed to her some horrifying version of their altercation and she wanted to put her tuppence in.

Cool air; cool head; cool tongue.

Stone also still needed to unwind, and walking always helped him to do that.

He made his way down to the canal and sent a reply telling Claire to call him. He planned his moves in the conversation like he would craft an interview with a suspect. He decided he'd begin with showing concern and reassurance, and listen carefully. Then he'd say how impressed he was with Steve's passion and feeling to protect Jack, and that he was humbled. Most importantly, he'd keep back the card about trying for a baby unless he needed it. He would wait to see…

… and then his phone rang. He answered.

'It's me,' she began.

'Is everything okay?' he replied, tentatively.

'Be honest with me. Did you see Steve earlier?'

'We went for a drink.'

Mike could see the puzzled expression on Claire's face.

'What time was that?' There was a quiver in her voice.

'Lunch. Claire – what's wrong?'

'He's not answering his phone or replying to texts. What did you two talk about? What did you say to him?'

'To be honest, we were talking about Jack. Steve was really pissed with me about not…well, let's just say he had his opinions.'

'He's around. He supports us. He supports *me*. And Jack has really taken to him, so…'

'Claire, I know. To be fair, he said his piece and I agree with him. And I agree with you, he does really care about Jack.' He paused. 'And you.'

A pregnant pause filled the airwaves between the two of them and it seemed like both of them were avoiding raising an unspoken topic.

'Did he mention anything else?' Claire finally asked.

Like a petulant child, Stone held back. 'Such as?'

'Don't do that with me, Mike. I bet it works with all the scumbags you interview, but I'm not one of them, okay?'

'He said you two were trying for a baby.'

'And how do you...*feel* about that?'

She didn't say it with any level of bitchiness. But it still came with a slap, and a shiver went down his spine. 'Well?' she pressed.

'You said he hasn't called.'

'We had an argument and I haven't heard from him since. You're now the last person I know who spoke to him.'

Now who's beginning to sound like a detective?

But he was also beginning to see her point about Steve's apparent disappearing act.

'He's probably gone on a mini-bender; the battery in his mobile died, and he'll stumble in really late. You know what blokes are like.'

'You think so?'

He had no idea. 'Yes! I do.' In truth, Mike was beginning to hope Steve had got himself picked up for being totally off his face.

They carried on talking for a short while longer, and much to Stone's surprise they even managed to talk about their son without shouting and point-scoring. Without setting any firm dates or times, which had so often caused problems before, they did at least commit to do something about his current poor efforts with Jack.

'Are you outside?' Claire asked.

'Yeah, I'm just having a stroll down the canal.'

'You're obsessed with that place. You always have been.'

'It's quiet.'

'It's dirty.'

133

A comfortable silence.

'Don't worry, Claire: he'll be home later. And if he's not back later, send me a text and I'll get a bored constable to call around to see if he's been handed in anywhere.'

'I'm not sure how reassuring that is.' Mike thought he heard just a hint of a smile in her voice. 'Thanks.'

They ended their conversation feeling better about each other than they had for a long time and Mike made his way back to this apartment, strangely relaxed. He put it down to having had a chat that didn't involve work.

His subconscious put it down to something entirely different.

* * *

It was just gone one in the morning when Mike got a text from Claire to say that Steve still hadn't got home and she was going to bed. He replied, asking her if she wanted him to get someone to do a ring-around to see if they could find out anything. It had taken her a little too long to reply, but when she did, it was clear she'd calmed down enough for her panic to turn to anger.

'no let the bastard mayk his excuses 2mrow,' was the reply.

Mike thought for a few moments about what to send back. In the end, after several drafts, he settled on: *'Ok. no problem.'*

'thankx. Jack sends his love.'
'Tell him I send mine back double.'
'Nite.'
'G'night.'

Chapter 14

The Birmingham City stadium was very close by, and it was one of the most notable landmarks outlined by the dawn light when Stone gave the area a quick scan.

The white tent erected around the body glowed against the dusky background as he walked a controlled route up to the crime scene. The whole area would be subject to a fingertip search later that day, so it was important not to contaminate even the remotest square inch of grass in the park.

A bleary-eyed Stone had taken a few moments to focus after getting out of his. Considering this had been his planned weekend off, two early starts had felt very unwelcome. But the thought dissipated quickly when he put his minor woe into perspective.

He caught sight of Carter and headed in her direction first.

'Is there something you meant to tell me, Stone?'

'Such as, ma'am?'

'I've already squeezed it out of your constable.' She looked at him with one of her dark eyebrows arched inquisitively. 'A serial killer? You didn't care to share that theory with me.'

'I had nothing to substantiate the theory, ma'am.'

'That doesn't normally stop you! Besides, you do now.'

Stone looked at her and then immediately went to the SOCO van to get the Smurf outfit, before making his way over to Khan and Bolton. 'What have we got?'

'Dead female, sir.' She paused. 'You're going to need to look – I'm not sure I know how to describe it yet.'

'Sands, if you need to take a walk for a minute, just do it, okay?' The fact that she didn't disagree, as she usually would, did nothing for Stone's nerves.

Khan was waiting outside the tent, poised to open it for him. Everyone seemed to be waiting an extra beat before each action, but Khan still opened the tent without any sense of ceremony or grandeur. It was more like everyone was waiting to see his reaction.

Stone nearly recoiled at the sight. A woman sitting up with her back to a tree, her knees up and spaced apart, posed as if in the full throes of childbirth.

There was a baby's head covered in blood, eyes open, facing upwards at its mother with a ridiculous, pouting small mouth. The head had a waxy, plastic complexion.

'Is it just the head?' Stone asked Khan. The constable seemed not to hear the question.

It was answered by another voice. 'Unfortunately not, Mike,' Reg Walters replied. 'From a preliminary examination, it appears there is extensive bruising and damage to the woman's genitalia, and even though you know that I am averse to guessing and theories, I'd say the rest of the doll has been forcibly inserted.'

Stone was stunned into silence for a few moments before he simply clicked into coping-by-working mode. 'Do we have an ID yet?' His mind suddenly flicked back to the loss of his work card.

ID. Shit. Must sort that out.

'No ID yet, sir,' replied Khan, appearing to have snapped out of his own trance-like state as well.

'What else can you tell me, Reg?' Stone asked.

The pathologist joined the professional tone. It was almost as if they were all trying to draw on a collective strength. 'Female: approximately twenty-five to thirty years of age. Injuries evident to the lower abdomen and genital regions – internal and external. Bleeding from lower injuries and small pooling of blood on the surrounding soil suggest that she was still alive when first… placed here. Pale complexion of the face suggests she has not been moved since the point of death. I also noticed small piercing injuries to the inner arm which will require further examination, but at this stage I would think they are the result of hypodermic needles. Bruising around these small injuries suggests that…'

'He drained her blood, didn't he?' Stone interrupted. Reg said nothing. 'Has rigor set in yet?'

'It's beginning to, but again the lack of blood in the body will greatly disturb the timing and duration of rigor,' the pathologist replied.

'Mr Walters,' Khan joined in, 'if she is not in full rigor, why is her head upright and looking out? How is that possible?'

'You may want to have a look at that.' He took them over to the tree and pointed to her neck at the base of her skull. 'You can just about make out a metal rod here, entering the rear of the neck, and into the tree.'

The woman's body had been most decidedly posed. Normally the sheer weight of the skull and brain would make the head slump forward or to the side, but it seemed that here, the weight was being taken by a large building nail or something similar.

'Harry, very carefully look around the ground about eight feet from the body,' Stone said. 'You know what you're looking for?'

He did. Khan started looking around the mud for signs of a camera having been placed there to take a picture or video. 'Found something, sir.' He pointed out three small indentation marks in the ground, in a triangular shape.

A tripod had been steadied in the soft soil, leaving indentations too uniform to be naturally occurring.

Both men then looked at each other, as if knowing they had thought the same thing, and began scouring the ground close to the body. Stone checked with the SOCO team too.

'Not a single footprint, Harry.' Stone knew that clear footprints weren't a given for all crime scenes, or indeed for most, but the lack of any signs of movement made the whole scene a little bizarre.

'Sir, how would you get the body here, pose it, and leave no prints or drag marks at all?'

'I think it's more that he made a concerted effort to remove them, as if they interfered with the picture he was framing,' Stone replied quietly, half distracted by another thought. He buried his hands deep in his leather coat pockets and stood entirely still for a moment, waiting for that voice to come.

Suddenly he gestured to two of the SOCOs: 'You two – hold open the tent for a moment, would you.' Stone moved to stand just in front of the body. He wanted to see what she had been positioned to look at. He called over another of the SOCO team and asked them to take a panoramic photo from the point of view of the victim. The woman with the camera looked at him as if he'd lost his mind, but still did as he asked. Stone asked if she could email him a copy of that when she got back to the lab.

He didn't know yet what it was, but she was clearly posed to look at something. Stone scanned the panorama himself. All he could see was the housing estate, the floodlights of the Blues' ground, the tops of buildings, and signs from an industrial estate.

'Harry, Sands,' Stone addressed them both. 'Listen – what can you hear?'

They all listened intently for a few uncertain moments. 'Traffic from a main road,' Khan said.

'We can't hear it now, sir,' said Bolton, 'but we are close to a train line.'

Stone nodded. 'Yes, we are.' He paused for a moment, then clapped his hands loudly in order to rally everyone to action. 'Right, I need everything from Forensics on a rush for this. Reg, I need this body pushing to the top of the list. This killer is talking to us. He's telling us something.

And I have a distinct feeling this is *not* the end of his story. We also need to look at old and cold cases and find out if Grace Peters was even the first.'

Stone and the other detectives all left the scene of the crime together and began to make their way back to their cars and the office. What had been a complex single murder case to solve, where they had no evidence to hold a prime suspect, had suddenly become a possible serial killer case.

That meant they were no longer trying to find someone who had done something, but rather trying to prevent someone from doing more.

Chapter 15

Reports came into the Aston station about a missing woman fitting the description of the victim. The clinching phone call came from a Mrs Irene Harris, whose granddaughter had rung her up in a panic when she'd woken up to find she was home alone. Her mother, Samantha, Irene's daughter, had apparently vanished in the night.

'We're not going to be able to keep a lid on this for long, Mike,' said Carter as she led him into her office.

'Well, no,' he replied. 'Firstly, we need to go and inform Ms Harris's parents of her daughter's death.'

'What the *hell* is going on here?' Carter's outburst was a general one, and not directed at Stone. Yet. 'We need to know where Aaron Peters and Malcolm Glenn were last night. If we released a potential serial killer...'

Stone felt the prickles of a criticism. 'Both of those men were under suspicion, but we had nothing to hold either of them on last night. Now, we need to check their alibis for last night – that's fine – but what's more important is to see if we can find a link between the two women.'

'Make that a priority,' Carter barked, as if only to assert an authority. 'I need something I can give the press – something factual. The sooner we give them details, the sooner we can try to draw attention away from the bloody media frenzy this will stir up. Anything common by way of MO yet?'

Stone thought carefully. 'So far, ma'am... both women, similar age, but different height and hair colour. Both had injuries of a sexual *or* childbirth focus. Both bodies were posed. Khan and I think they were photographed by the killer. And, I'm not sure yet, but location has something to do with it, too.'

There was a silence between them for a moment. Carter sat semi-slumped in her chair whilst Stone stood, leaning against her immaculate glass meeting table, with his hands in his pockets. That's when a thought seemed to flash across Carter's face.

'Where's your ID card, Mike?'

'About that,' he began. 'I think I might have lost it sometime yesterday, around lunchtime.'

'Oh, shit, Mike, I don't need that adding to the pile. Have you reported it yet?'

'That was on the to-do list for first thing this morning, ma'am.'

'Do it *now*, Mike, because you are grounded until it is replaced.' She put a hand up to stop his objection. 'No, Mike. I can't have you visiting families or questioning suspects, or even outside this station on duty, without that card. I know it seems anal but you know how sneaky little defence lawyers will find any technicality to throw out interview or witness statements based on procedural issues. That means we are up shit creek until you get it done.'

'Sorry, ma'am.'

Carter drew a line in the air with her hand, which was her way of saying that was the end of the issue; a line drawn underneath it; move on. One of the things Stone respected about her was that the gesture was genuine. He also respected that the same hand would be connecting most forcibly with your backside if you screwed up in the same way again.

'Mike, we need to go joint lead on this one from now on.'

'I can handle it, ma'am,' Stone protested.

'It has nothing to do with ability, Mike, it's about accountability and image. DI is not a high enough rank to cover a serial, and you damn well know it.'

Stone hated it when she was right *and* wrong at the same time, but got away with it thanks only to her rank.

* * *

Everyone gathered in the incident room as Stone and Pete Barry populated the wall with new details of the case.

143

Barry had already received information from the SOCO team that could be added, and Stone had insisted a map be placed on the board to mark the locations of the murders. Location was an important factor in murders or other serious offences.

Without a pathology report, Stone knew there were going to be lots of questions that could not be answered, but this briefing was about reshaping the investigation. As he turned around to face the room, he noticed a growing number of detectives and officers in there. Carter had made immediate calls to all local teams to send in a proportion of their CID staff in to work with Force CID as a kind of temporary secondment.

Unfortunately for Stone, this new addition of personnel included his less-than-favourite DS Sharp. Stone made a mental note to ask Bolton and Barry to keep tight reins on him.

'These two murders are connected, and I stake my reputation on them having been committed by the same man,' Stone began.

'Or woman?' Greer threw in his usual unhelpful contribution.

Stone was not impressed. 'Which is exactly why Barry is going to find the most shit-boring, paper-pushing task he needs a gobby detective to do, and hand it straight to you, Martin. Okay?' Room settled, he continued. 'DS Bolton and DC King went to see the daughter of the first victim, Grace Peters.' He left the sentence hanging for one of them to give some feedback. King took the cue.

'Well, besides the completely obvious shock and upset, sir, something came up about her relationship with her dad.' She looked at Bolton, but got the nod to carry on. 'The relationship isn't good. I thought she might ask to see him, but as soon as he was mentioned it was clear from Sophie and her grandparents that he is not a popular figure. We didn't press too hard, but he's not *dad of the year* material, that's for sure.'

Stone considered that for a moment as the room rumbled with a mixture of agreement and cynicism. 'Okay, thanks, you two. Sorry to sound like a broken record, but can you do the same with the daughter of the second victim. I want to know if anything strikes you as a connection. Do they know each other? Check school histories, and so on. We need to build an MO – are they part of it?'

Notes were being scrawled down.

Khan raised his hand. 'I'll follow up the FAPAS link, see if there is anything in that.'

Stone nodded. 'We'll call Malcolm Glenn back in on that front if we need to. I also want two others to work with Harry on finding out more about that organisation. Who joins it? How do they join it? How much do they know about each other? I want to know everything about it. I also want someone else at the family courts checking up a link there.'

As Stone handed out the various tasks, a uniformed officer came in to deliver a message to Carter. Stone could see the look on her face as she pulled Sharp aside with another detective from the West and Central CID.

At the same time, Khan took Stone to one side, holding a file folder on Malcolm Glenn. 'Sir, you need to read this,' he said with a darker look on his face. Occasionally the young detective liked to hand over files as if they were top secret documents in a crime thriller. Stone assumed he must watch too much TV.

'What is it, Harry?'

'Malcolm Glenn's name has come up on a search of Social Services files. He was in care when he was younger due to the death of his parents.'

Stone's interest was piqued: 'Go on.'

'Well, I'm having a bit of trouble getting through the social worker who has pulled the *confidential file* excuse on me, quoting court orders and so on. Glenn isn't a prime suspect and I don't think we have the grounds for a warrant yet.'

'Leave that with me,' Stone said, throwing the folder on his desk. 'If needs be, Harry, we will pull him in again and ask him to volunteer the information, and then if he misses any details out…'

Khan got the point and made a note to get in contact with Glenn again.

Carter let Stone finish the briefing, and then waited for the hubbub of activity to begin before she called Stone into his office and shut the door.

'I don't like that look, ma'am,' Stone said.

She didn't reply.

Carter sat down at Stone's desk and leaned forward, interlocking her hands and resting her top lip on her thumbs. There was a profound quality to her thought that concerned Stone. Finally, she spoke.

'Mike, I need to ask you something, strictly off the record – for now.'

'Go on.'

'And I want you to answer me honestly.'

'Oh, for pity's sake, ma'am.'

'I'm not pissing around here, Mike. I shouldn't even be having this conversation with you.'

Stone took a deep breath.

'When did you lose your ID card? And I want it as close to near certain as you can damn well get it.'

'Why?'

'Mike – answer the question.'

'I definitely had it when I left here at lunch yesterday. I remember taking it off as I went into town: close to one o'clock. I noticed it was gone by the time I got back – around one-forty. Front desk will be able to confirm what time.' He waited. 'Why? What is this?'

'Who is Steven Simpson?'

A very heavy weight hit Stone from above and he felt his shoulders tighten.

'He's my ex-wife's boyfriend.'

'And when did you last…'

'It was him I was seeing in the Crown, okay? He came here, mouthing off about something personal. I told him to piss off and I'd meet him for a drink at lunch, which I did. In the Crown, so it was away from here. We talked, we left, and when I got back here, I noticed I'd lost the card. I even phoned the landlord to ask if it had been handed in.'

Carter paused again. She was clearly weighing something up.

'Is there any chance he took it during that meeting?'

Stone thought for a moment. 'No, I don't see how. My coat was on the back of my chair the whole time.'

Carter dropped back in her chair with a deep and heavy sigh. 'We got another call, Mike. Another body.'

He didn't want to ask. 'Steve?'

She nodded. 'That alone would be enough to cause me concern, given what you just said.'

'Well, it's shitty, yes. I knew him, yes. I won't hide any of that. So, what is the big problem here?'

Stone's volume was increasing enough to draw attention from the incident room.

'He has your ID card clenched in his fist, covered in blood. And his body was found on a stretch of the canal not so far from your apartment.'

The implications were clear – and Stone had yet to mention the fact that his last encounter with Steve had been an argument.

'You don't think I…' Stone began.

'What I think doesn't matter, Mike. There is a material link between you and a dead body. Not to mention the personal link.' Carter sighed deeply again, and it became clear what she had been weighing up a few moments ago.

Stone waited.

'I've got no choice, Mike. You're suspended from all duties until further notice.'

That was the hand again.

That was the slap.

Chapter 16

His frustration was at boiling point as he slammed out of the station. It took a lot to genuinely knock Mike Stone, but this had done it. *He* had done it.

How did this fucker get my card?

Stone knew instinctively that this third body – his ex-wife's boyfriend – holding his ID card was far too much of a coincidence to be just a *coincidence*.

Just as his hand got to his car door, he glanced three cars down to see Sharp, who looked up, smiled like a Cheshire cat, and threw him a pathetic mock salute.

Come here and I will smash that smarmy fucking smile the other side of your face.

His raging expression caused Sharp's smile to falter.

Stone got in his car, cranked his stereo up dangerously loud and pulled out of the station car park. Initially, he drove round to join the inner ring road in the direction of his apartment. Then he took a quick lane change and swung onto the roundabout by the old fire station and headed back into the city. Taking a winding, turning route through Digbeth and Highgate, he worked his way to the south side of the centre. He often took deliberately complicated driving routes in order to block out everything and focus on the driving. It didn't work taking open roads like motorways, because he found he could switch back to thinking mode as he drove or sat in traffic. Stone just needed five minutes of utter distraction, as if to reboot his overactive brain. The only way he knew how to achieve that was to plot as complicated a driving route as he could improvise.

It wasn't an aimless task. Keeping up to date on the city streets, including roadworks and diversions in place, could mean gaining a few seconds in pursuit of a suspect one day. All things considered, it was his own form of Continued Professional Development.

Or at least that is how he justified it.

He headed out of the city centre towards Edgbaston, resisting the temptation to stick his blues on and get to where he was going a bit more quickly.

After ten more minutes of driving, he finally got to Cannon Hill park. Leaving his car on double yellow lines, and placing his 'On Police Business' card in the window, he went for a walk. The park was like the canals: one of his walking and thinking places.

He'd put off the thinking for long enough. His mind began to race.

Why hadn't Claire contacted him again when Steve hadn't shown up that morning? Why didn't he tell the Carter about the argument at the Crown? Why didn't he mention the conversation with Claire? Who the hell stole his ID card from his coat pocket? How might he get hold of the CCTV at the Crown?

Stone hated not having control.

A new thought suddenly flooded in and blackened his mind like a huge cinema screen. On that screen, in stark, bold white lettering:

Who is going to tell Claire about Steve?

* * *

Sharp and DC Michaels arrived at the scene of the crime on Livery Street shortly after leaving Aston. They got out of their car and stood on the canal bridge near Snow Hill station, looking down at the white tent set up to hide the body, surrounded by a gathering of SOCO. The large archway was a well-known feature on the Birmingham canals and had featured in TV dramas numerous times. This time, however, the drama was real, and the grand size of the arch seemed more ominous than historic.

There was a gathering of officers at the top of the rusty white-painted metal staircase, accompanied by a particularly busy Reg Walters.

'All right, Reggie,' Sharp said. He seemed to have an innate talent for saying the wrong thing most of the time.

'It's Mr Walters, thank you very much, detective,' Reg said, knowing all too well that the arrogant sergeant did not outrank a civilian pathologist. He also didn't outwit him – but that was an issue of genetics and education.

'Well, let's make sure we do this right, Mr Walters, since this body implicates your good friend Mike Stone,' Sharp smirked.

'Detective, might I clarify a few things for you?' Reg began, not looking at the sergeant, or waiting for a reply. 'Firstly, if you were in fact doing your job properly you should not be attempting to cloud my objectivity before I have seen the deceased. Secondly, I require more respect to be shown to the dead. And finally: piss off.' He looked at the sergeant sternly. 'Oh, and one more thing: until I release this body and this scene, *I* outrank *you*.'

There was a palpable tension as the men made their way down to the canal. Reg went into the tent, and although he knew he had to remain completely objective, every bone in his body was telling him, urging him, to find something that ruled Mike Stone out of any suspicion.

The first thing he noticed about the body was the colour of the skin and the staining of the blood on the face and under the chin. He made a mental note to record his thoughts on that. The body was pushed right back into one of the smaller arches that ran down the side of the canal, parallel with the water, but at least twenty feet away from the edge of the tow-path. The whole archway itself could easily span a two-storey house, and the grandiosity made it seem more like a Victorian rail station than a through route for the canal. Albeit an impressive one.

The man's body was lying on its back and had evident wounds to the throat and neck, most notably a horizontal cut across the neck that had clearly severed the main arteries. It was the kind of injury that Reg Walters rarely saw. In fact, in his twenty-year career, besides accidental injuries, he had barely come across that kind of deliberate cut a handful of times.

But that wasn't what caught his eye. It was the other cut, which ran vertically from between the collar-bones to an inch or so from the chin, that seemed out of place. He knew that he would need to check much closer to confirm, but his gut instinct, and years of experience, told him that injury was inflicted after the first. It was, from a killing perspective, entirely unnecessary.

Walters then took a moment to reflect on his own abhorrent thought about 'necessity' in killing. Reg Walters was a highly intelligent and educated pathologist, having chosen to turn to medicine after graduating from Oxford with a First in Philosophy. It was his exploration of philosophical musings on life and death, and the human condition, that often helped him look at the victims' bodies as studies rather than people. It wasn't a matter of being cold; it was more a different way of coping with some of the most depraved things he came across as the result of human free will.

It was also true that the pathologist respected Stone greatly, and would even go so far as to say there were times when he was in awe of the way the detective could thread together the narrative of a victim's death, explaining the *why,* albeit with an uneducated eloquence. But in the absence of Stone, the pathologist would need to have a private go at theorising for himself. Since the vertical cut was unnecessary for the purpose of murder, it could only have been there for a different reason. That injury was for show. It was there to tell a story.

It was all about Mike Stone and his tracheostomy scar.

Given the state of the two other bodies he had attended over the past few days, even Reg Walters – civilian pathologist, not a trained detective – could see that the injury suggested a link. Adding the discovery of Stone's ID card into the mix, he couldn't help but think that something especially odd was going on.

Besides the depraved physical atrocities.

Reg could see that the body had been moved after the initial cut to the throat and that the victim had been face down when the throat was cut. He had then been turned over after a significant amount of blood had already been drained, not too different from the way a butcher might drain an animal.

'Apparently, the man's wallet has sat next to the body,' Sharp said. 'It still contained all the cards and money. It also had Mr Simpson's driving licence – which is why we already know his identity.'

'Has anything else been moved?' The question was directed at a nearby SOCO, who confirmed that they were still waiting for him to release and remove the body. Reg spoke to one of the photographers and ordered a range of photographs to be taken of the body in its context as Carter and Khan arrived on the scene. They got up to the tent just as Reg was testing the liver temperature of the body.

'I'll need to do a proper check, but the cut to the throat seems to be the most obvious cause of death at this stage,' he explained, without even looking at his audience. 'Judging by the level of rigor setting in, and by the liver temperature, I'd say that this poor chap expired somewhere between 10pm and 2am. But that is a wide and flexible estimate at this stage, taking into account weather conditions and the location.'

'So, what was the delay in it being called in?' asked Carter, of no one in particular.

'I'd say that it was a matter of chance, ma'am,' said Sharp. 'Given its position, it's not so obvious as to stand out, so unless someone actually approached this particular small archway, I think it's possible that it might be missed for a few hours.'

'Ma'am, you might also want to take a quick look at what is protruding from the gentleman's inside coat pocket. I haven't touched it, but I did notice it when I moved the clothing to get to the liver.' Reg asked one of the SOCO team to take a box out of the pocket.

It was an unused pregnancy test kit.

'Reg,' Khan jumped in, 'just to check, your estimate for time of death: could it be any later?'

'It could be, but I doubt it. The body has really begun to settle here after it was dumped.'

'You mean he wasn't killed here?' Carter sounded stunned.

'Why, no, I very much doubt that,' Reg replied. He took a small torch out of his pocket. 'That kind of neck wound would, at least initially, provide quite a substantial arterial force, and there just isn't the blood-spatter and pooling to support a hypothesis that he was killed here. Loss of consciousness would have been very quick, death within a minute or so.'

As Carter began giving Sharp a range of instructions, Reg took Harry Khan aside.

'You have an interest in photography, don't you, DC Khan?' A knowing look between the two men was enough to ensure that the young detective understood the pathologist was intending to communicate something to him more privately. 'Don't forget to stand about eight feet from the body... and get a *good look from there,*' said Reg with a wink.

Khan did so and was unsurprised to notice that the body did seem, from that viewpoint, quite staged. It had not been dumped quickly and left; it had been arranged, legs slightly parted, with the belt buckle and top button of the jeans undone. Most significantly, three small indentations marked out a triangle in the dusty gravel.

A tripod.

Khan asked for a panoramic shot of the body to be taken from that viewpoint, and then turned to Reg, asking quietly, 'Why would a killer risk setting up a tripod?'

Reg smiled. 'I take it you don't know so much about photography? To get a shot like that in low light conditions, such as at night-time, you either use a very bright, attention-drawing flash, or a very slow shutter speed. Something like that requires a tripod.'

The pathologist released the crime scene, gave instructions to the SOCOs, and made his way back up to road level. All the time he was thinking: 'This body had all the signs that were meant to communicate *with* Mike Stone, not *to implicate* him.'

Chapter 17

Mike Stone sat in his car a hundred yards down the road from Jack's school. There was at least an hour to go before he could pick his son up for the first time in…

Too long.

He already had his tablet connected to the internet, ready to do some of his own research into the fathers' group FAPAS and Parental Alienation Syndrome in general. The term was a new one to him, and even though Khan had given him a quick summary, he really felt he needed to know more about the issue. He was sure that it was somehow connected with the case he'd just been thrown off. Even though it wasn't clear whether Malcolm Glenn was their key suspect any more.

The first thing Mike noticed was that PAS was beginning to gain some traction – and more so in the US – even if the gender bias in UK family law was still profound. However, for all the support it was getting, PAS wasn't getting a serious enough hearing in courts and custody cases.

He paused for a moment, thinking how grateful he was that Claire had not dragged him through that kind of mess.

The question remained: would it form a part of the MO of a serial killer? It could be a key aspect of how the killer selected his victims. Stone was well aware that 'jumping the gun' would be an understatement in this case, but given the connection between two dead females, both murders staged with a theme connecting to childbirth, this link to parenting was too much of a coincidence to be ignored.

PAS was about one parent getting the child to hate the other parent. His mind cast back to Claire. Regardless of the many, many arguments he'd had with Claire, she had always been decent with the way she spoke to Jack about him. He knew his son missed him, and he knew his son was being affected by his absence.

But he also knew that this fell squarely on his shoulders, and unless he did something about it soon, he would begin building walls between them that might never be broken down.

The loss of a father was something Mike Stone knew far too much about.

His mind ticked over the thoughts of Jack for a while until a new idea about the case crept back in. A task that he would normally delegate to Harry Khan, since he was a lot faster with social media than Stone could be bothered to be.

He made his way on to Twitter and quickly found the FAPAS group. Rather than sign in with his own account, he went through the hassle of creating a new email account and using that to set up a new Twitter logon. He shuddered at the thought of what he was doing – setting up false accounts to pursue people and elicit information. It sounded far too much like the work of an online paedophile than it did of a police officer. But at the same time, he also knew that what he was doing was vital in some way, even if he couldn't yet work out exactly why.

When the accounts were ready, he followed the right Twitter users, joined in with the conversations, and began introducing himself. He came up with a quick back-story, and thanks to a small amount of undercover work he had done in the past, he knew that the best lies to tell are those where you use as much truth as possible. As much as was safe. He needed to disclose that he was based in Birmingham, knowing that location was important to the links between the current victims.

Mike posed as someone who was really quite new to the issue and was desperate for some support. His character had been divorced for over a year and couldn't understand why there was a growing tension between him and his fictitious son, whom he hadn't seen at all for six months. His ex-wife was doing everything she could to prevent contact. He also decided to invent a growing custody battle. With a quick bit of online research, he was able to find the name of a local firm of solicitors and cite them in his story.

After just half an hour, he had already built up a miniature secret world. The ease with which he was able to build a convincing lie sent a shudder down his spine for a moment.

And that was when his mobile rang.

'You fucking, shitting bastard!' Claire hissed at him in a stunted, whispered shout. It sounded like she didn't want to be overheard.

'Claire, I…'

'Why didn't you tell me? Why didn't you call me? You said…'

'It's complicated.'

'It is always complicated with you, isn't it?' She was sobbing.

'I am so, so sorry, Claire.'

She gathered herself. 'I need you to do something for me. And I do not *care* what you are doing now. I do not *care* if you are interviewing Fred-fucking-West! You drop what you are doing and you get over to your son's school and you pick him up. Thirty minutes.'

'Okay, yes, of course.'

'No excuses, Mike. Just do it.'

'Claire, yes. I am already there.'

'Where?'

'At his school, waiting for him to finish.'

There was a stunned silence.

'Why are you there already?'

'I can't be involved in Steve's case because of my personal connection. Which is also why I couldn't tell you myself. So, when I found out what had happened…'

Mike Stone, the hardened detective inspector, who had seen so many horrific sights in his time – especially over the past few days – and learnt to weather them all, suddenly found it hard to hold back the lump in his throat.

He imagined holding her tight, still able to remember those times. The smell of her hair, the precise shape of the crook of her neck. The exact distance between her shoulder-blades as his hand would hold her close.

And he waited.

'They're still here,' Claire said, sounding drained.

'Which ones?'

'A tall woman with dark hair. And a shorter, older-looking one.'

Bolton and, he assumed, DC King. 'I'm glad it's those two, Claire,' Mike said. And he was being honest, although at the same time a niggle in his mind wondered who had been sent to speak to the daughters of the other victims, and why the reshuffle had happened. He knew it would have been a deliberate move from Carter, and he cursed her under his breath.

Then Mike refocused himself. 'I'll bring Jack home.'

A thought crossed his mind, and he wondered why it hadn't done so already.

'Claire,' he said, with perhaps a little too much caution, 'do you want me to, perhaps, keep Jack with me for a bit. Bring him home in a while. I don't mind – if you want him straight…'

'No, bring him straight home.'

That stung more than Mike thought it would. Had her trust of him eroded that much already? Or perhaps the reading he'd been doing just before this call had coloured his emotions.

Claire waited a moment before she added: 'Maybe later Jack will need it, though. If you're not too busy.'

The conversation ended shortly after that last sting in the tail.

When Mike hung up, he could see the parents beginning to gather around at the gates, and he decided to leave it as late as possible to get out of the car. He couldn't stand parental playground gossip, and he knew that he would be the subject of comment and curiosity. Besides, he wasn't sure if many of the staff or parents would remember who he was if he just walked up. It made a lot more sense to just wait until he saw Jack.

Unexpectedly, Mike's stomach began to fill with that uncomfortable feeling of 'butterflies' – a term he'd never understood, given that the beautiful creatures seemed to be used as an analogy for fear and anxiety.

Sometimes vomit-inducing.

It struck him that he hadn't thought to bring a present with him and he chastised his steering wheel for not reminding him.

His heart stopped when he saw Jack.

He got out of his car and crossed the road. It took a few moments for Jack to notice and register the man walking towards him in his long leather coat, and for a terrifying moment, Mike was concerned what Jack's response was going to be.

Smile, Mike, you idiot.

Thankfully, the smile was reciprocated, and Jack ran to his father as if he hadn't seen him in years. They embraced tightly, and for a moment all the tension in the world disappeared.

Chapter 18

Besides, in her view, he was bloody stupid for not reporting his ID lost.

As she sat at her desk, preparing her draft of a speech to be sent to the Force media team ahead of their press conference, Khan knocked on the door and hovered outside. He had to be told twice to come in.

'Sorry, ma'am,' he said, squeezing in through the door he'd only half-opened, for no particular reason.

'Don't apologise: you haven't done anything wrong. Yet!' she replied. 'What is it?'

'Just need to run something past you, ma'am.'

'Harry, just get in here and sit down.' Carter knew what was coming. It would be about Stone. Nevertheless, Carter liked Khan, so she thought she'd give him the benefit of the doubt. 'So, what is it, Constable?'

'Photography, ma'am,' he began, leaving a little too much time before he continued. 'DI Stone had a theory – as did I – that the killer was recording the murders on camera. No idea if video or still, but nevertheless, definitely taking pictures of some kind, and most probably as a trophy, or a way of reliving the events.'

'Is there any evidence to support this?'

'Yes. At the first scene, there was a void on the chest of drawers in between the otherwise carefully rearranged photos, and the body had been posed in the right way for it to be on show for a camera placed there. It's in the report.' Khan had Carter's attention, so he continued. 'Then, with the second body, there were three equidistant indentations in the soil, about eight feet away. I've got information back from SOCO confirming that they're compatible with the size and spacing of the legs on a camera tripod.'

'That sounds worryingly close to a supposition, not evidence, DC Khan.'

'Yes, I know,' he said, slightly rattled, but also excited by the next piece of evidence to back up his theory. 'But I also think the body this morning… is the work of the same killer.'

Carter just looked at him.

He continued. 'That's based on the posing of the body, and the three similar indentations in the ground nearby, which, according to SOCO, match those found at the second body. So, if we assume the killer took a photo of the third body, in darkness, without a flash, they'd need to know how to take dark photos.'

'What's your point?'

166

Khan was caught off guard by the question. 'Have you ever seen Stone use a camera, other than the one on his phone?'

Carter leant forward on her desk, resting her chin on her hands. She wanted to say, *'Brilliant! Yes! Call him back in!'* but knew that she couldn't do that without a bulletproof reason.

There was a knock at the door, followed by the immediate entrance of a detective in a rush. Sharp came in with a degree of haste that suggested something serious, but a smile that belied his urgency.

'Ma'am, I think you're going to want to see this,' he said, holding a USB memory drive. 'CCTV footage from cameras in the city centre.'

Carter took the drive and plugged it into her computer. Locating the file quickly, she opened it on her large office monitor.

The video file began playing and Sharp took over the presentation. 'Here you can see the victim, Steven Simpson, entering the Crown pub in town. Nothing else happens until just over an hour later, when look who turns up. Stone. Now, if we scroll ahead –' he did so with the touch-screen controls '– we see an entirely different thing.'

And Carter did have to admit, the footage was pretty damning. It showed Stone dragging the victim outside and forcing him up against the wall. Not the most action-packed scene, of course, but it was certainly clear that the two men had parted on very bad terms a matter of hours before the victim was later murdered not far from Stone's apartment.

'It's a circumstantial link at best, ma'am,' Khan said, attempting to downplay the issue.

Sharp decided to continue. 'However, I checked with the landlord of the Crown, who confirmed that Stone had been there with the other man. He also said that Stone had told him the man was drunk and likely to cause a scene.'

Carter's eyebrows raised.

Sharp continued. 'Another detective also saw an earlier altercation.'

Carter almost jumped. 'Who?'

Sharp looked at Khan.

The chief superintendent exploded. 'Why the bloody hell haven't you mentioned this already, DC Khan?'

He was stunned, and looked between the two of them – Carter red-faced and raging; Sharp smirking with arrogance. 'Because I thought…'

'Thought?' Carter was incredulous. 'Thought? Why would this require any *thought* whatsoever, constable? You know we have to be completely above board, and treat every piece of evidence…'

Khan stood and raised his voice uncharacteristically loud. 'Excuse me, ma'am, but due process or not, why do I feel like I am the only one who isn't trying their damned hardest to screw Stone over completely?'

'What the hell do you mean by that?' Carter shot back.

'I just sat here and gave you concrete reasoning why we shouldn't even be entertaining the notion that he was involved, but instead you're listening to what is little more than gossip from Sharp.'

A frosty pause settled on the room.

'Sergeant: thank you for the information. You're dismissed,' said Carter calmly, without even looking at him. She waited for him to leave before speaking to Khan. 'If we ignore any piece of connecting evidence, we place ourselves, Stone, and the station in a very risky position. It could end up looking like a cover-up.'

Khan nodded and went to exit the office. When he got to the door he turned back and added: 'It's always helpful to be reminded that these days we put liability above loyalty.'

As he closed the door behind him, he shuddered. A mixture of fear and exhilaration; adrenaline coursing through his blood.

* * *

It had been a long time since Mike Stone had played the part of the father and not the detective. He had to admit to himself that he loved it.

He missed it.

It didn't take long for Mike to drive his son home from school, and the ten-year-old chattered away excitedly for the whole journey. Despite his original nervousness about it, Mike loved the journey, loved listening to his son talk about school, his friends, the picture he'd drawn, and any number of random tangents that children of his age tend to bounce around.

Not a single mention of his recently missed birthday.

When they got to the house, Mike stopped the car and switched the engine off. He turned to look at his son and smiled. Jack was a fairly small boy for his age, with short hair and a round face with cheeks that dimpled distinctively when he smiled. His deep eyes were a strong hazel in colour, and, together with the thick eyebrows, there were times when he was a miniature spitting image of his father.

'Whose car is that?' Jack asked.

'Looks like Mum'55s got some visitors,' Mike replied.

'Are you coming in?' said the boy, bubbling with enthusiasm, and apparently forgetting his first question.

'Jack, before we go in,' Mike began, carefully. 'First thing, you give your mum a great big hug and kiss, right?' The boy rolled his eyes, but smiled and nodded.

'Is Steve at home too?'

Mike's heart jumped up into his throat. He stopped and thought for a moment about what he could say to prepare the boy. His son had learnt about death the usual way children do. The first time had been the loss of a goldfish, which had resulted in a dignified small 'goodbye' ceremony in the garden. The second had been the demise of a guinea pig, Truffle, which had required a full-blown family funeral when Jack was only five. That one had been harder, as Truffle – or Ruffle, or Rulluf, or Fluff – had been a pet that Jack could hold, and stroke, and occasionally lose under the sofa.

Mike realised he had no understanding of how to deal with helping his own son through such trauma. He'd delivered the standard death message to other families, countless times, but had always been able to walk away from it quickly after. This time it was his own son who would need putting back together, and especially if Jack was anywhere near as close to Steve as the man had suggested.

He had delayed the inevitable as much as he could, and they both got out of the car. Jack ran up to the house and banged on the door, and shouted through the letterbox to his mum. Mike followed up behind, slowly, unsure as to whether he would be invited in.

The door opened and Claire grabbed hold of Jack and held him tight as if she hadn't seen him in a week, a month – even a year. She held him so tight he began to giggle and squirm free. Holding back tears from bloodshot eyes, she looked up and gave Mike the nod to come in.

As they went in, Claire took Jack into the large kitchen-diner that they'd built after they moved in. She went about finding something for Jack to eat, which gave Mike a few moments to look around for the detectives, who had clearly decided to stay out of sight at first. He caught sight of Bolton and King sitting in the living room and gave them a silent acknowledging nod. Everyone seemed to be enacting a quiet dumb-show that had obviously been devised for Jack's return.

Coming out of the kitchen, Claire told Jack to go up to his room and change out of his school uniform. With an uncharacteristic treat of a chocolate bar in one hand, the boy tried to drag his dad upstairs with him, but Mike told him he'd follow in a minute or two.

Finally, the coast was clear and the charade could be dropped.

'Mike,' said Bolton. King nodded as if to tag onto her colleague's greeting. They both got up and made their way back into the kitchen. He was not quite sure of the reason, but it seemed that the business was being conducted in the kitchen. Mike felt slightly reassured, in that as much as he knew the room had three detectives and one civilian victim – it also had four parents in there.

'Do you want a cuppa, Mike?' Claire broke the silence. Mike turned to look at her and his heart tripped over a beat and fell flat. Even through the roughly tied-back hair, the worn-out makeup, the reddened eyes, Mike was looking at the mother of his son.

Who was he kidding? He still loved her.

'Yeah, sure,' he replied.

'Sir, can I have a quick word?' Bolton said in as calm a manner as she could. 'You don't mind, Claire, do you?'

She just shook her head, and the two detectives stepped out into the hallway.

'Her neighbour has been round and will be coming back in a minute. You don't need to be here.'

'Don't, Sands: just don't. Carter suspended me, as you well know. So, at the moment, I am a civilian who just picked his son up from school. Or am I a suspect now, too?'

'Sorry, I didn't mean…' Bolton looked uncomfortable.

'Look at me, Sands. Do you *really* think I had anything to do with Steve's death?'

Bolton was genuinely annoyed that he would even ask her. 'I *am* worried about you getting further… implicated. You know it's all about how things look. And you being here – well…'

A little voice pinged from the top of the stairs.

'Come on, Dad!' Jack said. 'Come see what I got for my birthday.'

'Be up there in a sec, mate,' he replied, giving Jack a wink. He turned back to Bolton. 'I'll go when *Claire* tells me to go, okay?'

They both went back into the kitchen where Claire was sitting with King, each nursing a cup of tea. His cup was also on the side. A reminder that this wasn't his home any more.

'How are we going to tell Jack?' Claire said. 'It's going to break his heart – he was getting really close to Steve.'

Mike felt a pang of jealousy, quickly followed by heavy guilt for thinking ill of a dead man. 'We can do it together, if you want,' he said to Claire.

'There's no easy way to do it, Claire,' King said. 'It's the plaster approach. A quick tear away, then kiss it better as much as is needed.' Spoken from the mouth of a mother, not a trained detective, Mike thought.

With a heavy heart, Claire stood, looked at her ex-husband, her son's father, and then they both made their way upstairs. Claire held on to Mike's hand, tighter than she had done for a long time.

Bolton looked at King and they shared the same thought: Stone should not have been there. A thought that was confirmed when her phone vibrated, and she took the call. It was Carter calling her for an update and asking her to return to the station. To say she wasn't impressed that Stone was there would have been an understatement.

'Get him out of there, now,' said Carter.

'Ma'am, I know he's suspended, but he's not a suspect, so we can hardly…'

'We have CCTV of him having an argument with the victim just hours before he was killed. And I am sure you don't need reminding where the body was found?' As much as she trusted her DI, and believed him, Bolton had to admit that it really didn't look good.

'I want you to bring him back here to the station, sergeant, is that clear?' Carter said. 'Don't accept *no* as an answer. Remind him it is in his best interest. Leave King there as Family Liaison for now.'

'He's not going to want to come, ma'am.' Bolton tried to emphasise the point.

'I don't care if he wants to come or not. If he refuses, arrest him.'

But Bolton knew that Carter couldn't hear the sound of a boy's tears from upstairs, and she truly dreaded even attempting to drag the father of that child away. It was one of those times when her role as a detective on duty was seriously clashing with her other role…

… as a human being.

She went up the stairs, following the voices, and managed to catch Mike Stone's eye. She had to admit to herself she was seeing this man – this stern, often cold, hardened man – in a completely different light.

Nevertheless, his glare made it clear that he knew what she was about to say. Had he not been suspended, it would have been enough to pull rank. But rank was not the issue here: it was his career, and possibly his freedom, that was under threat.

Mike got up and stepped out onto the landing space, pulling the boy's bedroom door closed behind him.

'Sir…' she started, faltered, but continued: 'Carter really wants you to come in and I don't think it would be a good idea to ignore her.'

'Well, that's just tough. There has been a death in the family. I won't claim I was close to Steve, but can you hear that? He's my *son*, Sands.'

'You don't have to persuade me, Mike, I'm completely with you on this. But she told me if you refuse...' The sentence ended itself.

Mike laughed. 'That's just a bluff, Sands. And you can tell her I said that.'

Bolton had no choice. She had to phone Carter back. And she got an order she never wanted to hear.

She was to arrest Stone on the charge of obstruction.

And if he wouldn't come with her voluntarily, she could send a van round.

When the sergeant spoke to Mike again and told him what Carter had said, he told her to go and wait downstairs and he would be down in five minutes.

Mike went back into his son's room.

Claire was holding Jack in her lap and rocking him back and forth. She knew the look that Mike gave her, but rather than admonish him, she simply mouthed, 'Thank you.'

'Things are going to change, Claire,' he whispered. And with that he planted a kiss on his son's head, and carefully kissed her on the cheek.

And left his son's room.

He silently moved down the stairs, avoiding the creaking floorboards. He paused by the opening to the kitchen-diner, listening carefully to the two detectives and waiting for his cue. He knew he was about to put them in a difficult situation, and he also knew that he was betraying their trust.

Mike slipped past, opened the front door and left the house. Getting into his car, he paused only for a second to wonder if he was doing the right thing.

He knew he had to face Carter at some point.

But first he had a gut instinct to follow.

Mike checked the rear-view mirror as he drove away, but he could see no signs of pursuit. At the same time, a thought crossed his mind, and a voice whispered over his shoulder. He had a sinking feeling that this whole situation was playing right into the hands of a dangerous killer.

You're not just telling me a story, are you? I'm becoming your story.

Chapter 19

The Boy

The boy woke with a jolt.

He had no idea how long he had been asleep, but he was freezing cold and his whole body was shaking violently. He could smell the dampness of the air around him and had the bitter aftertaste of vomit in his mouth. The inside of his nose and the back of his throat were burnt dry. Even through the numbness of the cold, he could feel a slight breeze chill his face where the tears had been running down from his eyes.

The boy listened carefully to the world around him. All he could make out were the faint rumbles of what sounded like a car every now and again. But the voices and shouts had gone.

Had they given up trying to find him?

How long should he stay hidden under the dark steps?

Why did his eyes sting and his stomach hurt?

The boy hadn't eaten for… he didn't know how long. But he didn't think he felt very hungry. It was just something that told him he should eat.

And he was so cold.

He looked all around, but there was barely any light besides a faint glow from outside his hiding place. His clothes were soaked through, and he needed to get out of there, find somewhere warm and dry. But, at the same time, he wanted to stay inside the tunnel.

It felt safe.

Everyone had always warned children at school about how dangerous the canals were, and how they shouldn't play near them. And they should never, ever jump in them. But he wasn't *playing*; and he'd *fallen* in, not jumped; and he actually felt quite *safe* under the bridge.

He decided from that point on, the canals would be one of his safest places.

But he was still… so… cold.

Chapter 20

Stone parked his car on Newton Street just outside the coroner's court. It was already dark but the city was still very much awake. He didn't know if the pathologist would still be at work, but he thought it was worth a try. After all, Stone knew that Reg would have had a busy day with two bodies to do post-mortems on, and he was never one to go home leaving unfinished business at work.

He also didn't know if Reg would necessarily be aware of his suspension, but he did know that Carter knew the pathologist all too well.

She has told him.

Stone made his way down the small driveway to the back door of the building. It had a code and buzzer entrance, which would be his first hurdle to get past. He looked around to check if anyone could see him. Here in the city centre, there were a lot of officers around, and he had no way of telling just how serious his arrest warrant was. By this point, it could have gone all round the Force, so all he could do was rely on his faith that Carter was serious, but never melodramatic.

He pressed the buzzer and waited. A voice came on the other end and he asked for Reg Walters. The voice took a few moments before it came back to ask who was calling.

Those few moments had been enough to be filled with a short conversation between the buzzer voice and Reg, to check who it was. Which meant that Reg was expecting a visit from him. Stone had always liked the idea of being mysterious, like an old film noir detective. In truth, he knew that most bricks had more finesse and subtlety.

The door opened and an assistant stood in the doorway with her coat and bag. She acknowledged Stone and there was a brief moment of tension. Stone couldn't tell if she knew something, if he was giving off some kind of smell of the accused, or if she was merely taking a moment to remember who he was. But she let him walk past and in through the door with only a mild smile. Stone hoped that didn't mean Reg was on the phone to Carter asking for back-up.

That's when Reg came out of the side office with a look on his face that spoke volumes.

'Sorry, Reg,' Stone began. 'I know I shouldn't be here – but…'

'Well, inspector, let's start with the fact that I *don't* think you are a psychopathic killer.' He paused. 'Well, I don't think you're a killer, at least.'

Reg didn't smile, but Stone did take a little reassurance from the flash of dry humour from the pathologist.

'That said,' Reg continued, 'I'm not sure exactly what you think you can get out of me, or what the bloody hell you are doing here.'

'I need your help.'

'And how am I going to help you, Mike – that is, unless you want me to dot the *i* and cross the *t* on my own P45?'

Rank, or vocation, had been dropped. This was man-to-man, it seemed.

'What can you tell me about the second body?' Stone asked.

'Would that be the second body of the case, or the second body of the day?' Reg was clearly intent on making much out of the inappropriate nature of their discussion. 'Don't put me in this position, Mike. You see, I have one of two choices, and both end up shit for me. I either tell you what you want to know, lose my job, maybe even go to prison for aiding and abetting a wanted man… or I don't help you and spend the rest of my days wracked with guilt if everything goes down the pisser for you and I'm stood in the dock with my balls in the grip of a rather nasty barrister.'

Reg walked into his office and sat behind his desk. Stone followed and leaned up against the wall just inside the door.

A silence hung in the air between the two men for a moment.

'Okay, how about this,' Stone began. 'You can't tell me anything. So, what if I say what I'm thinking, and if I'm right, you say nothing? If I'm wrong, you simply say no, and that way you won't be lying when you tell Carter that you told me nothing.'

Reg took a moment to consider the idea, and then, toasting him with his mug of tea, replied: 'The best way to lie is to keep as close to the truth as possible.'

Stone smiled. 'The second body had a pregnancy test somewhere on or around it.'

Reg said nothing.

'It was negative.'

Reg said nothing.

'Cause of death was the same as the first body – he drained her dry of blood.'

Reg said nothing.

'The body was clear of unexplained DNA.'

'No,' Reg replied.

Stone was stunned. The men glared at each other. Stone exploded. 'Fuck this, Reg, I am not a mind reader, I need to know. Tell them I stuck a scalpel to your throat or something.'

'But that would be a lie, Mike.' Reg smiled.

'At this rate, it might not be. I might not hold it to your *neck,* though,' he said, nodding a little lower.

Reg relented. 'Semen. The rape kit showed, amongst all the other severe penetrative damage, signs of sexual activity that could only have happened within a few hours before time of death.'

Stone took several moments to process this. He looked over his left shoulder, in search of that secret voice, but it wasn't there this time. 'Early indications were that she was a single mum: no signs of a relationship with a man were found at her place.' He paused for thought, now pacing a little restlessly, talking aloud to himself more than to Reg. 'But it can't be the killer. It's not him. It's not about rape.'

'The sample was sent to DNA as soon as I found it,' Reg said. 'I put it on rush for analysis and comparison on the basis that there could be a connection to…' He paused for a moment to carefully choose his words. 'A connection to any other male on the case, or in the system.'

'And?'

Reg didn't reply, but clearly had an answer. He appeared to be weighing up the costs of telling Stone what he knew.

'Come on, Reg. By your silence, I can tell that it can only be significant. I know it isn't my DNA, so I'm not worried about that.'

'For fuck's sake, Mike, this is my career.' He was standing up, back turned to Mike.

'It's another man on the case, isn't it?' Stone tried. Reg was silent. 'Well, let's see, that means it has to be, so far, Aaron Peters or Malcolm Glenn.'

'No.'

Stone was stunned. There were no other viable suspects. No other DNA samples would have been taken for sampling.

'Reg, I swear I am going to get one of those scalpels."

His eyebrows hit the ceiling. 'Well, at least now I can say you threatened me with a scalpel and I won't have to be lying.' He smiled, before burying his face in his hands, and finally groaning as he ran his fingers through his medium-length, beautifully conditioned hair. The kind of well-washed hair that matched his accent.

'The DNA is a match to the only other DNA sample I took today,' Reg said. 'And before you ask, no, I did not fuck up the samples; and yes, we can turn it round that fast when needed.'

Stone had to think for several moments before that voice whispered from over his shoulder.

'You are kidding?' he said. Reg wasn't. 'Steve Simpson? Steve Simpson's semen was found in the second victim?'

Reg said nothing.

Stone repeated the question, but Reg still said nothing. Until…

'And just to complicate things further,' the pathologist continued, as if to pose a great riddle, 'Steven Simpson died between ten pm and midnight, whereas Samantha Harris died between around two am and four am. So, it appears that your second female victim had unprotected sexual intercourse with a dead man… and despite being dead, he still ejaculated. Which means your timeline is all over the place – or Samantha Harris was a really dead-good fuck!'

Knowing that the latter was just the dry wit of the pathologist, Stone now had to work out why, and how, Steve Simpson came to be having sex with the second victim.

It also meant Stone's theory that the killer was making this into a kind of personal, intellectual game was gaining serious ground.

How do you win a game when you don't even know the rules?

Chapter 21

Stone walked away from the coroner's court wondering how much longer he was realistically going to be able to keep up his petulant child act. As he turned the corner onto Newton Street to head back to his car, he found a marked police car parked up beside it and a uniform officer calling it in.

Carter had been deadly serious about the arrest warrant.

He knew this meant his car registration had been picked up on the officer's ANPR. The poor officer, who barely looked a day out of training, seemed somewhat confused on the radio. Stone decided that the lesser risk would be to walk back the other way. It was, he thought, very unlikely that this youthful PC would recognise him.

That still didn't stop Stone picking up the pace as he walked in the opposite direction. As he turned left onto

Steelhouse Lane, he pondered the idea of popping into the Jekyll & Hyde for a much-needed quick pint. For a moment, he wondered why Reg Walters didn't use this as his regular post-work pub, but then thought it was perhaps a little too much for someone in the medical profession to risk that level of irony – especially when dead bodies were the main business.

Even more problematic, however, was the sight of Sharp walking up the road in his direction.

What the bloody hell is he doing here?

Stone wondered if Sharp was on his way to see Reg. But if that was on official business, why had he not parked in one of the staff spaces round the back? Stone spent a moment too long mulling over the question before turning around; Sharp had seen him, and immediately called his name. Instinct kicked in, and Stone ran.

Why are you running, you damn fool?

Stone picked up the pace down Steelhouse Lane, passing next to the children's hospital, hoping he could outrun the sergeant and get back into the hustle and bustle of the town centre.

That's when he heard the screech of tyres behind him, followed by the growl of a revving engine. Determined to escape what he was sure would be an unmarked car, he began scanning for places to get off-road quickly.

Stone's heart was pounding in his chest, and the adrenaline was pumping.

Just as he dodged to cross the road in an almost suicidal move designed to scare the driver into another swerve, the car came from behind and screeched to halt right in front of him, sideways on. He had no choice but to vault the bonnet of the car and bounce off the windscreen.

Landing badly on the road, he rolled and let the momentum get him back on his feet. That's when he heard the voice.

'DI Stone! Get in!'

He recognised the voice but couldn't pin it down in his mind, so he turned. The first thing he saw was Sharp about fifty yards away, gaining ground quickly.

'Stone! Get – in!' the voice shouted again.

And then he saw the driver.

Malcolm Glenn.

He had no time to think, but felt a sense of dread as he ran to the car, got in the passenger side, and felt the vehicle jolt into action before he'd even closed the door.

After regaining his breath, the thought dawned on him that he was now in a getaway car being driven by a man who was still considered a possible suspect in a murder inquiry.

If he'd dug himself a hole by not going in to see Carter, he now found himself carving out a canyon.

* * *

The two men said very little in the car, which was fine by Stone as he needed to catch his breath and try to work out what was going on. Malcolm Glenn was focusing on driving as fast as possible to get away, whilst remaining as inconspicuous as possible.

What Stone was struggling to understand was why Sharp had been there, on his own, at almost exactly the right moment. Sharp could have been on his way to see Reg Walters, but since Reg had already passed the post-mortem details on to Carter and Barry, Stone couldn't understand what the sergeant had been doing. Of course, it *could* have been a coincidence.

'I don't think we're being followed,' Malcolm Glenn finally said.

'Good,' Stone replied. 'Now, forgive me for sounding unappreciative, but what the fuck are you doing?'

'I was cutting through town when I saw you running, with that guy chasing you, and picked you up. I thought you were in trouble. Who was the other guy?'

Stone was not convinced by the story, but decided to leave it for the time being. He knew he had to limit anything he said, not least because he was still very sceptical as to Glenn's reasons for involving himself in such a way.

'Another detective,' he said.

'Oh shit! That's not gonna look good, is it?' Glenn seemed worried. 'Hold on… why was he…?'

Stone cut him off: 'Long story. Where are we going?'

Malcolm seemed to think carefully about his answer before giving it. 'I'll level with you, Mr Stone. This is also quite opportune, because I've wanted to talk to you, but without drawing attention to myself. You know. Without calling the station or turning up there. Off the record kind of thing.'

This sounds interesting.

'What do you want to talk to me about?'

'Fancy a drink?' Malcolm said. When Stone didn't reply, he took it as a yes and carried on driving away from the city centre towards the Perry Barr area of Birmingham. He kept to the smaller side roads, away from major CCTV cameras that might locate them, until they got out of Birmingham completely.

Malcolm eventually pulled into a pub on the outskirts of the neighbouring town Walsall – close enough to Birmingham, but far enough away to allow them to feel somewhat safe.

The pub was a reasonably large establishment that gave over half its floor space to the restaurant area, serving carvery menus all day, every day. It was dressed on the outside like a poor pastiche of medieval style, using the cheap brickwork and mock woodwork typical of the nineties. The doorways to the building made an attempt at being aged, framed with darkened, chipped wood, but it still had that clearly manufactured, chain-pub plasticity that slightly cheapened the experience.

As the two men walked in, Stone went straight to the bar as Malcolm went to find somewhere secluded to sit. Stone followed soon after with two pints of lager and a lemonade. He hadn't gone for crisps or nuts, although tempted, as it had felt like a kind of betrayal.

'Go on then,' Stone said.

'I know I'm a suspect. Hell, I'd suspect the ex-husband who is stuck in a custody battle. And because of that, I know you shouldn't be talking to me at all – well, at least not outside a little room with a tape recorder.'

'Trust me, Malcolm, this conversation puts us both at great risk,' Stone replied.

'But you have to hear me out.'

Stone wondered why he was in agreement with this man. Something was telling him that although the meeting was surprising in its timing, he'd fully intended to have it himself, especially since he'd looked up more about Parental Alienation Syndrome earlier that day.

'Malcolm, I'm going to give you the benefit of the doubt, but you have got to help me out here. There's a lot I don't understand.'

A long pause held between the two men.

'Do you have kids, detective?'

'Call me Mike in here, please. Technically I'm not a detective right now. Hell, I might not be one again after today's antics.' Stone weighed up the risks of sharing personal information with him. 'And yes, I have a son.'

'What would you do…I mean, how far would you go to protect him?'

'That's a stupid question. You're a father, Malcolm; you know how far we'd go.'

'And do you do everything you can to support your boy?'

This was getting a bit close for Stone. 'I know I need to do more. I don't need my ex-wife to tell me.'

'But what if you couldn't? What if your hands were tied and every time you pushed harder, you were made out to be worse?' Malcolm appeared to be struggling. 'You can't go to school events like plays or open evenings. But if you protest, you are told that you're causing arguments and it would ruin the atmosphere for all the parents and children. So, you don't go, in order to keep the peace. And when you don't go, you're blamed for not being there, not

190

supporting your child. And your absence is used against you.'

'What about your daughter?' Stone asked. 'How does she feel?'

'That's the worst part. My daughter would be told I didn't show up because I didn't care. She wouldn't get birthday cards or gifts, because – as they would tell her – I had forgotten to send them. I wouldn't be at parents' evening because I didn't care about her education. I even heard my ex-wife put on the crocodile tears down the phone for no reason, just so she could say to my daughter that I had made her cry, and she didn't like talking on the phone to me.'

Stone suddenly came to appreciate the efforts his ex-wife put into keeping her own frustrations to herself, and making sure his son still had a positive image of him.

'After enough time, enough of the stories, enough of the tales about the big bad wolf of a daddy... they begin to believe them.'

Stone nodded gently as if he was beginning to understand. 'And that's Parental Alienation?' Malcolm Glenn was clearly struggling to hold back the tears as the two men shared a bit of silent drinking. Finally, Stone voiced another thought, knowing it would make him sound more like a detective again. 'Forgive me for sounding like a copper, but do you have any proof of this happening, this brainwashing?'

Glenn grunted a semi-laugh at the notion. 'That is the worst part. It's extremely hard to prove. I had a text once from my Sophie asking why I didn't care any more. She has no idea how *much* I care because she is constantly being told the opposite.'

'You do realise you've just given me a pretty rock-solid motive for…'

'Yes, I know, Mike. But do you really think I would give that to you if I'd actually killed my ex-wife? Would it make sense to risk getting locked up and then never seeing my daughter again?'

Stone had to admit he had a point. 'But what if you thought you were so good at it that you would not get caught? Surprisingly, a lot of criminals think they know how to beat the police.'

Glenn's voice cracked a little more. 'Last time I saw my daughter – months ago – she just looked at me. She looked *through* me. No smile. I have no idea what goes on in her mind when she thinks about me. I don't know how she feels about me as a dad. I don't know what she's been told. They won't let me see her now, even with her mum being…' He took a moment, wringing his fingers. 'For all I know, she's been brainwashed so much she is now thinking I don't even love her enough to show up when her mum is dead! Do you know how that feels? To know your own child has lost faith in you?'

'No, Malcolm. To be honest.'

'I'll tell you. It makes me feel every ounce of anger, rage, and anything else that stacks up a motive to kill my ex-wife. So when I am accused of it, it's like a catch-twenty-two. I either lie to you about the little things, or downplay how I really feel, and then you think… you know I'm a liar… and so I could be the killer. Or I tell you the absolute truth, like I'm telling you now, and I sound like…a killer with hell of a motive.' He raised his arms in the air in a gesture of helplessness, and then dropped them to the table. 'Either way, I lose!'

Stone's detective eyes were never switched off, and watched every movement of the man's body language. His gut told him the what he was hearing was truthful. But as always, his brain kept ticking over niggling thoughts.

And his mind flashed a picture of Jack.

'Malcolm, I need you to tell me everything you can about FAPAS.'

'What do you want to know?' he said, sitting up, almost relieved by a bit of emotional respite.

'It's an online group, isn't it?'

'Yeah. It's like a mutual support group for everyone who has similar issues. Someone…some people to talk to who truly, truly understand what you are going through. They don't judge you or doubt you or need you to prove what you say. You don't need to run away from them, or to hide from them.'

Stone felt thankful that the more he heard about FAPAS. the less he felt he *needed* them for himself.

He continued. 'Is there any way someone could get personal information out of members? How do you join?'

'You have to either personally know one of the admins, or send a message to the team to ask to join. It's a closed group.' Malcolm stopped to process a thought, taking a drink to bridge the short silence. 'What kind of personal info?'

'Names, addresses, information about how custody battles are going.'

Malcolm thought carefully, shaking his head. 'Not unless they were able to convince an individual to share that kind of information. But why would anyone do that?'

'This is important, Malcolm. Have *you* told anyone personal information about you, your ex or your daughter online? Anything at all?'

'Do you think there's a connection? Between FAPAS and Grace's death?'

'Consider it an angle, a lead. Suppose there's a killer out there who is killing women because of issues to do with child custody – maybe – and he chose Grace because he...'

'Got to *me*?' Malcolm suddenly looked incredulous. 'Are you saying you think this is my fault?'

'No, that's not what I mean...'

'Yes, it is! You think I somehow gave away personal information and some psychopath has used it and killed my ex!' He was trying to keep his voice in check, spitting his words through gritted teeth.

'No, Malcolm, listen to me. What I want to know is – let's say he *chose* you; chose your ex-wife. How would he do that? How would he know any of what you told me in order to make that choice?'

Malcolm calmed down and thought about it. He shook his head: 'I don't know. What makes you think...' He trailed off. Looked in Stone's eyes. 'There's been another, hasn't there?'

'I can't tell you anything.'

'You don't need to. You would not have asked me that unless there had been. You aren't just fishing for motive here – he's done it again, or you think he might. Don't you?'

'Okay, listen, it is *essential* that you do not tell anyone this – don't mention it to anyone at all. Okay? Don't even repeat it out loud.'

Malcolm looked almost excited by this secret disclosure, like he felt he was being deputised in some way.

Stone continued. 'I'm just considering it a potential lead in that the killer is selecting victims in some way connected with PAS or custody battles. Certainly something that is anti-women.'

'I want to ask you something, but I will understand if you say no.'

This didn't shake Stone at all, as a lot of the things he was used to, as a day-to-day part of his job, seemed very big and shocking to the layperson.

'What did… he… *do* to Grace?' Malcolm asked, carefully. 'I don't want to sound weird, or like a sicko, and I don't want complete details. But…'

'I can't give you any details.' Stone watched as Malcolm swallowed heavily.

'Did he rape her?'

The voice over his shoulder shouted at Stone not to answer the question. 'No.' He ignored it.

'You're certain?'

'As my science friends will say, certainty is a big word. All I would say is I don't think this is about sex, so I doubt he raped her. That's not to say he wouldn't have been sexually aroused by it.'

'Did she suffer?'

Stone's pause and silence spoke volumes. Glenn sat back and put his hands in his pockets. It was a kind of defensive posture. Rather childlike.

Another chilly silence held between the two men.

Glenn's focus suddenly shifted to a point over Stone's shoulder, and his expression changed. 'What the hell?' He shot up from the table and ran towards the door of the pub.

Stone desperately scrambled up and followed Glenn round to the car park. As he turned the corner, he found Glenn wrestling with a man holding a camera. Without thinking, Stone jumped in to drag Glenn off the photographer, swinging him away and pushing him backwards, knowing that allowing him to commit an assault would not help anyone. The man with the camera had also scrambled to his feet and made off into the car park before Stone could get a good look at him.

He instinctively ran to the side of the road, away from the car park, with the intention of getting as much time to look at any escaping car as possible. Taking out his phone and fumbling to get the camera app open, he just about got it to record several seconds before the car sped away. It was a dark red saloon that he recognised, but also knew there could be no way to prove any direct link to the killings. He needed more.

Stone walked back over to Malcolm, looking at the very shaky and rough video on his phone.

'Did you get a good look at the number plate?' Stone asked Malcolm, as he checked the outside of the building for CCTV.

'No, sorry,' he said. 'But I can go one better than that.'

Stone looked at him.

'I think I know who it was.'

Chapter 22

Stone got Malcolm Glenn to drop him off in the city centre not far away from where he had left his car. He assumed Carter would have had it towed and impounded. The two men parted politely, and, despite the incredible irony, Stone recommended to Glenn that he didn't travel too far, just in case the police were to call him back in.

The detective then walked up Newton Road towards where he had parked his car. Much to his surprise, it was still there. After doing a careful sweep of the area, he also satisfied himself that no one had been left on hand to watch the car. He knew Carter well enough to be sure she wouldn't waste money on a surveillance effort just for him.

Next on his agenda was to get Khan on the phone. It was a risk phoning the young detective, but Stone thought it was one worth taking. If he could test anyone's loyalty, he felt Harry was the most likely candidate. He had already run off on Bolton, and probably got her into some serious hot water, so he didn't want to press her again. On the first attempt to call Khan, he withheld his number.

'Harry?' he said, as soon as he heard the line click open.

'Who is this, please?' said a concerned voice.

'Stone. Can you talk?'

'I can talk, yes. Can I talk to you? Not if I want to keep my job.' The level of sarcasm was uncharacteristic of the young detective, and Stone began to wonder how much of a knuckle-rapping he'd been given already.

Everyone is always so desperate to keep their job.

'Don't hang up, just listen. I need to send you a short video file that has a car in it and I want you to tell me if you know the owner.'

'Is this some kind of game?'

'Look, Harry, I have no idea what is going on, and I am sorry I'm being all shifty…'

'And bloody stupid for not coming in.'

A fair point.

'Harry, it's a theory I'm working on that I need to bounce off someone, off the record. And I need someone I can trust,' Stone pleaded.

'Why not ask Bolton?'

Another fair point. Christ – he's grown a pair.

A silence held for a moment.

Stone didn't know whether to tell Khan he had already spoken to Reg Walters, and was pretty sure he knew enough to clear himself of any *crime* – but maybe not a disciplinary.

Khan broke the silence. 'Are you going to send me this video file or not?'

Stone smiled to himself. 'Thanks, Harry. I'll hang up, send you the file. Just text me back what you think. I know I don't need to tell you to keep this to yourself.' Stone thought could hear Khan's eyes rolling in his head.

Stone was making every move up as he went along, and his ultimate goal was to get back onto the case, which he felt needed him. Or was it he who needed the case? There were many more leads he could give Khan to check up on, but this one was particularly personal and peculiar.

As he started his engine, he checked his rear-view mirror. And there it was.

You persistent little shit.

The dark red saloon was parked up a good two or three hundred yards away. There was a vague shadow that suggested someone was sitting in the driver's seat. Stone turned his own engine on and waited to see if the other car would do the same. It was a cold night and Stone knew he could keep an eye out for the exhaust fumes even if he couldn't hear the car from where he was.

The red saloon also started its engine.

Stone slowly moved away and rolled his car to the end of Newton Road, all the time watching his mirror for the saloon's moves. It too crept, keeping a good covert distance. Stone slowly turned left onto Steelhouse Lane, and once he was sure he was out of sight, he pushed hard on the gas, swung the car right, into a side road, and parked up very quickly just in front of another car. He waited a few long seconds until he saw the red saloon drive past at pace. Stone couldn't help but let a thin smile creep across his face.

I won that one, my friend.

That's when he got a text.

'Call me. Mobile.' It was Harry Khan. And that text meant that Stone's suspicions had been confirmed.

'You know whose car it is, don't you, sir?' Harry said.

'Judging by your tone of voice, yes, I do,' he replied. 'But keep it to yourself for now, Harry.'

'You have got to come in. This is stupid.'

'Have you had the post-mortem report back from Reg yet?'

'Yes; and forensics on both bodies.'

'And you're keeping the Jedi informed on everything, right?'

'A bloody mess, sir. The timings are off on bodies two and three.'

Stone stopped him. It was a test. 'So, you think the same guy killed Steve Simpson?'

'Like you always say, sir, don't trust coincidences – look into them, assume they mean something. Body three is riddled with the same MO. Okay, different gender and all that, but the whole thing about it being posed, put on show. Also, cause of death might have been different but it was still themed around loss of blood. Reg Walters said the body was moved.' Khan seemed to be rattling off the entire case without even thinking about it. 'There were marks that indicate a camera tripod in the gravel, about eight feet from the body. And, one more thing, sir. Steve Simpson had an unused pregnancy test kit in his coat pocket.'

Nothing Khan had told him was new or different, but a picture was beginning to develop in the background. Stone likened it to the old days of tuning a TV with an aerial when he was young. Starting off with that snowy effect, then turning and turning a tiny little black cog, occasionally seeing the snowstorm begin to take a blurry shape. After a while that blur would develop into defined people moving around in a kind of snowy silhouette, then suddenly a slightly clearer one. Finally, it would snap into a black and white picture with rolling horizontal lines before eventually you'd grab it in full colour.

This case was still in the blurry snow stage. But it was beginning to gather a bit more shape.

Stone continued. 'Have you tracked down the ex-husband or partner of victim two yet?'

'Please don't ask me for his details, sir.'

By the time they'd put the phone down, Stone had got what he wanted.

Chapter 23

Stone had to finally bite the bullet and go back to the station. However, he was now armed with more information, and a worrying lead with which he felt he needed to tread very carefully. His suspicions were confirmed when he saw the dark red saloon in the car park. All he needed to know was whether the lead was already common knowledge to the rest of the team, or whether Harry had kept his word and held on to that information.

He quickly went over to check the number plate. It was the same vehicle. There could have been a completely logical reason for what he was thinking, but that would mean another coincidence – and the coincidences were multiplying at a worrying rate.

Stone hoped he could play this card close to his chest.

At least he knew that Carter had plenty of evidence to show there was no need to keep him suspended from duty. Unless, of course, she wanted to make a big issue of his episode of evading arrest.

He was hoping she might overlook that, given the circumstances.

Stone met Carter down in reception, but it felt less like a ceremony and more like the beginning of the Green Mile. To his relief, she took him into a side meeting room rather than a formal interview room. However, it did cross his mind that it might simply be for a warm-up round before the real bout began more formally in her own office.

'I thought it best if I just come in and talk to you,' he said, somewhat sheepishly.

'Well, how bloody noble of you, Mike. What are you going to pull out of the hat next? An apology note from Fred West?'

'No, ma'am,' Stone said, 'but I have got a recipe for humble pie from Mary.'

The spot of humour did nothing to warm the atmosphere.

'Don't say anything, just shut up and listen,' she said. 'I don't know how much of this you've been squeezing out of your colleagues...'

Stone tried to look innocent.

'Oh, don't give me that, Mike. I know what loyalty earns you. Their silence might save their own arses, but it might not save yours. We have more from Reg on the second body, which just makes no sense. We also have DNA from the third body – which Khan has been trying to convince me is from the same killer – that makes a sodding nightmare of the timeline.'

'That's where I might have some more ideas,' Stone said, 'to help tie things together, at least a little.'

'Do I want to know where or how you came about this information?'

'I was suspended. So, I stayed away from work, as you told me to. If other civilians happened to be in other public places at the same time, I couldn't help that, could I?'

There was a long silence between them. Stone felt a flash of guilt: he could see that Carter really was putting her neck on the line for him. Even if her head wasn't completely taken off, you could definitely hear the blade being sharpened.

Stone wondered if it was the right time to play his extra card, but decided to keep it in his hand until he could give Carter more assurances. If she was going to cover his arse, he thought it was about time he started returning the favour.

Even if he couldn't tell her about everything he was doing.

His mind played tricks on him. His ex-wife flashed in; followed by Jack.

'You need to be debriefed,' Carter said as she handed him a new ID card on its lanyard. 'Don't make me have to strangle you with that!'

Stone didn't say anything, but just gave her a respectful nod.

No bollocking? No warning – or final warning. That was too easy.

* * *

There was a semi-mocking cheer when Stone buzzed himself through the door into the incident room. He waved it off with as stern a look as he could muster, even though he did quite like the attention. He'd never admit it to anyone, but it did feel good to be wanted, even if the show was in jest. 'I'll give you all fifteen minutes, then I want a full briefing.' He turned to Barry. 'I'll catch up with you before the briefing, Pete.'

Pete gave a mild smile with a characteristically non-committal nod. A lot of officers had great respect for Stone, but knew better than to air their opinions on that matter too loudly or publicly.

Loyalty was one thing. Self-preservation was another.

Stone went into his office, sat down at his desk, and tipped back contentedly in his chair, knowing he had only a few seconds until the first knock at his door. It duly came, and he groaned a sound to say: 'come in'.

Bolton came in with an uncharacteristic smile on her face as she said: 'Welcome back to work, sir.'

He looked at her.

She closed the door behind her and then turned on him, a completely different woman. 'You complete and utter prick! I will rip your balls off if you do that to me again.' She paused. '*Sir.*'

Ouch. But fair.

Stone smiled at her. 'Have I missed much?' he said.

'Well, I'll let the briefing bring you up to speed on the nitty-gritty, but there are some nuggets,' she began. 'We

208

did get some foreign DNA inside victim number two that belonged to…'

'Victim three,' Stone jumped in.

'Which brings into question…'

'The timeline.' He was enjoying getting his own back after the amount of times she had done this to him.

'We are now pretty sure, thanks to Harry, that victim three died before victim two…'

'And that his body was moved or dumped after death.'

They both looked at each other. 'But there is something else I have been considering – well, Harry and I have both been thinking.' She paused for a moment to run her hair over her ear.

Stone noted the bags hanging under her eyes. He realised she had just referred to Khan as 'Harry' – which she very rarely did. Stone wondered just how many extra hours the two of them had put in on his behalf. He weighed that up against how many additional hours that meant she had *not* spent with her own children.

A heaviness hung on his shoulders.

'We now have to work out how he moves and transports his victims,' Bolton said. 'The first one happened in her home; the second was placed in a public park. How did he get her there? Undisturbed. No one saw anything. We are trawling CCTV like crazy but it could take days or weeks to come up with anything. And the third victim. How did get it down there without anyone noticing?'

There was another knock at the door and Khan came in, sporting a cautious smile when he looked at Stone.

'Bolton has just been telling me about your new dilemma, Harry.'

'Sir?'

'How he moves his victims around.'

Khan thought for a moment. 'I think it might have something to do with trains.' He went over to the map of the city that was roughly stuck to the wall of Stone's office. Despite all the technology on offer, Stone always liked to have hard copies of the city map in view. Context and location were important factors in so many of the most serious crimes.

'Look at where we found the first body,' Khan began. 'By the train line – closest station was Gravely Hill. The second body, near the Small Heath line – Bordesley station. The third victim was clearly very close to Snow Hill station. Of the three of those, if we take the third victim as the most overt direct communication to us – ' he looked at Stone '– especially *you*, sir, surely we cannot ignore the proximity to train lines.'

Stone decided he had to highlight a slightly obvious point, even if it did hurt a couple of egos. 'You seem to have ruled out a car already. And, to be honest, there aren't many places in this city that are far from a train line.'

The point was made. The silence was telling.

Stone continued, 'I agree that the victims must be caught or transported, or taken somewhere specific. Nothing is left to chance with this guy. Steven Simpson does not frequent that canal bridge right under a train line, but I do. So, I agree. We should consider it a possible part of the MO, and as yet another coincidence we can't afford to ignore.'

The three detectives went to join the rest of the staff for the briefing, and Stone noticed that the team had grown still more. This case was now being treated as the most serious multiple murder enquiry in a long time. Although the official line was non-committal on whether this was a serial killer, there was no doubt amongst the CID specialist team that that was what they were dealing with.

What was bubbling under the surface, however, was the few extra cards Stone was playing very close to his chest. It wasn't a matter of trust, or anything to do with being embarrassed about being wrong, but he wanted to amass more evidence before he dared to say something that could have wide-reaching impact and possibly expend valuable resources on a false lead.

And yet, as the briefing churned out the details, and jobs were being handed out, Mike Stone's mind was wandering back to his son and ex-wife.

Again.

The thought lingered in his mind that the death of Steve Simpson might not be the end of their involvement in this case. He hoped his imagination was running away with him…

'Mike,' Carter said with an unusual softness of tone.

'I'll start drawing up an action plan on the new leads,' he began to reply.

'Go home.'

Stone was stunned by the response and couldn't quite work out the reason behind it. 'Go home?'

'I'm about to do the press conference on the case, which is going out live on TV and local radio, and I don't want you involved with that anyway. I've got a DCI on the team now who can act as joint lead with me. There is nothing solid you can do this evening that we can't handle. Go home now, come back fresh tomorrow.'

'What is the bloody point of me sitting on my arse at home whilst the rest of the team...' He took his cue to stop and listen from Carter's look.

'You bloody fool. I don't mean your God-awful man-pad. Go *home* and see Claire and your son. Mike, this is a very rare occasion when you will experience compassion from me. Don't waste it.'

For the first time in a long time, he didn't argue with his superior officer.

Chapter 24

As Stone drove away from the station, he turned the radio on to listen to Carter take a press conference on the murders. Her voice was calm, professional, and unnervingly clear. Her tone carried the weight and seriousness of the issue without melodrama. She knew what she was doing.

Her address had the intention that had been agreed by the whole team: to show that the Force were throwing all of their resources at the case; that they were following the murderer; that they were hearing him. It had to portray confidence that the murderer would be caught, but still emphasise the need for vigilance.

Carter alluded well to the weakness the CID team currently had and turned it into a strength. She commented on the movements of the murderer around public places – quickly stating there was no need to panic.

She reminded the public to continue calling in to report anything that stood out or concerned them, be it an unusual car in their street, or the unusual behaviour of people hanging around otherwise quiet places. And fundamentally, if they had a loved one or member of their family whose movements were not as expected – late home from work, not turning up at the pub – not to ignore it, but to double-check, if only to be double safe.

'Panic plays into his hands, but so does complacency. Vigilance and calmness is how we shall stand,' had been the final message of the conference.

Stone was impressed. Of course, some people will take any opportunity to panic, and the papers will pick up on it and make it sound like Jack the Ripper has come out of retirement, but the police force would remain steadfast and professional.

He turned the radio off when he got to Claire's house, and sat silently in his car. Once again, he felt a nervousness creep up on him and he couldn't quite understand it. Or rather, he didn't want to admit to the feeling that he knew exactly what it was.

It was what he'd felt when he first got to know Claire and he'd begun his systematic approach to earn her smiles, her laughs, and ultimately her heart. It was what he'd felt when he used to sit in his car and rehearse what he would say when she answered the door, just to make sure he came across as keen enough, but not sleazy; tender enough, but not needy; strong enough, but not overbearing.

Yet, more than ten years later, with a marriage and a son behind them, there he was again. Which meant, as far as he was concerned, he knew exactly what he was doing, and knew to tread carefully. He decided, above all, he must focus on Jack. After all, no matter what Mike's feelings were, Claire and Jack had both suffered a massive emotional blow, and common decency alone precluded him from making any kind of move on a woman in such a situation.

But he also knew it meant it was really, very seriously, time to step up when it came to his son.

Mike got out of his car and walked up to the house. It was the three-bedroom house he had bought with Claire when she was pregnant with Jack. A nice, suburban property in the southern area of Birmingham that was reasonably quiet by Mike's standards. He had to live as close to possible for work, but didn't want to bring up a family in the city centre.

He had wanted a garden. She had wanted a spare room. He had wanted a garden to eat barbecues in the summer and drink with friends. She had wanted a good kitchen. He had wanted a garden in which to spend time on a quiet weekend with a book or some music, hiding away from the world. She had wanted enough storage space, especially when the baby came. He had wanted a garden...surprisingly a lot, for someone who was never a real 'outdoors' or gardening person.

The house had a small porch attached to the front that gave coverage from rain in those essential 'find the key' moments. Mike stood in the porch and noted that it still needed some DIY attention that he had never got around to.

He'd already found his key, and although he'd been invited to use it when he pleased, something just didn't seem right. It was his house, but not his home any more.

He paused long enough for Claire to notice him through the glass of the front door and come to open it. Mike looked at her rather pathetically, showing her the key and shrugging his shoulders like a nervous boy asking out his very first date.

A moment passed between them where no words were needed, and as her eyes filled, Mike stepped into the house and caught her weight, almost picking her up in his embrace.

* * *

The camera's shutter clicked in rapid succession. Frame after frame was caught of the inspector returning to the house. It seemed odd to see the man who always carried himself with such confidence approach the door to what used to be his own home with such nervousness.

He'd seemed like a schoolboy knocking on the door of his girlfriend's house for the first time. Delicate, fidgety, with a head gently hanging, as if it belonged to a dog that had angered its owner.

* * *

Jack shot down the stairs and leapt at Mike and his mother when he heard the front door close. He tried to wrap his arms around both of his parents before managing to squirm his way in between them. It was a sickly-sweet, ideal-homes scene, but Mike couldn't miss the smile on Claire's face as she turned to go into the kitchen, no matter how hard she had tried to hide it, leaving him to pick up his son and stumble off into the living room.

The boy bombarded his father with questions. Was he staying for dinner? Why do cats purr? Could he stay after? Had he seen 'something or other' film? Could he help with homework because it was maths, and he hated maths? Are cats better than dogs?

When could he stay at dad's again, for a weekend?

And what about fish – are they better than cats?

Claire had obviously been thinking about a pet for the boy. A distraction?

Mike's mind wandered to all those army dads who go away for months on end, leaving their wives and children behind. When they get home, they must get the same barrage of attention, he thought. But they've been in a different country, often in dangerous places, fighting wars to protect people. He might well be fighting local, smaller battles, and he might well be in the business to protect the public, but it was hardly comparable.

So, what was his excuse?

Mike got Jack to carry on drawing his picture of a high-speed police chase whilst his mum finished cooking dinner. He had to promise he'd stay for the meal before Jack would agree to carry on drawing by himself while the adults had a chat in the kitchen.

'They still won't tell me what actually happened, you know,' Claire said.

Mike knew what she meant. She wanted the gory details. It wasn't a morbid curiosity – in fact it was quite a common thing with victims. They felt a need to know the details of the death of close ones in order to process them, to gain some kind of closure. Perhaps what made it worse for Claire was that she hadn't been the next of kin to Steve, as she wasn't married to him.

'Why wasn't I called to identify the body?' Claire asked, a little more quietly, to make sure their son didn't hear.

'His parents were called. And…' Mike was really trying to avoid a line of conversation he didn't want to go down.

'Those two women detectives,' Claire said, 'they told me it wasn't a case you were working on.' She paused. 'It was a murder, Mike. You're an inspector. Why weren't *you* working on it?'

Mike thought carefully about his answer. 'As soon as the connection was made between Steve and me, that was it. There was no way the chief would let me anywhere near it. Call it conflict of interest, or something. It's no different from a doctor in a hospital being prevented from doing surgery on someone they know.'

Claire looked at him. She wasn't convinced; she knew Mike too well to be fooled by a cloak of official policy answers. She took her cup of tea to the back door and looked out onto the garden and patio. Mike could tell there was something on her mind. Something she hadn't yet asked, or put to him. Part of him wanted to press and find out more. Part of him wanted to wrap his arms around her, to hold her close.

But a bigger part of him could feel a drop in the temperature in the room.

'What did you two talk about when you met in town, Mike?' she asked. The pause hung a little too long for Mike to retreat from it. 'Did you argue?'

'Yes, we argued. He told me you two were trying for a baby and I flipped. I'm sorry.' He waited for a response.

'We were trying. He wanted to. Not because he didn't love Jack, but because he…'

'Wanted to be a dad. I do understand why he would want to.'

'And you were threatened by him.' It was a statement, not a question. It wasn't delivered with venom, but it tasted sour.

Mike nodded.

'Did your argument with him…' she paused, and Mike knew what was coming. 'Did it have anything to do with him – with what happened?'

'No.' He rethought it. 'Maybe.'

Claire swung round and glared at him. 'You were meant to say no and leave it at that, Mike. Christ! So, you tell me, Mr Detective, did you get him killed? And before you say anything, I don't care what you think – thought of him, I *loved* Steve.'

'I know, Claire.' He fumbled to work out what he could say without crossing lines that hadn't even been drawn yet. He could run rings around a suspect in an interview room, but Claire turned that ability to jelly. 'Claire, it might be possible that the killer chose Steve very carefully and deliberately to communicate…with me.'

'Is that some kind of celebrity-detective fucking ego?' Claire began busying herself with the cooking, which she had finally got around to, later than normal. Having lost her appetite, she was merely doing it to make sure Jack kept eating.

'The killer stole my ID card and put it in Steve's hand when he left his body.'

'But why you, Mike? Why *you*? If Steve had to die because of you…why *you*?'

And that was the crunch question. Mike had made the connections easily enough. He had accepted that the psychopath killing people had made a deliberate effort to communicate with him. He'd even considered that the killer must have witnessed the fight between him and Steve in the pub and somehow overheard the mention of a baby – hence the pregnancy test left in Steve's coat pocket. But what Mike had not yet worked out was why.

Who had he wronged? Even if he took the FAPAS connection into account, there was no custody battle, animosity, or anything close to Parental Alienation Syndrome between him and Claire. Claire was still waiting for a reply.

'Well, Mike? Why do I…why does *Jack* have to suffer *again* because of you and your bloody job?' A pause. 'Again.'

This sting was palpable. Mike sat down as Claire turned away to dish up the fish fingers and chips she had cooked for Jack, taking them through to the living room and letting the boy eat them in front of the TV. Another minor bribe that would not normally be allowed.

Again.

The serious car accident that had left Mike critically injured and threatened the lives of Claire and Jack had been the result of a revenge attack from a bailed suspect.

The suspect had identified his car and deliberately rammed it at a junction just as the three of them were setting out on a rare short-break holiday. Stone had just managed to swerve so that the oncoming car hit his driver's-side front panel rather than the other side where his wife sat, or the back where their young son was sitting. But that had resulted in him sustaining injuries so severe that paramedics had inserted an emergency breathing tube into his throat at the scene of the accident.

He was lucky to have suffered few long-term injuries, other than a persistent pain in his knee and hip that only flared up in very cold weather. After a few months of rest, he finally went back to work, once he'd been given the green light from his doctor.

The physical green light.

The damage to the relationship between him and Claire went deeper, and after many arguments about putting his job before his family life, eventually Mike decided to leave, if for no other reason than to ease the constant tension in the house that was doing no end of damage to Jack.

And clearly, for Claire, that tension had never quite eased.

Claire came back into the kitchen and began washing up, busying herself as she waited for his reply.

'I don't know, Claire. I really don't know – and I hate that. It didn't make any sense – *why me* – it was a departure from the others...' He realised what he had said a split second after he'd said it.

'Others?'

At that moment, Jack ran into the kitchen to show his dad the high-speed car chase. Mike immediately switched away from the subject and looked at the picture, heaping on the compliments quickly and ushering him out to go and finish his dinner, promising to be there in a minute to steal a chip and a fish finger.

He hoped the interruption would let him off from answering the question. No luck. Claire's steely eyes still wanted an answer.

'We are working on a *theory*, and it is just a *theory* at this stage,' he lied, 'that Steve's death might be linked to the two other deaths over the past week. Only because it's so rare to have this many murders in such a short space of time. There might not be any connection at all, Claire, but we cannot ignore a possibility of a link between other deaths I am investigating and one that was clearly aimed at me.'

She was not pleased by the answer, because she knew there was something, or many things, that he could not and would not say. Their relationship had always been one that required her to accept that she simply could not know all about his work.

'How much danger are Jack and I in?' she asked, giving him no room to wriggle.

The hairs stood up on the back of his neck. 'You're not in any danger.'

But he'd taken a split second too long to answer that question.

'I would never, ever risk your safety, Claire. Or Jack's.'
But he *had* risked it.

They changed the subject and Claire carried on preparing some more chips and fish fingers, which they agreed to just throw on a big plate and share, since she still had no appetite.

She might have been able to go on autopilot for Jack, and to keep functioning for his sake, but when it came to looking after herself, that plan had gone out of the window completely. Mike made a mental note to get DC King to pop round again in the morning.

Mike spent some much-needed time with his son, and put him to bed for the first time in a long while. He tried to reassure the mother of his son that they were not in danger, but offered to have a car watch her house – which was a brave move to take without checking he could fulfil such a promise. Budget cuts did not leave room for police protection duties in all cases. But given Carter's tone earlier that evening, he was pretty confident he could twist an arm to get what he wanted from the department purse this time.

It didn't answer Claire's question about why she would need such protection if they weren't in any danger.

* * *

Jack's room hadn't changed at all and Mike noticed that most of the toys, posters, and even cuddly toys that he had given his son were still on display. No matter what he thought of Steve Simpson, the man had not tried to elbow his way into the boy's relationship with his real father. It seemed that, despite their argument, Steve had actually been the antithesis of a PAS-enabling step-parent.

He sat with his son for a while, looking at the various toys on the bedside table. Jack had never developed much of a policeman fantasy, and perhaps Mike had discouraged that, so he was surprised to see some crude plastic police action figures amongst the debris in the room.

And then he saw the mobile phone.

It was one of those cheaper models from unknown companies that could be bought from any supermarket. He picked it up and pressed a few of the buttons to see if it was switched on. It was.

What would a ten-year-old want with a mobile phone?

In reality, children much younger than Jack were walking the streets with some of the latest models. He'd even had to deal with a case of robbery where a child younger than Jack had been seriously beaten just to get his mobile phone. The attackers had been caught – fifteen and sixteen years old.

The sixteen-year-old literally pissed himself in fear during the interview.

Mike scrolled through the contacts and found only a few names. One or two he recognised as Jack's best friends from school, whom he'd heard about earlier that evening. Then there was 'mum' and 'home' – again unsurprisingly. There was also 'Steve', and Mike recognised enough of the numbers to know that it was Simpson's number.

But no 'Dad.' No one was to blame for that except himself. He added his number and saved it. Then he found the number of the phone to copy into his own.

With each new thing he discovered, Mike felt another step away from his own son. As he looked down at the sleeping boy, he made a silent promise, a silent vow. One that he had made many years ago, and broken. One that he now had to rebuild.

Mike set Jack's phone to silent for a moment and took out his own to send him a text.

'See you soon. Love you. Dad.'

He waited for the message to be received before placing the phone carefully back where had found it. Jack stirred in his sleep and appeared to Mike as if he was frowning. He gently placed a hand on Jack's chest and quietly hummed a tune that crept in from deep in his subconscious.

'It's raining, it's pouring,
The old man is snoring…'

Jack's expression seemed to soften and relax. Mike kissed his son gently on the head and left the room silently.

* * *

As Mike left that evening, he had no idea how long the case was going to drag on for, and how much danger his family were in. All he did know was that the perpetrator had made a bold statement that he himself was in the killer's cross-hairs – not just as a DI, but as a man and a father. It would take a lot more than a card held close to his chest to protect his heart from that kind of injury.

Chapter 25

He'd woken up almost every hour that night, and by six in the morning he decided to give up on sleep and just get up. Insomnia struck Stone quite often, but that night had been particularly harsh.

His mind had been buzzing with an excitement from the night before, thanks to having spent more time with his son than he had done in a while, and having made some kind of connection with Claire again. He wasn't so naïve as to be thinking about happy families too soon, but still the evening had left him with a bounce in his step.

A bounce that had quickly become a thud, given what was turning into the most complex multiple murder case Birmingham had seen in years. He had appreciated the time off the night before, but he also felt out of touch with the case and was itching to get into work early.

As Stone approached his car in the gated car park behind the apartment block, he noticed the envelope under the windscreen wipers. Without breaking his step, he reached inside his coat pocket and took out two latex gloves.

It was an impulse.

Stone knew that he had to assume the envelope was linked to the case. That meant the envelope was evidence, and since his face was all over one piece of evidence – his old ID card – he didn't want his fingerprints all over another.

The envelope was neatly adorned with his name in full: 'For the Attention of' – not FAO – 'Detective Inspector Mike Stone, of Birmingham Force CID.'

I know you know where I work, you prick.

He carefully opened the unsealed envelope and slid out the A4-sized gloss-paper photographs. His immediate thought was that in this digital age of emailing photographs, this kind of offering was too much of an artisan statement to be ignored.

It didn't take him long to work out what the photos were, or where and when they had been taken. One of them was of a man standing outside a house with a porch. He was wearing a black leather coat and holding something small and reflective in his hand. The door to the house had been cut out on three of its four sides, and allowed to flap like an opened advent-calendar window.

The second image was even clearer. It was of Mike Stone standing in the cemetery at a headstone, which had also been cut to flap open. Stone estimated from the angle that the photo was taken from much further into the cemetery, and therefore almost certainly by whoever had left the envelope.

The was no question for Stone that the photos were connected to the case, but they didn't show a clear enough connection to be classed as evidence. The only proof was that there was some connection between the detective and whoever took the shots.

A connection that Stone was sure he needed to work out.

Quickly.

* * *

Stone sat in his office staring at the map of Birmingham, hoping in vain that some big epiphany would spring out at him. That eureka moment didn't come, and still hadn't done by the time Khan knocked on his open door and came in when there was no reply.

'Sir,' he said wearily, 'I really think we need to talk.'

Stone knew exactly what this was about. The dark red saloon and its owner, and why that owner was carrying a camera around and taking pictures of Stone. And why those pictures had not been handed in to Carter.

'How did he find me in Walsall, Harry?' Stone asked.

'He has his contacts, and I have mine. It just so happens that one of those contacts was the same person who accidentally let it slip that he'd received an '*off the record*' call from Sharp the other day.'

Stone gave Khan a look that was enough to ask who the contact was, and although he was initially reluctant,

Khan finally told Stone who it was in the technical team that he knew so well. And who would be his go-to man for all things technical, such as mobile phone tracking.

Especially if he needed it doing on the QT.

Stone took out the envelope with the photos. 'Don't touch them,' he said, 'I need them fingerprinted, though I daresay nothing will be found.'

Khan had a keen eye for photography that gave him a slight advantage over Stone. 'Taken from quite some distance, sir, probably with a longer lens. It's very clear it's your house.'

'But it's not my house, is it?' Stone replied. 'That's the point. It is me, standing outside the house that used to be mine. It's not just a photo, Harry; it's a statement.'

'Saying what?'

'That he knows where my family lives. And that I can't protect them all the time.' He paused and finally said quietly, almost to himself: 'Saying that the door is open.'

Khan's eyes darkened at the sinister overtone of the threat. And then he looked at the second photo.

'Well, that's morbid, sir.'

'Isn't it just?'

'Any idea when it was taken?'

'Saturday – whilst you were getting some chips.'

Harry Khan didn't say anything, just mouthed a silent 'oh' that spoke volumes of the cogs turning in his mind. 'You have to take these to Carter, surely, sir.' He paused for a moment. 'One thing I don't get: what's with the door on the gravestone?'

Stone stood up from his desk. 'He's saying my past, and my life with Claire, is an open book.' He walked over to the internal window looking into the open-plan office buzzing with activity. Looking through the cold-grey vertical blinds, he let his eyes hang on Sharp for a while, and let his mind wander.

If this is you playing silly-buggers, I'm gonna...

A flashed image of the woman on the bed in Erdington curtailed Stone's imagination.

But the very idea that there could be someone with such cold audacity working amongst those detectives not only gave Stone a chill down his spine. It also made him question who he could trust.

'What if the killer isn't working alone, Harry?' Stone quietly asked, without turning to look at him. 'Sharp hasn't handed in his photos to Carter, and he knows that I could approach her at any time. That takes some balls.' Stone turns from the window and focus on a spot on the floor. 'Let's assume the worst: that it *is* him.'

Khan let's a wry smile slip for a moment. Then the impact of the suggestion really hits him. 'Sir? Really? Is DS Sharp a suspect?'

Stone continued. 'That third body: Simpson, holding *my* bloody ID card. That was all about showing he could fuck with me forwards, backwards and sideways.'

'I did think it was rather odd that you were seconded to help him on a poxy robbery case, and then he conveniently turned up to help here, after the second body.'

Stone began to scan the floor with his eyes as he slowly shook his head, as if he was trying to piece together a difficult jigsaw puzzle. He suddenly turned and opened his office door with a bust of energy like a second wind. Stone called Bolton over and turned to Khan she was making her way over. 'Harry, I want you to get Malcom Glenn and James Harris on the phone.'

'The two ex-husbands? Um, right, okay…'

'I want to meet with *both* of them, *and* others. Gather together all the local fathers who are members of FAPAS or similar groups in this area and are currently going through custody cases. Arrange a private meeting. Tell them it is *us* that need *their* help. If needs be, hint at the possible danger their child might be in. Guarantee discretion; suggest possible anonymity; but *promise* nothing.'

Khan looked decidedly uneasy with the suggestion. 'You're asking me to call two possible suspects in a murder case and ask to meet up for lunch? For a chit-chat?'

Stone's glare made it clear that this wasn't a request.

'No, Harry, I'm ordering you. So, it's only my ass on the line, okay? Give them my direct number. I don't want them calling through to here and being put on the line to…' He didn't need to finish the sentence.

Bolton got to the office right on cue and Stone gestured her in without saying a word. She noticed the photo, but Stone knew she would have too much decency to bring it up. Khan took his instructions and went off to fulfil his duties. There was a reluctance, almost a nervousness in the way he moved that gave Stone a pang of guilt at just how far he was pushing the young detective's loyalty.

'What do you think?' Stone said, nodding at the photo.

Bolton took a good look at the photo. 'I think someone is really trying to get to you. I think it is working. I think that's why you haven't shown these to Carter or Pete yet. And I think that yapping dog is going to need to tone down his enthusiasm a bit – it's making me a little nauseous.'

'You leave Harry alone,' he smiled. 'He's a good copper. He's loyal, too. And he'll go far if his loyalty doesn't cost him his job.' Stone took a moment to listen out for that voice over his shoulder, but nothing spoke. 'I need you to just go along with me on this, Sands. I'm shooting from the hip, and I need you with me making sure I don't blow my balls off, okay?'

'No one is *that* good a marksman.' She threw him a quick wink and took her place leaning against the wall behind his desk. Stone called Sharp over to his office and took his seat.

When Sharp came into the office, he closed the door behind him, and took a seat opposite his senior officer without being asked.

You're a cocky little shit, but I ain't gonna bite.

'Well, now that you're comfortable, sergeant, I want to pick your brains about the third body,' Stone continued. Sharp looked at Stone, then Bolton, then back at Stone, and waited. 'Talk me through it. I mean, talk *us* through what sticks in your mind.'

'Why?' Sharp asked.

'Humour me.'

He fidgeted in his chair, opened his suit jacket out a bit more, and straightened his tie. It was a set of ritualistic movements designed to delay and to prepare. As Stone

233

always put it: *those who intend to tell the truth never have any need to prepare.* The rituals were a sign that either an outright lie was coming their way, or a concealment of the truth, or parts of it.

'Dead male was found in…'

'Cut the formal speak here, Chris. Just take me through it.'

'Okay.' He flattened his tie again. 'The victim was lying on his back. Body was shoved right up into one of those small archways with his head and shoulders kind of propped up against the wall, as if he was sitting up a bit to look. He had an ID card…' He paused for a moment, unsure as to whether he should speak about the elephant in the room. 'He had your ID card in his left hand, all covered in blood.' He fiddled with his own ID card as if to demonstrate what one looked like. Another thing liars did: over-exaggerate simple actions or details. 'His throat was slashed both ways. Doc Walters said in the report that —'

'Stick to what you saw at the scene,' Stone cut in.

Sharp nodded, and continued. 'Bloodstains on his chin and cheeks didn't really fit. I mean, the blood would go everywhere, sure, but it looked like it had run *up* his cheeks, like he'd been the other way up when the wound had been inflicted.' A pause. A thought. 'Oh, and he had an unused pregnancy kit in his coat pocket.'

Bolton decided to jump in. 'What about his face, Chris?'

He looked completely confused by the question. 'I don't understand what you mean.'

'Expression?'

'Well, he was dead,' laughed the sergeant, until he realised he was the only one who found that funny. 'His eyes were wide open. Yeah, that was quite striking. Not that they were open, but that they were wide open.'

'What colour were his eyes?'

'Brown,' Sharp answered. Perhaps too quickly.

'Take a look at these,' said Stone, suddenly handing him the photos.

Sharp instantly reached into his pocket and produced a handkerchief before touching the first photo. After a few moments of studying it, he said: 'Is that you, sir? Why are you showing me a photo of you standing outside…a house?'

Stone left a pause to hang in the air.

'What's with the door being cut out?'

Stone let the pause continue to hang.

'And, oh, look – another one of *you*. In a graveyard – and another little door.' He laughed, a touch uncomfortably. 'Someone making a really morbid advent calendar of you, Mike?'

Stone looked at Bolton. She was staring at Sharp intently, her arms folded, her gaze driving daggers into his skull.

'Well, thanks for that, sergeant,' Stone said, suddenly standing as a teacher might at the end of an awkward meeting with an overbearing parent.

'Is anyone going to tell me what this is all about?' Sharp replied, without standing up.

Bolton just shrugged her shoulders as if to say she had no idea.

For a moment, Sharp had almost looked flattered that he'd personally been called in for an opinion, had it not been for a look on his face that showed he clearly knew that *something* was going on.

'How old are Sophie Peters and Rebecca Harris, the daughters of victims one and two?' Stone asked. Bolton took out her notepad, flicked a few pages, and confirmed they were both ten years old.

'How old is your son, sir?' she asked.

A chill ran down Stone's spine. Jack had just turned ten years old, and the look on his face was enough to say as much.

'I want you two to go back over to the family courts. We are looking for all active custody battles in the Birmingham area. There will probably be a fair number. Narrow that search by age of child, and gender of child. Try and find any other similarities – focus on victims one and two for patterns. We also need their addresses. Everything you can get.'

'We aren't profilers, sir,' said Sharp.

'No, but you are a *detective*, aren't you?' Point made. 'Also, get onto local family solicitors. Find out if there are any major disputes – particularly messy cases. And yes, I will be chasing with warrants if we need them. We need to build a picture here, guys.'

Sharp left quickly but Stone called Bolton to wait a minute. 'So?'

She didn't need any more prompting. 'He's hiding something. And he practically recoiled at being handed the photo, despite the fact he saw you touch it.'

'What about the photos, though? How did he *react* to them?'

Bolton took a moment to think. 'To be honest, his confusion about the doors being cut out seemed genuine. But, in a way, he didn't seem thrown off by the subject of the photos.'

That was what worried Stone – he had *not* expected that reaction.

'Isn't a brown envelope and printed photos a little...old-fashioned?'

Stone gave her his best *go on* look.

'Email, sir. I know the killer isn't going to send you an email from their personal *killer at psycho dot com* account, but it isn't hard to use a public computer and an anonymous, untraceable account, is it?'

'Actually, Sands, it is easier to send a physical photo with no trace than a digital one these days. But I had the same thought. And I think *most* of the message was to be found in the fact that it was left on my car in a private, locked car park. The killer is making a statement that he can get to me.'

'And your family, too.' She knew he would have thought about it.

The thought hung in the air.

Stone sent Bolton on her way, and as planned the night before, asked King to pay Claire another visit. He knew it should be him, but he just couldn't afford that much down-time on a case.

In truth, that voice over his shoulder was telling him to keep his distance.

Chapter 26

The Boy

After waiting for some time under the canal bridge, the boy finally crawled out into the complete darkness. Cold and tired from the shivering, he clutched his aching stomach in hunger.

He made his way a few yards down the tow-path and looked all around, eyes adjusting but still blurry and stinging from the dirty water. No one was in view and the whole area seemed deathly quiet. There was some distant background noise from the world that all seemed to be about ten feet above him. As his small fingers clung onto the brickwork, he could barely feel the sandy texture through the frozen layers of numbness. Getting warm had become his priority.

The boy carefully made his way up the same freezing steel steps he'd been hiding under. Each step burned at his thighs and knees as if he'd been running non-stop for hours. He kept tugging and pulling at the icy handrail to help himself up, desperately trying to grip with his numb hands. Every step was a reminder of the night so far: his soaking wet trainers, and what felt like grit and dirt between his toes. His whole body was heavy with dirt, shaking with cold, and tired with pain.

Making it up onto the path, he felt a sudden light breeze hit him like a block of ice and his arms shot around his body in what seemed like a futile attempt to draw warmth from an invisible blanket.

Just along to the path and across the road to his right stood the four concrete monsters leering over the canal. They stared back down at him knowingly, having watched his whole plight in escaping his pursuers and falling helplessly into the water.

Yet they still drew him in. He began to walk towards the first of the tower blocks to see if there was anything to be found. Some lights were on, dotted at different heights up the walls of the towers. They looked as if they could be the building's eyes or smile, but only if contorted and deformed – monster-like.

It seemed to take an eternity to reach the first building, and he began to feel ice-cold darts drop on his head and the back of his neck. First slowly, then gathering pace and weight. The boy walked up and leant on the cold, rough exterior of the building. It was as if it had been painted with sandpaper, designed to keep anyone from getting too close. He looked up into the dark grey sky, squinting as the ice-drops attacked his face. The tower seemed to grow and lean over him as if he had shrunk into a tiny version of himself, dwarfed by the world. The building was solid, immovable, unfeeling, uncaring.

He wondered if he should return. If he should turn around and go back to…

But his need for food and warmth pushed him on, even though he had no idea where he was going.

The boy slowly followed the wall up to a window on the ground floor. The light was on, and as he got closer he could just about make out sounds coming from inside. They were the familiar chiselled noises of clashing crockery and cutlery; the orchestra of a busy kitchen. Someone was standing right there at the sink. The boy crouched down to walk under the window, but his legs were so very cold they couldn't hold the semi-standing position for long. He quickly scurried past the window and stood up again when he was sure he'd got past.

He waited and listened, trying to work out if he had been seen or not. The sounds of plates had stopped, replaced with the noise of his heart thumping again. Had he been discovered? Would he need to run? Was the chase on again?

The boy quickly ran the remaining length of the building and looked around the corner. He could see a dark overhanging wooden shelf poking out from the wall, glued on at about double his height. It must have been the doorway.

He waited.

His heart pounded louder; his breath scratched harder across the back of his sore throat. The rain began to pummel down on his shoulders.

Satisfied that the coast was clear, and keeping tight up against the sandpaper-wall, he made his way down the side of the building.

Coming to the opening for the doorway, he stopped and peered round to make sure the coast was clear. He looked through the narrow-slit windows that ran from floor to ceiling and were made up of wooden jail-style bars, separated by that glass that looked like school maths paper. It was the wire-mesh glass that the boy had attempted to break with stones many times, with no luck.

It looked so warm inside with the yellowed lights gently heating up the hallway. The boy grabbed the handle to see if it would turn, and much to his surprise, it did.

As quietly as he could, the boy tugged on the metal handle and slowly pulled the door. It was cold and heavy, and made a loud squeaking howl as it began to open outwards. The boy manoeuvred his body around the door and slid in slowly.

When he was halfway through, a huge, hot hand grabbed hold of his wrist. Instinctively, with his other hand, the boy tried desperately to pull himself from the grasp of the building. But the building was too strong and the hand dragged him inside, with his dry mouth refusing to let him make any noise. He felt a second hand grab the neck of his t-shirt and both hands swing his body into the freezing internal wall. His head smacked against the solid concrete. Despite already being freezing cold, the boy felt a cold flooding feeling creep up his body until it got to his head. The sensation crawled round to the back of his head and focused until it suddenly burst into a pinpoint spot of burning pain.

The view of the figure holding on to him blurred as the corridor darkened. The boy's eyelids grew heavy and fluttered as they began to close.

A darkness swallowed him up again, and the last thing he felt was a sudden weightlessness as he slumped into the man's arms.

Chapter 27

The cold morning rain battered the roof of the white concealing tent which had been erected hastily by the SOCO team at their arrival on the scene. The small tent looked like a strange kind of circus act as numerous Smurfs came in and out with plastic evidence bags.

An out-of-uniform, off-duty PC was being praised by Carter for a little bit of forensic initiative. He had been driving past the small wooded area when he'd seen the body, and had attempted to preserve some forensics by covering the ground nearby with some plastic sheeting he'd had in his boot.

Stone stood with Bolton, Khan and Sharp, waiting for the all-clear to come from Reg Walters. There had initially been another on-duty pathologist assigned to the scene, but Stone had called Reg personally to ask him to come down. It wasn't standard procedure, but Stone didn't want any absurd red tape getting in the way of moving the investigation along. Reg was the best pathologist anyway, and the last thing he needed was some rookie who wasn't ready to see the next level of depravity the universe was about to throw at them.

There was no doubt whatsoever, even at a distant glance, that this was exactly what Stone thought it was. These women were being treated like art installations set up to tell a story, each with their own setting and props; their own character and narrative; their own picture.

The body was sitting in a wheelchair in a small park-like area overlooking the Queen Elizabeth Hospital. It was early in the morning, so there was little traffic or public about on the road that ran close to the hospital and the nearby Birmingham University. Stone thought this was a saving grace, as something told him that press interest would result in quite a crowd developing when the sun came out fully.

For now, the rain came down and Stone looked up to the sky and mumbled that he completely agreed. Not a religious man at all, he didn't know who he was talking to. It was more a comment on Mother Nature's reflection of the mood down on the ground.

Reg Walters waved in his direction and the four detectives, already suited in the Smurf outfits, made their way over.

'Bloody hell, inspector, what's this? I know the weather is bad, but it's hardly apocalyptic enough to bring the four horsemen.'

'All right, all right, Reg. What have we got?'

Reg suddenly looked a little more morose than normal. He simply turned and took the four detectives into the tent. They had to clear the SOCO team out so that all five of them could fit inside.

That's when Stone saw the reason for Reg's morose look. The woman was sitting in a wheelchair wearing a hospital gown under a dressing-gown. She was black. Stone had no problem with equal opportunities, but he allowed himself a private joke about serial killers trying to fulfil representation quotas.

He stifled a smile, knowing that his joke would not be appropriate just yet; but also knowing that it really was just his way of coping.

The woman was sitting upright, and even though Stone couldn't describe her as looking pale – he was really stuck on that humour – he could tell by the complexion of the skin and the colour of the lips that she was pale in a very different way.

She was drained.

'She was also holding this,' Reg said, holding up a plastic evidence bag with an A4 piece of paper or card. A photograph. 'It was positioned as if she was sitting looking at it. I got SOCO to photograph it in situ before bagging it.'

Stone took the photo, but he paused for a moment before looking at it.

The black and white photo was of a man and a girl in bed. The man was naked, but the girl – who could only have been about ten years old – was wearing pyjamas. She lay on her back, asleep, whereas the man appeared to be lying on his side, looking at her, with his arm reaching over so that his right hand was on the girl. The picture was not overtly sexual in nature, but the man's hand was placed over the girl's lower abdomen, just a tiny bit too low to be comfortable.

'What's he trying to say, sir?' asked Bolton. 'I never thought we were dealing with a paedophile here.'

'We're not,' Stone replied, confidently.

'But…' She stopped. Something was clearly burrowing away, hiding behind the frown.

'Come on, Sands, out with it.'

'This is the third victim – fourth when you include Simpson – and you cannot deny the inference of this photo, sir.' She continued: 'How the hell is he doing all this, with such escalation in MO, so quickly? How is he able to pick them, plan the killing, carry it out, leave no trace, and vanish into thin air?'

And all with no witnesses.

Stone sighed heavily as he turned to Reg to signal for him to give them the low-down – the initial observations.

Khan had had to retreat from the tent by this point: the combination of the body and the photo proved to be just a little too much for him to stomach this time. Sharp simply stood and shook his head.

The heavily swollen abdomen of the body was clear to see. It was as if a patient had been wheeled out and left here to die. Her hands were cupped under her belly. Her face was plain, completely emotionless. It was if time had stood still for her.

And her unborn child.

Another child had been photographed lying in a bed with a young man apparently gently resting a hand in exactly the same place.

'And it looks like this one is a double murder, sir,' said Bolton.

'Not at all,' replied Reg. 'She wasn't actually pregnant.'

'Reg, I don't want to ask the obvious question, but…' Stone trailed off.

'I won't suggest you feel for yourself, but the first thing we checked for once her death was confirmed was if there was any sign of life from the foetus. However, she isn't pregnant. Despite what it looks like at first, Inspector, that abdomen is absolutely solid. Whatever it is filled with, it is not a human foetus. And before you ask, I have no idea until I can get the body back for the full PM.'

The air was thick with a strange mixture of shock and confusion. Stone let the pathologist continue.

'This victim has needle marks to both inner elbows, just like the others. Her head has been attached to a board of wood just like the body of Ms Harris, but this time using a single nail hammered through the back of the wood and into the top of the back of the neck, at the base of the skull. This blasted weather and the apparent blood loss makes time of death difficult to pinpoint, but I would plump for the early hours of the morning, between midnight and 4am, maybe. Liver temp is hard in these conditions, but even given the cold, wet weather, it still has some warmth to it.'

None of the detectives opted to take a closer look at the body; they were willing to take Reg Walters' account of it. It was also important that they got the body transported inside as quickly as possible.

Stone and Bolton exchanged glances and nodded. They knew what they had to look for. Before leaving the tent, Stone took a good, hard look at Sharp. He wanted to know how he was taking this scene in. 'Sharp, have a chat with SOCO and find out if they've found any footprints and tyre tracks for the wheelchair.' Stone gave Bolton the nod to go with him. She also knew that meant she was to keep an eye on him. As always, he trusted her judgement, and if Stone's thinking was correct, Sharp had a problem with women – which, in this case, might work to Stone's advantage.

Stone met Khan outside the front of the tent and raised a hand to stop him apologising for a hasty retreat. They both carefully made their way along the pathway of metal plates, and Khan asked one of the SOCOs if they had found a set of three markings that suggested the use of a tripod. A faceless ghoul crouched down to show him exactly where.

'Three marks already measured and photographed for you.' She paused. 'Just like the other one, sir. And it seems like these were made pretty deep in order to really steady a camera.'

And perhaps to make doubly sure we'd see them.

Stone said nothing in reply but stood up and, with Khan, began to get a good view of the local area. The hospital was clearly right in front of the scene and Stone asked a SOCO to get another panoramic camera shot. He also noted how this area was a lot less overgrown than the grounds behind the stadium where they'd found

Samantha Harris. It would have carried a far greater risk of discovery for someone wishing to dump a body. Something told him that the killer would not have been so slack as to get himself caught on CCTV, but that would have taken quite some preparation.

Why is he increasing the risk?

Again, the question of the level of planning and preparation was casting a fog over this case. Stone genuinely could not fathom how anyone could achieve such a level and frequency of murder, and in such detail, all without being seen.

A worrying thought crossed his mind about just how long the killer might have spent planning this week. The voice suddenly whispered over his shoulder again.

'Sir,' shouted Sharp from the other side of the white tent. He was standing in a slight opening between two trees, looking at the ground. 'Two very faint tyre tracks; same wheel, and apparently parallel. I'd say probably the route of the wheelchair.'

'Where are the footprints of the person who pushed it, then?' asked Khan. 'There's no way, surely, she pushed herself.'

'There are some markings here.' Stone pointed out some indentations in the soft ground that were approximately shoe-shaped. He waved over one of the SOCO team with a camera.

'I've seen this before, sir,' the SOCO said as she took photographs using measuring set-squares to give size details. 'To disguise the print and size of the footwear, it's pretty easy to make a basic silicone mould which you can wrap around the shoes.'

'Is there no way to identify the print?' Stone asked.

'There's a database of shoe prints, sir, but not one for random shoe coverings. Unless there is something particularly distinctive about any such cover – and we aren't even certain that's how he did it – there is no way to identify even the size, except within a range of plus or minus maybe two sizes.'

Stone knew that such shaky evidence was of little use when it came to identifying a suspect, and even more useless when it came to proving a case in court.

Stone and Khan walked away from the body another ten yards or so towards Vincent Drive. As usual, Stone took in the local area: the sights, the sounds, even the smells. He scanned slowly until his eyes fell on something. He stopped and pointed it out to the younger detective: The University train station.

'My, my, sir, isn't that a coincidence?' Khan said, with a smile that told Stone he knew exactly what the next thought had to be.

The link to the trains was getting stronger.

'The question, Harry, is if we assume that his choice of locations is deliberate, what is he saying?'

'That he's doing all the killings near to a train station?' he replied.

'Or that he's using the trains.'

'Or the victims all use the trains, and that's how he chooses them.'

Stone slapped Khan on the shoulder in appreciation. 'Nice one Harry. Passes; regular journeys; current or previous employment. Whatever it is, Harry, I want to know.'

'Sir, I'm still setting up the FAPAS meeting; I don't have time…'

'Delegate, Harry – delegate. That is what you will need to show you can do before I put you forward for promotion.'

Stone saw Reg Walters waving him back over, so he left Khan to try to work out if Stone's last comment had been an instruction or a compliment.

Reg Walters wanted a private word. 'Mike, a quick thought for you.' He waited, clearly thinking about what he was about to say. 'It appears to me that the uterus has been forcibly expanded from inside. I don't yet know what with, but what I can tell you is that it would have been extremely painful. Really, extraordinarily painful. To be able to do that to a woman would be very difficult without complete sedation or some very powerful anaesthetic.'

'But so far there's been nothing on the tox-screen,' Stone replied.

'We send bloods off for tox on all bodies. But drugs like Rohypnol are not part of a standard screening. Nor are drugs used for all forms of anaesthetics. If I were you, I would order a specific test for this, Mike. The other bodies could have been arranged relatively quickly. But this one would have needed a lot more time, out of sight, and with at least some level of powerful sedation that required some experience or knowledge to use.'

'This has been planned very *carefully*, hasn't it, Reg?'

'Meticulously,' Reg replied, with his perfectly clipped accent.

Stone nodded, and kicked himself for not ordering extra tests on the other bodies. 'Does Rohypnol stay in the blood for long enough?'

'It can sometimes be traced up to sixty hours later. Other drugs can be detected in the hair.'

'What others?'

Reg took a moment, running a hand through his hair and resting it at the back of his neck.

'He could be using Propofol – that's used a lot, but isn't long-lasting. Nor is it a painkiller. He'd have to mix it with morphine, too.'

Stone's head turned to that voice over the shoulder, and Reg recognised the mannerism straight away. 'Three women. The first was all about pain to the womb. The second was about childbirth from the womb – the birth of a toy. This one is about filling the womb, stopping it being used. What's next?'

'Either it is the removal of the womb…' Reg suggested.

'… or it's about the early removal of a child from the womb,' said Stone.

There would be more bodies. And with each body, the depravity was escalating.

'Reg, have you seen anything yet to suggest that the person doing this has medical training?'

Reg seemed very reluctant to answer that question, clearly not liking the idea of the association of his own professional skills with those of a psychopathic killer.

'Answering without any ego, Mike, I'd say they are *not* a doctor or surgeon. But I wouldn't be surprised if they have some familiarity with the medical world or procedures. Maybe a nurse. But for God's sake don't let the media hear you say that.' Reg looked at Stone. 'Seriously, Mike, that comment stays strictly off the record. The panic it could cause would be substantial.'

Maybe that's what he wants. Panic.

Stone knew how much Reg was sticking his neck on the line in professional terms, sharing opinions as he just had.

After gathering the detectives together, Stone sent Bolton and Sharp with uniform to find out the identity of the victim and to start finding out who was in the photograph. Although he was pretty sure it would be the victim's daughter and current boyfriend.

Meanwhile, Stone and Khan had a meeting with a few members of FAPAS to attend. Now that they had a new body – and Stone had the strong feeling that this would not be the last – any lead he could get on the killer was essential.

He also wanted to see if someone else would be there, too, even if that person only watched from a distance.

* * *

Back at the station, a call had come through on dispatch from a frantic young man who could not locate his girlfriend. When the description was passed on to the Force CID team, it was picked up by Bolton and Sharp. Instincts, and a small bit of deduction, told them that hours of searching might just have been saved by a single call.

They arrived at the address in the Kings Heath area of the city just ten minutes later, shortly after a marked car had already got there. As the two detectives arrived at the house, the door was opened by a young man who, Bolton thought, could barely have been much over school age himself. Certainly, a little young to be with someone of the age of the victim discovered that morning. He introduced himself as Drew Massie, but Bolton had already recognised him: he was the young man from the photo.

The two detectives were invited into the semi-detached house, showing their ID to the uniform officer already sitting in the dining room. The other officer was in the living room with the daughter.

'So, anything?' said Massie.

'If you'd like to take a seat, sir,' said Sharp, about as coldly as he could. 'DS Bolton and I have come to see you because we take missing persons cases very seriously. We have a few questions to ask you, and it would be in your best interest if you answer them at this stage.'

Bolton saw the expression on the face of the uniformed officer, who appeared to be shocked by the abruptness of Sharp's tone. She decided to take over.

'Mr Massie, isn't it?' Bolton began.

The man nodded.

'Can you confirm the name of your partner, just to make sure we're all talking about the same person.' Bolton had also taken as tasteful a photograph of the victim as she could on her mobile phone, just in case she needed to use it.

'It's Danielle, Danielle Fallon,' said Drew. 'What's going on? Where is she?'

Sharp jumped in. 'We found the body of a woman who fits the description of your wife…'

'Girlfriend,' Drew corrected, and then realised what had been said. 'Body? *Body?* What do you mean?'

Bolton could have knocked Sharp out there and then for the callous way he delivered the message. It was important to just get it said, but some level of sensitivity was required.

The man just stood there, struck by the shock. Bolton watched him closely and took barely a few moments to know he wasn't the killer. His shock wasn't an act.

That was when Sharp surprised her. He took her out into the hallway. 'I don't think there is any need for two uniform *and* both of us to be here,' he said.

'What the hell, Sharp? Do you have something better to do that I don't know about?'

'Look, I can go ahead, speak to that pathologist and find out when we can ID the body formally.'

'Which we can do with a phone call either to his office or to the DI, yes.'

'But I can also get back to the office and start updating Sergeant Barry on details.'

Finally deciding it wasn't worth the argument, Bolton told him to just go, but to also check in with Stone. She decided that the job would probably be easier without him there, anyway. Especially since she now had the uncomfortable job of broaching the subject of the photograph. She made her way back into the room, finding the man sitting down with his head in his hands.

'When did you first think there was a problem, Mr Massie?'

'I woke up this morning. I couldn't find Danielle. But I also couldn't remember anything from last night. Anything at all,' the man said.

'Where were you when you woke up?'

The man looked worried. 'I was here, in bed. Why? What are you accusing me of?'

The PC decided to chip in: 'No one is accusing anyone of anything, sir, these really are standard questions.'

'She's right, Drew. So, can I also ask: where was the daughter, Shannon, when you first woke up and realised something was wrong?'

That was when the real fear shot across his eyes – just for a split second, but it was enough to get the young man on a back foot.

'She was asleep,' he stumbled. 'She woke up, she got up first, you see. Why does that matter?'

'I just want to try and put a timeline of things together. You know, at what time anyone realised Ms Fallon had gone missing.' Bolton was pressing slightly harder because she knew how important it was for him to tell the truth. If the wrong thing was said at the wrong time, he could end up being a suspect in something a hell of a lot more sinister. 'Well, I'll need to have a chat with her, anyway.'

'No!' He stood up, his panic growing. 'She's worried enough as it is. And when she finds out what's happened to her mum…'

Bolton could tell that Massie's priorities had changed, and he'd become more concerned about the danger of being considered a paedophile than with becoming a prime suspect in a murder. However, he hadn't got as far as working out that a paedophile might be suspected of killing the mother of a ten-year-old girl because she'd found out what he was doing to her daughter. Indeed, he didn't even know about the photographic evidence that could provide the motive for such a narrative.

Bolton suddenly wondered if she had missed her calling as a tabloid journalist.

'Drew, listen,' she said. 'Danielle's death is being treated as suspicious. Part of the circumstances also included a photograph that was taken, which I need to ask you about.'

'A photograph? What of?' He was almost dripping with the sweat that was building on his forehead.

'Officer,' Bolton said to the PC, 'could you go and check how Shannon is, please? Don't tell her yet, try to keep neutral. Prepare her for going down to the station, okay?' In reality, Bolton was trying to get her out of the room. When she had left, Bolton closed the kitchen door behind her and looked at Drew.

'Drew, this is strictly between me and you, off the record, okay?' He nodded. 'Where was Shannon when *she* woke up? What happened? And please, don't bullshit me, because I might be the only thing between you and a whole world of shit. Okay?'

Drew struggled for several moments at the change in the detective's tone. Bolton could see the tears well up in his eyes. He seemed genuinely, truly disturbed by what could be unravelling. She decided to take mercy on the boy, who would no doubt be running as far and as fast as he could by the end of the day. He wasn't her problem.

But another young girl now without a mother *was*.

Sandra Bolton was a single mother of two young girls. The very thought of them ending up alone, like the girl sat in the other room, terrified her more than anything else.

Everything she did was for her girls. She lived for them. She simply couldn't imagine not being there for them. She would give her life to save them – absolutely, and without hesitation. But she still found it hard to reconcile having to die for them, knowing that they would have to live with that for the rest of their lives.

Chapter 28

Carter had tried to insist on a more formal location for the meeting of FAPAS members that Stone had organised. He told her the men had refused to meet unless it was on completely neutral ground.

Which was not *entirely* true.

Stone had bent the truth slightly, but it was only because he wanted to try to bring the killer out into the open. He had considered whether he needed officers watching the venue, but in truth there wasn't the budget to start mounting surveillance teams for a meeting that was absurd by any real procedural purposes.

But Stone knew all too well that there was nothing typical about this case, and so he needed to employ some of his own strategies to start weeding out this killer. That meant playing right into his hands.

'You've spent a lot of time in pubs this week, sir. During working hours.' Khan was enjoying his little chance to jibe his senior officer. 'People might start talking, you know?'

'Let them talk, Harry,' he replied.

They waited for the fathers to start arriving, unsure what exactly they hoped to get out of them, but after what they had found that morning, a sense of urgency was certainly burning hot. They were up against a killer who clearly didn't need to go and find his next victim. Given the pace at which he was producing these victims, the killer had already done his homework, and Stone was having to scramble madly to catch up. Being one step behind was bad enough. Not knowing if he was even in the same race was even worse.

* * *

As the men gathered in the pub's back room, the mood softened slightly with the arrival of the first round, bought by Stone. Malcolm Glenn had bounced in and shook Stone's hand like they were old friends, or as if he'd been in some way deputised for the case. Stone even managed to convince Khan to have a pint – despite his protests of being on duty – in order to ensure that at least one of them looked 'off duty' enough for this to be an informal affair.

Although he was guarded about how the meeting should proceed, Stone was happy to allow Malcolm Glenn to keep playing the role of self-appointed deputy if it resulted in more co-operation from the otherwise suspicious participants. After all, a number of these men had been victims of false allegations, and so the police were not their favourite drinking buddies.

'So, why are we all here?' asked one of the men, loud enough for it to mark the beginning of the meeting. He was a large, burly man with a thick beard and dark eyes punctuated with grey sacks that told of too many sleepless nights. He sat next to Malcolm Glenn, and the two of them together looked like informal leaders of the group.

Stone took the lead. 'I'm going to tell you a limited number of facts, which you can take as facts, despite anything otherwise that you may have read or heard in the media. I am asking you to not release any of this information into the public domain. Don't discuss it on your forum, or via any social media.'

That ruffled some feathers. They didn't like the idea of being censored. Some rumbles of 'cover up' were muttered. He had heard from Malcolm Glenn, and read for himself, what these men had experienced: the constant pressure to 'shut up' or 'back off' or 'keep their distance'; imprisoned by court orders; shackled by injunctions and any other methods used to keep them away from the people they loved most of all in the world. So, having another arm of the law telling them something else they weren't allowed to do, Stone began to wonder if his opening gambit had been the right one.

'Guys, please, listen to the detective,' Malcolm Glenn chirped up, as if he were chairing the meeting.

'I'm a father, too,' Stone said, trying a new tack. 'I don't get to see my son as much as I want to…as much as I need to. I love him more than anything else in the world – just like you love your children. So, I am not some mindless cop trying to tell you what to do for no reason. The only difference is that the reason I can't see my son is my own fault. My own obsession with my work. My own weakness. I am to blame for my predicament, and I am the one who has to get off my arse and sort it out.'

Malcolm Glenn joined in. 'Mr Stone, if you are trying to gain our trust and respect, telling us you are a shit dad is probably not the best tactic.'

'Yes, I know. But that is my point. I have no excuse – no reason. You guys, on the other hand, have *every* reason to help. We have a killer on the loose who is out killing women: the mothers of your children. If they succeed in doing that, you *will* find yourself as prime suspects.' Most of the men looked incredulous. 'I'll be honest with you – in all murder cases, those closest to the victim are automatically suspects, because in truth, most of the time, one of them is the guilty party. So, let's not be naïve about this, okay?'

Stone left the men to get a rumble out of their system before he carried on.

'That doesn't mean we won't rule you out when it becomes clear that you had nothing to do with it. But still, imagine that sting in the tail. Even in her death, your ex-wife manages to get an extra stab in there. *Investigated for the murder of his ex-wife.* How good does that look in a custody battle? And if you think her death will get you any closer to your child, I'll trust you guys all know that the so-called justice system isn't as simple, or as fair, as that. If your ex-wife has really done a number on your children and on your reputation, the courts are more likely to stick them in care than grant you custody.'

There was a silence that told of their slow realisation that this odd detective had a point.

'So, what do you want from us, then?' said another one of the men, who had already made a large dent in his pint. 'I ain't killed no one. Yet.' There was a laugh. 'I am happy in saying if someone does that evil bitch ex of mine over, I ain't gonna shed no tears. But I ain't gonna kill her.'

'Well, you're not all here for us to ask you nicely not to kill your ex –that really would be an unreasonable request,' said Stone, trying to tune in to the relaxing atmosphere. 'But we think you might be able to help us catch someone who is – all jokes aside – pretty dangerous.'

'How? How do we help, detective?' another of the men asked, much less aggressively than the others.

Stone suddenly felt like one of those religious canvassers who knock on people's doors offering to spread the word of God, but never get let in, or given time to speak. It was as if he hadn't thought that far ahead, and his mouth suddenly dried up. This was one of those rare occasions when they looked to Khan for help.

'We want you to think really carefully,' Khan began. 'If anyone has joined your forum, maybe over recent weeks or months, who has stood out. Anyone who might have been really pushy, trying to find out personal information and learn more about your cases. Anyone who offered to meet up personally just a little too soon or too eagerly. Or maybe their story just doesn't ring true.'

'Most of our stories don't ring true, but they are,' Glenn said.

'We realise that,' Khan continued. 'That's why we want you to think of anything small and share it with each other, and listen to each other. If there's a pattern you've noticed, we need to know.'

There was another rumble of disapproval in the room.

Stone continued: 'You know that feeling you get sometimes when you swear you're being followed? That's important, too. Have any of you felt like someone has been watching you? Any random emails that seemed like phishing scams – especially if there was any mention of your situation with your children or ex-partners. Any odd sighting of someone with a camera. *Anything.*'

'Shouldn't you be doing this on Crimewatch, mate?' Malcolm Glenn added, but with a smile that told Stone the remark didn't really warrant a reply.

Stone took Khan out of the room for a moment and into the small main bar. It was a very small pub at the front. Just one thin room with cushioned bench seating along the entire length of one wall, and the tiny bar in the middle of the wall opposite. There was barely ten feet between: certainly not enough space anywhere, any private nook or cranny, for the two detectives to grab a private chat. They both stepped outside the front door.

'Sir: just a quick thought. If anything does come up, how are we going to be able to get this informal chat in a pub past the CPS? Hardly an established evidence collection method, is it?'

'You let me worry about that,' Stone said. 'Besides, at the moment, that's the least of our worries. We aren't collecting evidence; we're trying to catch a psychopathic killer.'

It was then that Stone thought he saw something. He didn't react at first so as not to give anything away. But he was sure his eye had been caught by a glint of reflected sunlight. Just a flash, bouncing off a mirror, a car window, or some other highly polished surface.

Like a camera lens.

Stone kept Khan talking for a few more moments as he scoped the area where he thought he'd seen the reflection coming from. 'Don't move, Harry. Stand still, and don't look, but I think we have an *onlooker*. And if my instincts are right, it's the same one that followed me and Malcolm Glenn out to the pub in Walsall.'

Khan's eyes widened and his heart pounded in his chest. Perhaps their meeting had brought someone out to follow them again. He began looking around, as naturally as he could, to see if there was a certain red saloon anywhere close by. Right at that moment, Malcolm Glenn's head poked out the door.

'Sorry to disturb you, gentleman, but we think we might be on to something in here,' said Malcolm.

'Excellent! We'll be back in a second,' Stone replied quickly. 'Malcolm, come and stand with us a moment, will you? Don't look around, but make out like you and my DC here are talking to each other as I go back in.'

The man did as he was told and Stone went back inside. He stood by the small bay window at the front of the pub and focused his gaze. He was sure someone was hiding in one of the industrial units some hundred feet or so from the pub, but he couldn't make out any details. He knocked on the window and called to Khan and Malcolm.

'Malcolm, you go back inside. Harry, you leave the pub, get into your car and go further up the road. Keep close watch and see if you can follow him. But do *not* get caught and do *not* approach him. Get him on your phone camera or video if you can.'

Stone returned to the back room, where all the men had gathered around a laptop that Khan had brought with him. It was logged in to the FAPAS forum. 'What's going on here?' he asked.

'We think we have something,' answered James Harris. 'This user here is relatively new. Only been on the forum for a few months, gives very little info about his own situation but is keen to know about everyone else.'

Stone had a look at some of the posts as examples and asked the men to point out any phrases that stood out. This particular user was notable for being incredibly helpful to everyone. Always there to lend an ear – or whatever the online equivalent was – and always offering to share a contact email address if people wanted to talk more about what was happening. Most of the men admitted that they had made similar offers themselves.

'Yes, but if you have done it before, what makes you think *this* guy is any more creepy or upfront than any others?' Stone asked.

One of the men finally said: 'Detective, I was chatting to him by email. I had to tell him at one point that I'd said more than enough and needed to protect my family's anonymity, just in case. But by then I had already told him my story, which included my wife's first name and my daughter's first name.'

'Sir, how old is your daughter?' asked Stone.

'She's ten, why?'

An icy cold chill shot through the room.

'You never said we were fishing out a fucking paedo,' said one of the other men, with a bubbling anger in his tone.

'No, no,' Stone said, 'we're not. There is no indication that the children themselves are in danger.' He knew this wasn't entirely true, given the photograph found at the last scene. In fact, he had even considered that, given the apparent escalation of the killer's MO, this could be a developing point. However, he knew that any mention of this would put fuel on to the wrong fire. 'But he *does* appear to target women who are mothers of children...girls... aged about nine or ten.' There was an uncomfortable pause. 'The children are *not* the target.'

Not all of the men were convinced.

'He's right,' said Malcolm, looking very uncomfortable, but glancing at Stone as if to give him some back-up. 'My daughter wasn't hurt – she wasn't even in her home when the... when *it* happened. He doesn't want the girls.'

'How many of you have daughters who are ten years of age, or at least nearly ten, or maybe just turned eleven?' Stone asked. All eight of the men raised their hands, slowly, reluctantly. 'And how many of you have been in email contact with this user?'

Seven of them raised their hands.

'That probably makes us all suspects, too, doesn't it?'

Stone knew that question pretty much ended the meeting. He'd pushed as far as he could with these men, so it was time to put the detective hat back on.

269

'None of you is being considered a suspect in any of the killings. However, I would like to say this to you all. This killer is intelligent and well prepared, and when I get a chance to catch him, I want to be able to move fast. He's good with forensics, too, leaves no trace. Well, almost no trace. I think he has made a mistake and left one of his fingerprints. He has no police record, so he isn't on the system.'

'So, you want our fingerprints?' one of the men said.

'Come to the station, volunteer your prints and DNA for this investigation. That way, when I catch this bastard, no one in the courts can claim I didn't follow procedure and compare possible prints. No slime-ball lawyer can get this murdering son of a bitch off on a technicality. We can use your prints and DNA to rule you out in seconds, and you have my personal assurance that they will be destroyed after the case is solved.'

Stone knew that wasn't entirely true, and he also knew that they had no such print from any of the scenes. But there wasn't even so much as a flinch from any of the men.

As the group started leaving the pub and Stone settled the tab with the jolly old barman, he called Khan on his mobile.

'No, sir, I haven't seen anyone. Are you sure you didn't…' Khan started.

'If you even try to finish that sentence, Harry, you'll be ending ownership to your own balls, too,' Stone finished. He stepped out of the pub and took a few moments to look around the area, in particular at the spot where he thought he'd seen his photographer. He couldn't shake the feeling that he was being watched.

Chapter 29

As soon as Stone got a foot into the briefing room, DS Pete Barry was under his nose with a printed file. 'You're going to want to read this, sir. It's from Walt Disney,' a nickname that only Barry used for the pathologist.

Stone took a couple of moments to scan the file.

Twice.

Then he handed it to the chief superintendent. Their eyes met after she had read it, and Stone thought for a moment he saw Carter's steely, experienced eyes begin to fill just enough to betray her powerful façade.

He was struggling himself with the contents of what he'd just read.

Stone took a few moments and then decided that he wouldn't give the usual fifteen minutes' warning before the start of a briefing. He wanted it right away.

He also decided to dispense with formalities.

And manners.

'So, what the bloody hell is going on?' Stone didn't bother to hide his frustration. 'It's like this killer is taking the piss out of us. He's watching us flounder around like idiots, and he is taking and killing innocent women right under our noses.'

The briefing room was stunned into silence. Stone looked around the room as if he was faced with a bunch of chastised schoolchildren. He brought up a screen and opened some photographs, going through them one by one. Each of the victims, plus photographs from various angles at the scene and from the post-mortems on each body. It was the most bizarre and grotesque of slideshows.

When he got to the fourth body, he stopped. 'The latest victim – number four – Danielle Fallon. Here we have a radical change in the MO. Forget any thoughts you had about these being sexually linked, people. Sexual perverts fixate on a type from around about adolescence. Sometimes they have mild deviations, but to go from short white girls to taller black women just does not happen when sexual preference is the driving force.' He waited for the thought to sink in – half waited from a smart-arsed comment from Greer – then took off his suit jacket and threw it over the back of a chair, ignoring it when it dropped to the floor. He was in full swing.

'The preliminary report from the post-mortem indicates that the killer –' Stone swallowed heavily '– filled that woman's uterus with what can only be described as a fast-setting filling agent, very similar to quick-drying cement. The kind of stuff you would use in DIY.' The gasps in the room were deafening. It was not often that an injury could so universally bring a room of detectives almost to the floor. 'Reg Walters has said that the injuries were inflicted when she was still alive, though he cannot tell whether she would have been conscious. If she was…it would have been excruciatingly painful.' All the detectives were noticeably struggling to hold their expressions, and for some it was too much.

'Sick bastard,' Bolton said, not bothering to whisper it. No one disagreed.

Stone let the disgust hang in the air, and then loudly clapped his hands once, snapping everyone awake. 'Right, we've soaked it in now. When you go home tonight, you'll hold your loved ones a little bit tighter today, we know that. But before we go home, let's work out how to catch this –' he looked at Bolton '– sick bastard.'

It worked. The room was suddenly energised with a bizarre positivity. It was the most inexplicable pep talk. Tasks were asked for rather than given, and there was a ferocious hammering of keyboards and telephone keypads.

Could do with the Rocky soundtrack for this lot.

Meanwhile, Stone stood at the whiteboard at the front of the room and moved photographs around, then stood back and stared. He scratched away at his stubble, wondering how he'd forgotten at least one day of shaving. His fingers found their way to the scar and his head tilted from side to side. Khan came to stand next to him as he looked at the panoramic shots taken from the point of view of the bodies.

'What do you see, Harry? What are we missing?' Stone asked him.

'Narrative, sir. He's telling us a story.'

'Chapter one – she looks at photos of her family, all looking happy,' Stone began.

'But where is the daughter?' Bolton stepped in.

'That's the pain,' Khan said, almost exploding with a realisation. 'She is looking at what she is hurting by keeping her daughter out of the family. *Cutting* her out?' His voice had that characteristic Birmingham twang, the pitch swinging upwards at the end of the sentence.

They all looked at each other. Bolton took her hair bobble out, let her hair hang loose for a moment and then retied it. It was a movement more ritualistic than necessary, but it took Stone and Khan by surprise, as she never did that publicly.

'Look at the second photo,' Stone said. 'In that picture, in that panoramic. What tells the story?' They scanned it, and Stone's head tilted to the left as if that voice was whispering over his shoulder. He saw it. Not the Birmingham City ground in view, but an altogether different sign. He tapped the photo and shook his head at the same time – partly at the tenacity of the killer, partly at what almost seemed like a sick twist of humour. 'The sign. *Toys 'R' Us*. A toy store. Match that with the doll inserted into her… he's saying that she treats her child like a toy to be played with.'

'And the pain caused by her treating her child as a toy or plaything?' Khan added, again as a question.

They turned their eyes to the third victim, Steven Simpson, and they agreed to come back to that since it stood out as different from the others.

And then the fourth victim. Bolton said, 'She's looking at the hospital, her hands placed under her belly, holding a picture of her daughter. Her womb filled solid with cement, almost like the most extreme of prevention of childbirth. Set like stone.'

'So, the story, as Harry calls it,' Stone said, beginning to summarise. 'The woman who causes pain; treats her child as a toy; must be prevented from just bringing a new toy home, when she is bored of her old toy, perhaps – think about how young her boyfriend was, too…' He looked at the others, who were strangely nodding as if they followed the most shocking plot they had ever heard.

'What's next?' Khan asked. 'The next victim: what is the next chapter in the story he is telling us?'

'Pregnancy tests,' Carter added, this time from over Stone's shoulder. 'How do they fit into your story? And where is the fourth victim's test?'

Stunned silence.

They all looked at each other. Even the third victim, a man, had a pregnancy test about his person. Stone walked straight to his office and hammered a number into the phone as the others all stood round looking at the pictures.

'Shall we run a book on where it's found?' Sharp's comment was somewhat unwelcome, and the others' glares made it very clear. 'What's with the looks? We're dealing with a killer who likes his messages; has a morbid sense of humour, if that's what you want to call it; has placed a pregnancy test with all the others. So, my bets are it is either secreted somewhere else, or it's tightly compacted in a ball of cold, hard stone.'

That's when they all heard the shout from the DI's office, and the slamming of a phone. Instinctively everyone made as if to turn and look very busy elsewhere, but not fast enough. Stone came out of his office and looked at them.

'Nowhere about the body,' he said.

'Told you!' Sharp said.

Stone launched at him. 'Do you have something you wish to *add*, Sergeant?' He walked up to Sharp and stood uncomfortably close. Stone's build was noticeably stronger than Sharp's, and although he had no real height advantage, there was a palpable physical presence emanating from Stone that made the others wonder if this could actually get quite messy.

'Sir, perhaps we should all…' Khan said, trying to add a bit of calm into the mix.

'You're ranked right out of this one, *Harry*!' said Sharp.

Stone spat out his words at Sharp. 'My office. Now.'

* * *

Had it not been for the standard softeners fitted to the door's closing mechanism, Stone would have achieved a great slamming of his office door. Instead, all he could muster up was a distinctly stronger closing.

'Sit down, shut up, and listen,' was his opening gambit. His sleeves were now rolled up and his tie had been loosened right down below the collar, whilst his eyebrows were fighting for the same space on the bridge of his nose as his frown deepened. His contempt for Sharp was plastered all over his expression as his top lip began to curl.

'Firstly, don't pull rank on *my* officers. Understood?'

'To be fair, sir, he is only a constable...'

'Fair, Sharp? Playing fair isn't a strong point of yours either, is it?' Even Stone wasn't sure how far he was going to go. 'Riding solo on the crest of the wave is likely to get you drowned. *Sergeant*.'

'If you have a problem with me, sir, maybe you should report me,' Sharp replied.

'I'm going to kick you into next week if you get in the way of this investigation.'

'What *exactly* am I doing so wrong, other than having an opinion?' Sharp said, with a smugness that would enrage even the calmest of officers.

Coolly, Stone stood up and leaned across his desk to the sergeant. Through his teeth, in a voice meant only for Sharp's ears, Stone made it clear: '*Stop. Following. Me.*'

Matching the tone and demeanour, Sharp replied: '*I'm. Not. Following. You.* Jesus Christ, Mike! You're paranoid!'

There was a knock at the door and Carter's head poked in. 'I hope you two boys are playing nice in here. I shan't bother you, though; I can smell the testosterone from here and I don't wish to drown at work today. Why don't you both wind your necks in and get on with the bloody job?'

With that, she left the door open as she walked away and the room fell silent. Sharp's face once again assumed that wiry, arrogant grin that wound Stone up so much. It was all Stone could do not to grab his head and smash it through the desk, but he figured two suspensions in one week was a bit much.

Sharp took it as a good time to leave, but as he got to the door he turned and spoke quietly.

'So, tell me, Mike: are we all going to get to be privy to your secret meeting with all those FAPAS dads? Or are you saving that until it's too late as well?'

Stone looked at a pen on his desk and seriously contemplated throwing it at the sergeant as he walked away.

He probably would have done had it not been for Pete Barry walking in.

Barry's face was as grey as a tombstone. Even his natural grimace was pained, and his grey hair seemed to have gone silver. This case, Stone thought, was getting to everyone in a bad way.

Everyone except Sharp.

'I've just sent you an email with a picture attached,' Barry said, standing in the doorway. As Stone went about reading it, Barry slowly walked into the office, hands in his pockets and his chin pressed hard against his chest. This was his thinking pose. He went over to the window next to Stone's desk and looked out at nothing in particular.

Looking up, Stone found himself comparing the colour of the man to the colour of the clouds outside.

'What is it, Pete?'

'Motive.' As the indoor sergeant, Barry had collated all incoming data on the case, including phone calls, reports, evidence logs and photos. When Stone got stuck on a case, he would often go to the cool, grey head of Pete Barry, knowing he could rely on the sergeant's objective viewpoint.

'Go on,' Stone replied, sitting back in his chair.

'I get what you were saying back there about how he is selecting the women, and how he's building a story. But I can't see a clean-cut objective. I can't find a rock-solid motive for what he is doing. Just saying 'killing to make a point' is not a strong enough motive on which to build a case we put to the CPS, sir. Something is missing, and it is the *why-factor*. In truth, we know a lot about the 'how'. We don't yet know why.'

Stone's hand went straight to the scar as he thought. Pete Barry was right. They had near as much ruled out any of the ex-husbands or current husbands, boyfriends, or close family who would usually feature as prime suspects. The situation was a catch-twenty-two: would a motive point them towards the killer, or would the killer point them towards the motive?

And one more factor still troubled Stone. How did the killer control these women? 'Is the toxicology report back on all the bodies yet?'

'Yes, it is, and it makes for interesting reading.'

'Save me the read and give me the details, Pete.'

'A combination of tiny traces of chlorophorm and a benzodiazepine were found.'

Stone frowned. 'Combination?'

Pete Barry smiled. 'Despite what films show, it is very difficult to render someone unconscious with chloroform alone. The classic tissue-to-the-nose, knocked-out-in-seconds scenario isn't really possible. It can take up to five minutes. And even then, you have to keep the dose up if they are to remain unconscious. It then takes quite some skill to maintain it without overdosing – hence the reason it was abandoned as a medical anaesthetic as far back as the 1930s. Whereas benzo drugs, like the popular Rohypnol, can take up to thirty minutes to kick in, but the effects can last hours.'

'Propofol?'

'Inconclusive. There were some traces that couldn't be identified with certainty. The only thing we do know is that a cocktail was used.'

Pete Barry was like a walking encyclopaedia, able to deliver remarkable amounts of information. Above all, he had a thirst for learning. In the rare times he wasn't given something to do, he would be scouring legal documents for case studies of applicable laws in a way that a solicitor or a paralegal might. People often asked why he didn't train to be a solicitor. His answer was always an honest, if quite amusing one: that he could do their job without needing to spend years at university, or end up wearing a bloody silly wig.

'But surely combining those drugs is ridiculously dangerous,' Stone continued. 'How has he managed not to kill anyone… by accident? If you can call it that.'

Barry shrugged his shoulders and walked to the door of the office, where he stopped and said: 'Who's to say he hasn't?'

The prospect of digging out unsolved cases and scouring them for links made Stone shudder. But the idea of assigning Sharp to that task made him smile.

He also had to pause for thought on the issue of motive, as well as a practical issue that had been concerning him for some time. Stone could not work out how the killer knew to put an unused pregnancy test in the pocket of Steve Simpson.

How much do you know, and how much are you going to tell me?
Before the final act...

Chapter 30

The Boy

His head felt as heavy as clay being pressed down into the rough pillow beneath it. After the weight came the feeling of searing pain in his back, but his memory had yet to wake up, and confusion set in.

Where was he? What could he hear in the distant background? What was the rough, damp-smelling, heavy sheet he lay under? He sat up stiffly on to his elbows, feeling every pull on his muscles as if they'd been tied into hundreds of knots. He looked around through blurred vision, just about making out a square-shaped room that was all yellow and brown and dark. There was noise coming from a TV to his right, not quite loud enough for him to properly make out. Barely able to move, the boy just about managed to pull one of his arms free from under the tightly tucked heavy blanket. He rubbed his eyes to try to regain some vision.

That's when he began to recognise the sounds. Water, plates, metal – someone washing up. Feet scraping on the lino floor, which seemed a familiar sound from somewhere in his memory. It was someone wearing slippers on a hard floor. But not the energetic tap and tickle of a child, or someone young, with energy: someone old and worn out.

He knew that *sound*; but he knew *these* slippers were not familiar.

As his eyes began to readjust, he was able to make out shapes and objects. The boy was lying on a sofa; his head had been on a pillow, and he was covered with an old blanket that was green and red and brown, all woven together but lacking distinction. A confusion brought on by age and many years of use, but with a damp smell that suggested none of that use had been recent.

The boy's body suddenly gulped at a yawn that came from nowhere, engulfing his whole being. His mouth and throat felt like he'd been eating sand and he noticed on the table to his right was a glass of water. As he reached over for the glass, he saw an old red washing-up bowl on the floor. He knew what it was for, but he couldn't remember using it.

His eyes scanned the rest of the table. A crumpled newspaper, a big black remote control, and a second glass. A smaller glass with some other brown drink, the one that grown-ups drank in large quantities.

He gently brought the water glass to his lips, but had to try to sit up at the same time. His first sip did not work out well and most of it spilt down his chin. What did get into his mouth seemed to go down the wrong way. Immediately his throat seized and he coughed the water back up, instinctively feeling a kick of fear at having made a noise.

The washing-up sounds stopped.

After a few moments, he could hear the scrape-and-slap and heavy thud of a man walking in slippers. He appeared to be approaching from behind, but the boy did not dare to turn and look, assuming this man should be feared. He wanted to jump up and run, but the heavy blanket pinned him down like a prisoner.

The tall figure emerged round the other end of the sofa and looked at the boy. His face was old and wrinkled, tired-looking, and shared the colours of the blanket. His hair had had no instruction in what to do and looked like he hadn't even run a hand through it in years, let alone brushed it. But through a thin fringe of matted brown-grey thistles, a deep-lined forehead told an anxious story of many frowns. A troubled forehead. The face hung lazily on a jagged set of bones and the chin seemed to be a comfortable home to silver bristles. Not a beard, just a texture. Beneath two dark eyebrows lay eyes which appeared to contradict the face with their softness. How could such a wrinkled, tired, angry-looking face hold such gentle, kind-looking eyes? Reassuring eyes.

The man nodded upwards ever so slightly, as if to say, 'You're awake, then,' but without using a single word. Slowly, the man moved to the front of the sofa and sat on the edge, right next to the boy, who realised he was still trapped by the blanket, and froze with fear. The man took the glass from the boy with his own massive left hand, and reached around the his shoulders with his right arm.

The boy's heart suddenly began to pound at his chest as if it wanted its own freedom and was determined to escape and leave him on the sofa, if that was what it took to be safe. He couldn't move, and he realised then that his eyes were fixed on the man's eyes. A stranger. A stranger whose terrifying branch was reaching around his shoulder, going for his neck, sure to strangle him. His memory kicked in and he remembered the hands as the ones that had dragged him into the building, grabbed him by the collar and smacked his head into the wall. The memory caused the back of his head to pulse with searing pain, in time with the escaping heart.

As the boy felt the touch of the powerful hand on his back, he felt his shoulders tighten as if to prepare for the attack. The hand sat between his shoulder-blades, and the boy could feel its movement, thumb and forefinger reaching, manoeuvring into the position he knew so well: ready to squeeze at the scruff of the neck. And as the thumb and forefinger came to rest at the base of his soft, ten-year-old neck, the boy tensed, bracing himself for the painful squeeze.

But the pressure came from the palm as the man slowly, tenderly lifted the boy just slightly, and helped guide the glass to his lips, instinctively knowing just how much to tip the glass.

As the boy sipped the water, his mouth regained some feeling. It became easier to swallow, and the water cooled his burning throat. For the first time, the boy took his glare away from the man's eyes for a moment, closed them, and just focused on the flowing feeling of clean, beautiful water. The last thing that had been in his mouth had been a combination of canal water and burning vomit, and now he felt, he tasted – really *tasted* – the freshness of water. He'd never really tasted water before, never thought of it as having a flavour. But this water tasted sweet and fresh in a way that promised to heal and revive every part of his body.

When he looked up again at the man's eyes, he saw the tenderness again. The man's face, cracked with wrinkles, stayed motionless except for the slightest raising of his eyebrows. It was as if he was smiling without moving his mouth. It was like he was saying 'you're okay' without speaking a word. The tension slowly left the boy's shoulders and neck, and he could feel himself resting his entire weight on this strong arm behind him, that thumb and forefinger gently supporting the neck as if he were a newborn.

The man slowly took the glass and placed it back on the table. He lowered the boy's entire body with his one supporting hand, back onto the pillow.

A strange mixture of sounds began to confuse the air. A soft, warm timbre, and a gravelly roll. The old man was humming a tune. Simple, repetitive, barely a few different notes over and over in the same pattern.

The boy couldn't quite place the tune, but he knew it from somewhere. His mind fogged and his eyes grew heavy once again: this time heavy with comfort and safety as he drifted gently back to sleep.

Chapter 31

Stone had worked late into the night at the office, with Khan and Bolton hanging on behind to help. Their motives weren't completely altruistic: the first two rounds of post-work drinks had already been assigned to Stone. It was a simple kind of overtime payment in the unwritten rule-book of Force CID. As the three of them sat in the back room of the Trocadero, there was a shared feeling of frustration at the lack of proper progress in tracking down the killer, or any solid leads on the suspect.

Or at least anything beyond the outlandish theories that weren't to be discussed.

'Isn't it normally the father that is the object of parental hatred?' Khan asked.

'That's not the point, Harry. The children have been turned against the father by the way the mother has deliberately prevented the father from seeing them,'

Bolton replied. 'So, our killer must have some history or unresolved issues with his mother.'

The two men looked at her.

'All right, Freud,' said Stone, 'that's quite enough.'

'Sir, why does it feel like we are just sitting around waiting for the next bloody victim to show up?' whispered Khan, with a rather uncharacteristic public display of tension.

It was at that point that Stone's eye was drawn to the main area of the bar. Leaning up against one of the many standing tables was Sharp. He appeared to be watching the football on the TV, but turned and noticed Stone looking his way. Stone tried his hardest to muster up every part of his communication skills to tell him where to go, but Sharp made his way over to the back room.

'Ears open, mouths shut, people,' Stone muttered to the two other detectives.

'Great to see you in here, sir,' said the sergeant, raising his bottle as if to toast an invisible comrade.

Stone nodded a reply but didn't say anything. This didn't stop Sharp from inviting himself to pull up a stool and join them. 'So, any developments?' he asked.

'Exactly what I should be asking you,' Stone said, finishing off his pint.

'No cases I've come across where use of chloroform or a benzo has been deemed the cause of death,' he said, with an inappropriate level of smugness. 'Seems kind of odd to me, sir,' Sharp continued. 'I mean, this killer we have is all about pointing us in the right direction. Dripping the clues to make sure we're following something. So why would he use a drug that we were less likely to see?'

Sharp finished his drink and placed his empty beer bottle pointedly in the centre of the table. He stood up, smiled and announced his departure, as if anyone else there would care. 'What a pretty picture you three do make,' he said, before turning and walking away.

Perhaps that is what annoyed Stone so much: that Sharp knew how much he pissed people off. Not only did he push their buttons, he seemed to revel in being able to do it so well.

Silence hung over the table until he was out of earshot. 'I fucking hate him,' Bolton hissed, not bothering to mince her words. The two other detectives with her didn't object or offer any disagreement.

Stone was left wondering what that little visit was all about. It was social, and it wasn't an opportunity to dig for information.

'I'm here. I'm watching.' Stone said, half to himself, half out loud as he gently rubbed the scar on his neck.

Bolton and Khan looked at each other, and then at him.

'Watching what, sir?' Khan asked.

'Oh, nothing, don't worry about it.'

But it was his only assumption. Sharp had merely wanted to let Stone know he was there. He wanted to know his presence had been felt. Not just by turning up, but also by offering some information that was of no use to the investigation, but was delivered on his own terms. A little nugget of his wisdom.

The placing of the bottle. The quip about the detectives being a picture. Stone's brain was going into overdrive trying to work out how much he was reading or over-reading into everything, but he put it down to his constant state of being on high alert.

He often felt like that, with his mind burning far too much fuel, firing on all cylinders, but seemingly doing it without his guidance or authority, and seldom coming up with something whole. Just pieces of one of those frustrating jigsaws with a picture of baked beans that were nearly impossible for anyone besides those with extreme insomnia, or the ability of a savant.

Bolton and Khan also finished their drinks and it was time for the next round – Khan's round. Stone thought twice about whether he should be going home to sleep, but before he could conclude his internal dialogue on the matter Khan had already scurried off to get the drinks. Stone knew that Khan hadn't settled on family life, still being quite young and fresh with ambition.

As for Stone: he seldom broke the cycle of working, eating and sleeping. Until recently.

'How's Jack?' Bolton hit the nail on the head in her usual mind-reading manner. She made Stone feel that when he was frail and old and trying to cross a road, she would come up behind him, take his hand, and walk him safely to the other side. 'You seem very distracted and I just wondered if your usually unflappable mind was becoming human and having a little wobble.' Her quip was not delivered with any criticism. More of a smile. An onlooker who didn't know the truth of their relationship might have thought she was flirting.

'He's doing well, considering what's happened.'

'And you?' For some reason, she was pressing harder that evening. Her maternal instincts were showing, and Stone put that down to the fact she was there in the pub rather than at home with her girls.

Why aren't you at home with your girls, Sands?

'Just putting the pieces together, Mike. This case has cut close to the bone for you, I know that.' She was talking quietly, showing a tenderness that was not part of the role she played as the sharp DS 'Jedi' Bolton. 'He knows something, doesn't he? He knows something about you; and you don't know what it is; and you don't like it.'

Stone's sudden need to strengthen the relationship with his son had been jolted into focus by the death of someone else who was close to taking that paternal place. The echo of the past was just too significant to ignore.

When Khan came back with the drinks, they all changed the subject and entered into mundane small talk. Stone asked Bolton about her girls, whom she flippantly dismissed as being fine and spending the night with her mother, called in as a last-minute babysitter. Then they moved on to prodding Khan about his romantic escapades – or lack of – and took great pleasure in making a few suggestions. The topic of 'Carter-the-Cougar' was a step too far for any of them to broach, however!

It was probably exactly what they needed for another hour or so. Khan's suggestion of going for a curry was quickly batted away, despite how welcome it would have been. In reality, Stone just wanted to get home and put his feet up, knowing full well that his mind would switch back to work mode as soon as he left his present company.

Chapter 32

Stone knew there was something wrong even before he closed his apartment door. It was a feeling in the air, like a smell, or the temperature, or an indeterminate sound. Something beyond definition, but a feeling nonetheless. He knew the feeling and what it did to people. His experience over many years in the police had taught him a lot about the strain placed on burglary victims who simply couldn't cope with staying in a house that had been broken into. It wasn't about security or sentimental value, or any other 'logical' reason.

Just a feeling.

He walked slowly down the hallway, all too aware that someone could still be there. As the hallway opened out into the living space, he scanned round and decided instantly that there had been no burglary. Nothing had been taken, but a feeling had been left. He stood entirely motionless, his hearing on heightened mode, his eyes searching. Gut instinct told him what he was facing, because Stone did not believe in coincidences.

That's when his eye was caught by the cordless phone on his small side table. Nothing significant about it stood out, and it wasn't clear at first why he had noticed it, other than the fact that it was in a different place. The stand had been turned so that it was facing the door. The intruder had known it would be seen.

You've got a thing about phones, haven't you?

Was Aaron Peters supposed to notice the phone when he got home in just the same way? To look at it and wonder until…

It rang.

The sound of Stone's phone was a shrill, metallic, imitation ring that he very rarely heard. Only cold callers used that number, as the whole world seemed to have switched to mobile phones altogether. He waited for the ring to cut out and the call to go to voicemail. This wasn't through fear or without reason; Stone knew what he was checking by waiting.

The ringing stopped and Stone wondered if the caller was leaving a message.

Then it rang again.

Which meant the caller was watching, or had at least seen him go into his apartment. Stone immediately went to the phone and picked it up, holding it unnecessarily tightly to his ear. He said nothing at all and just listened. The sound was faint, but the caller was definitely calling from outside judging by the background noise. Stone slowly walked over to the windows which covered the whole wall of the apartment, overlooking the north-east side of the city and the canal below. He took a cursory look around the area, but there was no one to be seen.

The call became the telephone equivalent of a Mexican stand-off: neither caller or receiver wanting to break the silence. Stone hung up and poised his thumb over the green button again. Waiting.

The phone rang again and he answered immediately. 'How long are we going to play this game for?' he asked, calmly. There was no response. 'I know you like your little games, so I'm wondering what this one is supposed to be showing me.' Another pause, which Stone let hang a bit longer. 'I also know you're watching because you have to, don't you? I wonder...' He began to pace around the room. 'I wonder what photos you've taken in here. Definitely one of the sofa where I sit to watch TV, right?' He started walking over to the bedroom door, noticing that it had been pulled completely shut – something that Stone never did.

When he put his hand on the handle, a surge of dread ran through him. What could be in there? Who could be in there? So he stopped. 'You want me to go in there, don't you?' Stone was sure he'd heard an intake of breath as his hand had hit the door handle.

'Let's make it a little harder for you to get your jack-off session, shall we?' Stone hung up, turned the phone off, and went back over to the window to close the blinds. Stone wouldn't admit it to anyone, but he was shaken as he took his mobile from his pocket and checked for missed calls. Part of him expected to get a call on it at any second. He wasn't at all surprised by the intruder having his landline number: while they were in the flat, they would have used the phone to call their own number and then returned the call. No doubt, he thought, from a pay-as-you go phone that couldn't be traced.

That's when the message alert tone came from his coffee table. But it wasn't from his phone. Stone made his way over to the table and took very little time to uncover a mobile phone. It was a cheap imitation smartphone, an obscure make. There was something familiar about the make that Stone couldn't put his finger on, so he stored the thought in his mind to deal with later.

He opened the received mail and noticed it was a picture message. With a sudden sense of dread, he clicked to open the message and watched as the cheap phone started to download a picture file. When it opened, his heart sank.

A woman. He didn't recognise her. She was sitting somewhere public, outside, in a spot that was relatively busy, judging by the out-of-focus background detail. But there was no clue as to who she was or where the picture was taken. Stone scrolled down and saw the text underneath the picture.

Do you know who she is? You will soon. Keep this phone.'

'You will soon.' Stone said out loud, as if to answer the question that he hadn't even asked yet.

Stone was looking at the picture of the next victim and the race had been set. Or it was quite possible that the race was all over already, and the only game now was to find what was left of her.

'No, you want me to believe she is alive, don't you?' he said to himself. 'You want me to hope so that you can watch that hope drain away.'

Stone knew he had to treat the message seriously, and as a serious threat to life.

* * *

'Well, is she still alive or not?' asked Carter. It was a strange situation for Stone to be in, having the boss standing in the middle of his apartment. He suddenly felt he should have tidied up a little; maybe whipped the vacuum round quickly, done a little dusting. He half expected the wandering SOCO team to be collecting dust samples for other reasons, and to see his home appear on an obscure reality show about how clean people's houses really are.

The thought then struck a strange note. To refer to his own home as a crime scene felt so cold.

Stone was pretty sure there was no point in the attention, but when he had told Carter about the call and the photograph, her reaction was inevitable. Even the slightest chance that the killer could have left DNA in his apartment was too big to let pass.

'To be honest, ma'am, it is impossible to tell if she is still alive, but something tells me she would be,' he replied.

'Why? Why bother to tell you?'

'He's treating it like a game. Remember, he's escalating the MO. Showing us a dead woman would not be enough of a challenge. I think he wants there to be some kind of race.'

The chief superintendent paced awkwardly. 'You think he has shown us who's next so we can play some kind of cat and mouse game to try and save this woman? Inspector, that is truly morbid.'

'And pumping several litres of quick-drying cement into a woman isn't?' Stone was quick with his reply. Perhaps too quick. 'If she was already dead, there would be no…risk…there would be no *excitement* in it for him.' He stood at the window and looked out onto the cityscape, carefully following the skyline of the buildings as a method of trying to concentrate his thoughts.

'But why *you*, Stone?' asked Carter, as she began to slowly survey the bachelor pad. 'What is going on with this whole case? He targeted you with the third body, and now he wants to play more games with you?' She suddenly turned to Stone. 'How did he get in here?'

The fact was that they hadn't yet worked that out. There was some scratching to the door lock, but none that couldn't otherwise be compared to the usual damage caused by keys. No one held out much hope of catching the intruder on CCTV around the building, having assumed that they were dealing with someone who just wasn't *that* careless. A note was made to look into it first thing in the morning, merely as a matter of regular practice.

'How do you want to play this, ma'am?' Stone asked Carter, aware of the need to move quickly.

'I'm with you on this, Mike. I think this is a challenge. He hasn't set a deadline. Is he going to kill her tonight or tomorrow?'

Stone thought for a moment. 'He seems to want to see us play the game.' Stone took Carter aside to talk at an almost whispered level. 'Let's disrupt his flow. Let's not get into a mad chase just yet – that's what he expects.'

'That's a dangerous game to play with someone's life.'

'No more dangerous that giving him the pleasure of watching us run around like headless chickens and killing her anyway,' Stone replied. 'Let's force his hand by sitting on this until the morning. It's only a few hours.'

Carter thought for a moment, and then sighed a reluctant agreement. 'But he'll kill her tomorrow night if we don't find her during the day.'

'He's not going to give us long after we start the race.'

'Don't forget, Mike,' Carter continued, in a darker, warning tone, 'he might be pitching this battle with *you* but we are all in this. Don't do anything stupid. You clear everything past me. Understood?'

'Fair enough. What do you want to do with the phone?'

'I'll have the team keep a trace on everything sent to and from that phone, but you keep hold of it,' she said. 'I don't know connection he has with you, if we *can* exploit it, we need to.'

Stone nodded. 'That way, he'll assume it's still *his* game we are playing.'

Carter took a moment to process an uncomfortable thought as she took the phone and looked at the photograph once more. 'We'd better not get this wrong.'

That's when one of the SOCO brought an envelope over to Carter.

'This was on the table, Ma'am.'

'What's this, Mike?' she said, holding it up.

'Where was that?' Stone replied, trying to avoid answering the question.

'Placed dead centre in the middle of your coffee table. Now, I know how obsessed you get with little things like that.' She gently parted the envelope open to peer inside, pulling the photo out just enough to catch a glimpse. She raised her gaze to tone and held it there as she took the picture out. Letting her eyes flick back to the image, she looked at it with some confusion.

Then something in the air changed. Stone saw it. The expression on her face dropped.

What have you seen?

'Where did you get this?' Carter asked.

'It was taped to a gravestone in the cemetery. Saturday.' Stone's reply carried enough weight to it to alert Carter that he had seen her expression change.

Carter ordered the SOCO team to pack up and clear out, since there was nothing to be found in the DI's apartment. They all knew that, so it didn't take them long to go, but Stone and Carter remained silent the whole time they cleared away. Carter asked for two uniformed officers to wait just outside the apartment.

'Why are *you* in that photo, ma'am?' Stone asked.

'I attended the funeral last year.'

'I can see that – but why?' Stone's question wasn't delivered with anger, but it was clear in its demand.

'You know why I never let you work on his case…'

'That is not what I asked, ma'am. And with all due fucking respect: don't patronise me.'

'Don't forget rank, inspector,' Carter threw back, with tone and volume rising.

'Screw rank: I'm talking about honesty.' Stone chose his words carefully. 'Why were *you* at *that* funeral?'

'Because *I* worked the case.'

'Bollocks.'

'Because I worked the *original* case, years before.'

'When…?'

She didn't answer, but turned the photograph over and read: '*You can't hide from hate.* What does that mean?'

Stone walked over to her and took the photo from her hand. It had been written on again. He looked at Carter. 'He's added that. It just had the other question when I found it on the gravestone. Can't hide from hate?'

'You're in this deeper than either of us thought, Mike,' Carter said, with more genuine concern in her voice than she had intended.

It caught his attention. Stone knew that the killer had achieved what he wanted simply by making his presence known. An early start was planned for the morning, leaving just a few precious hours to catch up on some sleep.

There was sense of dread beginning to hang in the air as they all wondered how messy this was about to get. Despite Stone's protests, Carter had uniformed officers posted outside his apartment for the rest of the night, based on the fact that she'd have to pay their overtime anyway, so they might as well make use of their time.

She had clearly been shaken by whatever realisation that photograph had given her.

As Stone put his head down for the night, he set out his usual stall of equipment on his bedside table, all lined up, ready to be swooped upon at the shortest notice. Except this time there was the extra phone added to the mix.

And that was the phone which received a late-night message.

'Goodnight, Mike.'

Chapter 33

The incident room was a hive of activity from first thing in the morning, with all the evidence gathered from the break-in being top of the agenda. Technical teams were busy scouring CCTV records, examining evidence, and digging into various phone numbers and accounts. Unsurprisingly for Stone, not a trace was left, and it still wasn't clear how the intruder managed to get into the apartment in the first place. The only evidence they did have had been handed to them quite voluntarily.

Carter had been onto the communications team and the photograph of the woman had been made public, with a request to help locate her as quickly as possible.

'We would like to emphasise that this woman is not in any trouble whatsoever, but it is urgent that she is located. She is not being treated as a missing person just yet, so it might be a neighbour, a co-worker, a friend or someone in your family who hasn't seen the picture yet. Or if you believe the picture is of you, please contact the police immediately.'

The picture was put out on social media, in the newspaper, and even on the digital screen in the Bullring shopping centre. The idea that this was a race was being taken very seriously. A call centre was set up and a whole corner of the incident room was turned into a temporary switchboard. Several calls were taken giving names for the woman, all of which were followed up immediately, just in case.

Stone was reorganising the main whiteboard with all the evidence to date, leaving space for a new victim. Some thought he was being too morbid and defeatist, but he knew that a killer like the one they were dealing with was hardly likely to bother giving away a victim before she was already dead...or close enough to death to ensure there was nothing anyone could do about it.

'So, you think he's already got her, sir?' Khan asked.

Stone just looked at him at first. 'What would be next in the story, Harry?'

Khan had a thought he didn't want to share, and Stone could see it. Either an outlandishly embarrassing idea, or something just a little too depraved to say out loud. 'My concern would be that at some point he is going to involve children in some way. Not just the mothers.'

Stone froze, eyes fixed on Khan. His mouth dropped open and he held it that way for long enough to make the young detective wonder what he had just said that was so shocking.

'How did I miss that?' Stone said, turning and running into his office. Khan followed him, still concerned he had said the wrong thing.

'What did I say, sir?' Khan pleaded as he watched Stone frantically search his desk for something.

'Names. The FAPAS men we met. Names, now!'

Khan rushed to the coat he'd hung over his chair and scrambled for his notepad. He found the list and began reading out the names.

'Sir,' a young PC shouted to Stone, waving a phone handset in the air. 'I have a caller who claims the woman is his ex-wife.'

'Name?' Stone demanded.

In almost perfect unison, the PC and Khan both said: 'Simon Daniels' – but it was only Khan who understood the importance of what he'd said.

Stone kept his eyes on Khan, but spoke to the PC.

'Why is this one standing out for you, Constable? Could it be just another nutter?'

'Sir, he says he met you the other day – he says you know him.' It was clear from the PC's face that she had been trying to be discreet about it.

Khan nodded. 'He's one of the FAPAS guys.'

'Is he still on the phone?'

The PC put the phone back to her ear. Her face dropped. 'Sorry, sir.'

'Well one of you bloody well get him back on the phone and put him through to my office. Now!' The outburst was uncharacteristic of Stone, and there was a momentary silence in the room, before everyone figured it was better, and certainly safer, to keep their heads right down for a while.

Stone's heart began to pound as he returned to his office. He was readying himself for the race. There was a feeling that maybe they had found her faster than the killer intended – or was this all too quick? The phone barely had a chance to finish its first ring before he snatched it.

'Mr Daniels?' he said, without pause.

As soon as he heard the man's voice, Stone realised which of the fathers he had been, and a knot tightened in his stomach.

Simon Daniels was the one father who had said that his ex-wife was pregnant. Stone had ruled her out as a possible victim because she was actually pregnant, and ruled Simon out as a suspect at the same time, due to the lengths the killer had gone to show the lack of pregnancies in the other women.

But Stone's theory fit it was true there was a pattern of escalation in the killings.

'When did you last speak to her?' Stone continued. 'Where does she work? Who else knows about her pregnancy – I mean, have you mentioned it on the forum?'

Each answer laid a heavier burden on Stone's shoulders as he began to piece the jigsaw together. The urgency was clearer tha ever before. But the one question that remained was: *where*?

Stone went out into the incident room and gathered everyone's attention.

'Okay, we have a possibility here. Our mystery woman is one Lucy Macintosh, currently married to a Peter Macintosh. Ex-husband Simon Daniels just called in to confirm that the photograph is a clear likeness of his ex. They have a daughter aged ten years. Listen carefully.' Stone handed out a list of tasks. 'I need someone to get over to the primary school where her daughter goes and get that girl supervised until her parents can collect her. Stay there with her, then bring her to the station as soon as a responsible adult registered with the school arrives.'

Hands went up and two detectives were dispatched with details.

Stone continued. 'I need a team to contact Mrs Macintosh's workplace now, and also any friends of the family. Simon Daniels is on his way in.'

Officers were shooting off in all directions.

'But where is he going to take her, sir?' Sharp asked.

'Who says he even has her yet?' Bolton shot back before Stone could even reply.

Sharp laughed at her reply, which earned him a few unwanted looks. 'Oh, come on, do you *really* think this psycho is going to give you a chance of beating him to her?' He picked up his coat and made his way to the door.

'Where do you think you're going, sergeant?' Stone said.

'To take a piss, sir,' Sharp said. 'A bit like this guy is taking out of you.'

Me? Not 'us'?

The stage had been set. The gauntlet had been slapped against the face, and the duel proposed. Their eyes met. Every atom of Stone's body told him to bury the sergeant's head into the nearest wall, but something held him back. Even Pete Barry had stood, prepared to break

309

up a fight. Stone's head turned slightly to his left, over his shoulder, and that voice came in.

'We'll find her,' Stone said, turning away from Sharp suddenly, 'and we'll work out where he was planning to take her.' He let Sharp walk out of the room.

Khan followed him.

'You can't let him fire off at you like that, sir,' Bolton said, with her voice clipped, but her rage evident. Her fists were clenched and her eyes dark in a way that would terrify any man no matter what his rank or size.

'Right now, Sands, I've got to locate that woman. Whilst Sharp is here – and believe me, he is grounded to paperwork – he can't do any real harm. I pick my battles.'

'But, sir…?'

Stone's glare snapped to Bolton: a sure sign that was the *end* of the matter.

For now.

'Sands, where's Harry?'

* * *

'What the hell do you think you are playing at?' said Khan as he stormed into the toilets to find Sharp splashing his face down with cold water.

'Watch yourself, *constable*,' Sharp replied. 'Besides looking like a brown-nosing little shit, you seem to be forgetting rank.'

'Your rank stinks as much as the shit that gets flushed in here… *sergeant*,' Khan retorted. 'You have a serious problem with Stone, we all know that. But doing it in public? That's low even for you.'

Sharp slowly and casually pulled paper towels from the dispenser and began drying his hands. He dried them so thoroughly, between the fingers, round several times, that it looked almost as if he was scrubbing up for surgery. 'Look, Harry,' he began, 'when you've got a bit more experience, you'll realise that Stone's way is not always the best way. He doesn't always get the results we need. And what's more, he's been too personally connected to this case right from the start.'

'Why should your opinion of him matter more than simply showing some bloody respect?'

'You'd do best to remember your place too, *constable*.'

Khan was floundering, his initial bluster all but extinguished. 'Just remember what your job is, and do that, Sharp. Stop trying to score points. You're being watched.'

Sharp turned on Khan, grabbing him by his jacket and pushing him hard into the wall. 'Stay the fuck away from me,' he spat through his clenched teeth.

The two men stayed motionless for a few seconds until Sharp released Khan from his grip, turned and left the toilets.

Khan took a few moments to gather himself, then left the toilets, turning right to go back to the incident room. That's when he noticed that Sharp wasn't in front of him. He turned just in time to see Sharp heading towards the stairs, and followed after him.

When Khan got to the bottom of the stairs, he headed towards reception, just in time to see the door shutting behind someone. Most officers and detectives used the private rear entrance to the station for both parking convenience and better access. But Sharp had taken to parking in the front car park, and Harry knew this.

Bursting through the front door, he could see that Sharp had a good thirty feet on him and was walking at pace. Harry had no choice but to break into a fast jog, thinking that a full sprint might look suspicious. He called Sharp's name, but the sergeant didn't even turn to look at him as he got his keys out and remotely unlocked his red saloon.

Harry picked up his pace and just reached Sharp's car as the engine started. He had no choice but to shout. 'Where the hell are you going, Sharp?' Harry stood in front of the car.

Sharp gave the engine a rev and Harry put his hands on the bonnet in a defensive reaction – not because he thought he had superhuman powers to stop a car, but as a reflex. That's when he saw the camera with a long lens on the passenger seat. And the high-grade binoculars. His glare drew Sharp's attention to it until the two men's eyes met again.

Sharp smiled slightly, put the car in gear, and took the handbrake off. He lifted the clutch to biting point and let the car jerk forward on the high revs. Harry backed off and stepped to the side, letting Sharp pull away with a slight screech of the tyres.

Khan put his hands on his hips as he stood there trying to process what had just happened. He was filled with anger, disbelief, and shock. His mind was awash with theories, suspicions, images…and confusion.

Chapter 34

The Boy

There was a flickering at the sides of his eyes as the boy slowly woke several hours later. A gentle murmur of voices he couldn't quite make out also came from the flickering, and as his eyelids slithered further open he could just make out the TV, out of focus, in the corner of the room just to his right.

Something was in the way of his focus, and his eyes had to adjust like a camera lens to see the glass of water on the table. Another clue to his foggy mind as to where he was. He could remember a comforting, supporting hand holding him up; a soothing drink of water, with the help of another hand; kind eyes smiling with their eyebrows.

And a tune. A familiar melody lingering.

The boy noticed that he was lying on his side, not so tightly tucked under the blanket that still smelt old with damp. All these feelings were drawing out a sense of familiarity as if it was safe, as if he was comfortable and warm.

He gently rolled his eyes until he could see the shape of the wrinkled man sitting in an armchair. The man was holding a small glass on the arm of the chair, reading something in his lap. The slippers the boy had heard before barely held onto the man's bony, hairy feet, which in turn clung on to very hairy, wiry shins. He wore long shorts and a dirty white t-shirt, all roughly encased in a dark-coloured dressing-gown.

The man raised his eyes from whatever he was reading, and looked at the boy. He repeated the same upward nod to acknowledge that the boy was awake again. The boy didn't know whether he should reply or try to say anything.

Then it dawned on him that he hadn't spoken a single word for hours… or was it days? How long had he been here? What time was it? Should he be asking all these questions? *Where* was he, and who was this man?

This stranger.

A knot of fear began to tighten in his belly, forming itself out of another sickly feeling. He moved his arm under the blanket to find his belly and only then noticed a sharp sting on his elbow, which made him wince. As he did this, the man slowly began a routine: glass on the table; a bookmark placed carefully and a book closed; the book very nearly placed on the table, but thrown the last few inches; hands poised on his knees first, then on the ends of the arms of the chair; and a body stood up in slow motion. He turned and slid in his slippers to the kitchen area.

The boy watched him closely as he went over to the stove and stirred something in a saucepan. He could just about make out on the side two bowls sitting on two plates. He wondered how he might handle the situation. Should he eat food given him by a stranger? He felt his stomach react to the thought of food, but he couldn't tell if he felt sick or hungry.

The boy decided it was time to move – to even see if he *could* move. He pushed himself up slowly and wound his legs, tangled in the blanket, round to the front of the sofa. Again, he felt the scratches that seemed to be everywhere about his body. His muscles felt like stiff, gluey toffee, and he longed for more time to rest. That's when he noticed a gritty, dirty feeling and the smell his clothes were giving off, and suddenly felt rather embarrassed by them.

The man threw a tea towel over his shoulder and walked back into the living room as the boy was sitting up. He left the room and returned moments later with a large, ragged old towel and held it out in front of the boy.

An offering.

The boy looked into the man's eyes to check: yes, the kindness was still there. Finally, the man spoke.

'You can wash… if you want.' He turned and pointed to another door that was slightly ajar. The bathroom.

The boy said nothing, but looked down at his clothes, wondering if there was any point in washing given what he was wearing.

As if reading the boy's mind, the man said: 'I can wash and dry them for you. No point putting on dirty clothes after a bath.'

That's when the boy noticed that the man had handed him not only a towel, but also some clothes. He wondered how any of the man's clothes would ever be the right size for him. But he stood slowly, saying nothing. Suddenly he felt a fizzing in his head and his balance began to falter. Without thinking, he reached his arms out slightly, and the man took them in his grip. Not a painful grip, not a squeeze. But a strong, reassuring hold that said *'take your time'* more than any words could have done. When the boy was steady again, the man let his grip go, placed his hand gently on the boy's shoulder, and looked him in the eyes.

Still kind.

He nodded the question. The boy nodded the reply that he was okay. And the man showed him to the bathroom, letting the boy walk in front.

Opening the door himself, the boy felt the warmth of the air and smelt the fruits of the clean soap. A hot bath had already been prepared, and was filled with bubble-bath.

Just the way he liked it. But not enough to smile.

He took a moment to look around the bathroom. It was all a washed-out yellow colour, dulled by years of living, but not dirty.

The man moved past the boy, sat on the edge of the bath, and dipped his hand into the water. He nodded, took

316

his hand out and flicked it dry. That's when the boy noticed more about the personality of the bathroom. He saw the various bath toys: yellow ducks, water pistols, and those wind-up toys with paddles that would spin around in the water.

A rumble of fear began to creep into the boy's belly again, and he suddenly felt very uncomfortable about using a stranger's bath. But how could he not? How could he turn down such an offer – he was so dirty and smelly. What could he do?

The man stood up and paused for a moment. The boy wasn't sure what was supposed to happen next. He knew what to do to have a bath…but not in front of a stranger. He didn't know if he had to *ask* him to leave the bathroom or…

But the man answered for him. 'Leave your dirty clothes on the floor. Those clean ones should be about the right size.' And with that, he walked past the boy and stepped out of the bathroom, turning back slightly and giving the boy another small nod. He closed the door behind him.

The boy listened as carefully as he could to the sound of the man's slippers. It wasn't until he heard the man walking around on the lino floor in the kitchen that he hurriedly undressed and carefully dipped his left leg into the bath.

His wounds stung with the water, which felt too hot for him. But he didn't want to turn a tap on to cool it down as it might make the man return, and he didn't want the stranger to come back in whilst he was…

That's when he noticed the small bolt on the door, and wondered if he should go back and lock it. He knew he would have to be quick, or the man would hear him and come back and open the door. Instead, he made the snap decision to get into the water quickly, bearing the sting of the wounds, and the mild scalding of water slightly too hot. He felt himself almost slip and his heart contracted at the idea of falling completely under water again.

He took a few moments to catch his breath, wincing through the stinging on all his wounds, as he moved to hide himself beneath the thick cloud of bubbles.

Finally, as his body adjusted to the heat, he felt himself relax. The last water his body had felt had been freezing cold and thick with dirt. The boy sat in the water for some time, gently splashing small waves and watching the water carefully, trying to fill his mind with nothing but the swirling of the bubbles. He looked around the bathroom and saw more objects that made him think. Bubble-bath in a bottle shaped like a dinosaur. Bright, multicoloured sponges and a pile of letters that he recognised as those magnetic ones that would stick to the side of the bath.

That's when the door handle moved. Just slightly. The boy's heart began to pound, and his instinct to run away was kicking in, even though he knew there was no escape. He cursed himself for not going back to bolt the door, and began looking around the bathroom as if he might find somewhere to hide.

The handle turned again... and the door began to open.

Chapter 35

When Khan got back to the incident room, he called Stone over to have a word in his office.

'Harry, *I'm* supposed to call you to *my* office, you know,' Stone joked, possibly in an attempt to lighten the mood after Sharp's outburst. It was important to him that his team remained energised and positive – that was the only way they could stick together and beat the killer.

But Khan wasn't taking to the humour.

'I think we have a big problem with DS Sharp, sir.'

'Leave him to me, Harry.'

'No, sir, you don't understand. I just had a run-in with him in the gents. He slammed me up against the wall, stormed out the station, and damn near ran me over in the car park.'

Stone was taken aback. 'Where the hell is he going?'

'I don't know. But the extra thing…' Khan faltered. Reluctant. Not sure of the potential consequences of what he was about to say. 'He had a long-lens camera on his passenger seat, sir. That and what looked like some pretty high-spec binoculars.'

The two men looked at each other, and neither liked what they were certain the other was thinking.

'I want you to take Bolton and track Sharp. Now.'

'Off the record?' Khan asked.

'Keep a record of everything you do, just don't put it *on* the record until we know we can. Make a call, Harry, to any of your contacts you need to track him down. Keep me updated, but only *me*, understand?' Stone left his office and told Bolton to go with Khan, no questions asked.

Bolton understood the tone in which the order was given and followed it without question.

Without missing a beat, Stone turned his attention to the rest of the room. 'We need to think about the geography of these killings.'

Stone brought up an online map on the projector and used a pen on the whiteboard to mark the locations of all the bodies. There was a clear pattern that everyone had considered but, until the fourth killing, no one had taken seriously. The connection was to be found in the train lines.

'It's not a typical pattern,' Stone continued. 'It's not a single line, or a circle. But on the map, the locations all connect with a loose line that suggests that unless we catch this bastard, we'll be finding the next body somewhere on the south side of the city.' He paused. 'I'd rather find a person than a body.'

The problem Stone had was trying to work out why trains were so important to the killer.

'There's no way he travels by public transport rather than car…not when he's moving the dead weight of the victim,' Stone said, feeling like he was clutching at straws. 'It just doesn't add up.'

'Or maybe he wants it to *look* as though he does,' replied DC King.

'No, I don't buy it. Too much CCTV. He's too smart, and he knows that *we know* that. He's banking on it.' Stone paused. 'But if he *wants* us to think that, then why? Why is it so important?'

There were murmurs around the room, which Stone left to stew like a broth as he returned to his office to check his phone.

Not his own phone.

'So, the race is on. Happy hunting. You'd better pray you make it in time.'

Stone took a few moments to consider his reply, picked up his phone and called Carter.

* * *

'What does it mean!?' Carter demanded.

Stone didn't dare shrug his shoulders or say he didn't know. He had to give *something*, an idea at least. 'I think it means he has her now and her life is in immediate danger. I think we have a matter of hours at most.'

That might have been an obvious thing to say, but hearing it out loud still brought that lump to everyone's throat as they sat around the glass table in Carter's office. They had put together a core senior team which included a detective from the investigation, one from Organised Crime's special team, and a sergeant from the Armed Response Unit. The intention was to put together a search strategy and a rescue or recovery operation.

'It is clear that the killer is using multiple unregistered phones, so the chance of tracking his movements that way is very slim,' Carter said. 'This might all sound a little Sherlock Holmes to you all, but we do know that the killer is deliberately providing clues to Mike Stone.'

'Why you, sir?' asked one of the Organised Crime officers, looking at Stone.

'I have yet to work that out myself. I don't know *why* he is targeting me, but he has been since the discovery of the third body in the investigation,' Stone said.

Much discussion was had about the murder that had literally had Stone's name on it with his ID card, and the intrusion into his own home. Stone was impressed, however, at the level of gusto with which Carter defended him.

'I want to make it very clear right now that Stone is under no investigation for any wrongdoing, and I insist that he is fully included in everything. Anyone with a problem with that can talk to me.' She glanced at him and he returned the gesture with a polite, but hidden, nod of the head.

Stone jumped in. 'This most recent text will contain a clue we haven't seen yet. I have the team looking at drawing up a logical search area, but we are looking for the smallest needle in the largest haystack here, and we are already several moves behind the killer. He knows that. That's how he wants it.'

'What's with the religious connection?' another voice threw in. Everyone looked at each other, and then back at the speaker. 'The text said: "You'd better *pray*..." Are there any other religious connection being made yet?'

There was a stunned silence and as everyone secretly admitted to themselves that they hadn't considered that point yet.

'Have any of the locations had clear religious overtones?'

Stone looked at Carter. Had they missed something? 'Not as yet, no. The locations have all carried a meaning, but none of those have been overtly religious. And for the record, I'm not religious, either.'

'Could a church be the next location?' another voice asked.

'I couldn't even say how many churches there are in Birmingham, but I would expect that there are too many to search, and far too many to keep watch on,' Carter answered, hoping to shut down any nonsense idea before it was even suggested.

'But what we can do,' Stone replied, 'is make all LPUs get out maps for their local areas and highlight all churches as a precaution.'

Stone knew the reference to religion or a church was tenuous. It could have been a nod to Muslim mosques, Sikh temples, or any other place of prayer. Since there was no set type of victim, there was no way of knowing.

'You say the woman he has identified as his target is pregnant,' asked the ARU officer. 'Does the killer know this?'

'Yes, he will know. One of the things he does is checks whether they're pregnant. The MO has been escalated with each victim, so there is no reason to presume that this would prevent him.' Many jaws dropped at that. 'I wouldn't put it past this guy for believing he is somehow sparing the child. Killing an unborn child would fit in with the escalation of the MO.'

Stone felt the weight of what he'd said as soon as he saw it reflected in the other faces around the table.

A mobile phone rang and everyone froze. Eyes turned to Stone, who had already begun to dig various phones from his pockets. The one that was ringing was his work phone. He checked the screen and felt that shudder down his spine.

It was Bolton.

He excused himself with apologies and stepped out into the corridor, knowing that the contents of that call *should* have been a topic for discussion in the meeting, but it was once again a card he was playing close to his chest.

'Sands, what have you got?' Stone answered as quietly as he could.

'Sir, he's off radar. He must have turned his phone off, and we can't find him after doing a cursory search,' she replied. 'Unless you turn this over to the chief super, and make this search formal, we have no way of tracking him down.'

Stone thought for a few moments. He knew what she was saying: to do anything more against Sharp, they would need to formally consider him a suspect. Getting Carter to agree to that would be impossible.

'I need you to stay out there. Check all the key locations – Lucy Macintosh's address, her work address, and her ex-husband's address. Pick him up and bring him in. Keep busy, but keep your eyes open.' Stone's confidence was wavering.

After he'd hung up, Stone took out his private mobile and reluctantly dialled a number to make a call he knew would be very risky. He needed to know Claire was okay, and that nothing was wrong or unusual for her or Jack. Perhaps she would have called him, but his gut instinct said it was time to check in with her. He couldn't put his finger on it – the impulse to check – but something in his subconscious…

That's when a cheap-sounding tone came from Stone's pocket and he hastily fished around for the phone. A new text had come through.

'Would you like a clue, Mike?'

Stone immediately clicked through the menu to read the number it was sent from and dialled it on his mobile. The phone rang a few times then cut to voicemail. Moments later he received another text.

'When I am ready to talk, I'll call you.'

Stone decided to send a text reply instead.

'Do you intend to kill them both?'

Something inside him told Stone that the killer would wait for a reply by text and then dump the phone. That reply would either jolt him if he didn't know about the pregnancy, or would at least let the killer know that they'd already worked out that part of his 'game'.

As Stone walked back into Carter's office to tell the team of the texts he had just received, the phone beeped again.

'I found three nails, two pieces of rope, and a clothes hanger on the road to Damascus. Meet me there in time and I promise to confess.'

Chapter 36

The Boy

Despite the hot water, the boy shivered as he saw the bathroom door begin to open. He felt utterly exposed and wondered if he should shout out to tell the man not to come in. But he feared that might anger him. He stared at the door and time slowed cruelly as it opened.

And then stopped.

'Sorry,' the man spoke, as his hand appeared, clutching something. 'I forgot to give you these, too.' Without opening the door any more, the man's arm reached in and dropped some underpants and socks on the floor just inside. 'Are you okay?'

The boy wanted to be polite and thank the man. Or say something that ensured he would close the door. He couldn't bring himself to speak, but managed to murmur a sound he knew – they both knew – meant 'yes'.

A moment passed, and then the man pulled the door shut. The boy let out a sigh of relief and for the first time felt that rumble in the stomach and building feeling behind his eyes. He knew the feeling. He knew it meant he was about to cry. But he didn't. He held back the tears and sloshed around a bit more in the water, washing himself as quickly as possible.

He got out of the bath carefully and quietly, and quickly grabbed the towel. The boy dried himself faster than he had ever done before, and far less efficiently than he usually did, but he wanted to be dressed as quickly as possible.

The clothes fit him surprisingly well, although they still felt a little too big. But they were dry, warm, and clean. The jeans had lost the tightness of being new, and the t-shirt felt rougher than it should, but in a reassuringly old, pleasant way. The thick jumper was made of wool or something like that – he couldn't tell – but it was warm. It had a distinctive pattern knitted into the front that looked a little like a big yellow face with its mouth open wide, just like the well-known arcade computer game character.

He looked around the bathroom again at the toys and the magnetic letters and the bubble-bath. He looked again at the clothes he was wearing and wondered whose they were, as there had been no sign of anyone else in the flat other than the wrinkly old man.

The boy took a few moments to try to hang the towel on a wall rack as best he could, but he had never been very good at it. He also gathered up his dirty clothes –

something else he wasn't normally good at – and went to the door. He carefully opened it and peered through the gap. At first, he couldn't see the man anywhere, and he moved his eyes slowly around the place in search of him, across the living room, and as far into the kitchen area as he could see.

Finally, a movement to his left grabbed his attention as he saw the man appear from another door. He was fully dressed in a mixture of browns and greens, and the boy wondered what had made the man get fully dressed.

The boy watched the man walk back to the living room area and pour himself another drink. Not much. Just a small amount, which he swallowed in one gulp of a mouthful.

Slightly reassured, the boy opened the door and walked slowly towards the living room. When the old man saw him, the boy stopped dead on the spot. The man walked over and held out his hands to take the dirty clothes from the boy, who handed them over dutifully. As soon as his hands were empty, he suddenly became aware that they had nothing to do and couldn't work out where to put them. He had always been chastised for putting his hands in his pockets or folding his arms, or keeping them in front and wringing his fingers. But letting his arms just drop by his sides left him feeling nervous and exposed again.

The man took the clothes into the kitchen and dropped them into a basket in front of the washing machine. He then turned his attention to the saucepan on the stove, stirring it a few times.

'Hope you like tomato soup,' he said, looking over his shoulder to the boy – who didn't really like tomato soup, but still couldn't tell if he was hungry or not.

The boy didn't nod or shake his head. After letting his eyes dart around slightly, he felt his face give the faintest smile as his eyes met the old man's again.

After a pause, the boy went back over to the sofa slowly, looking around the room properly for the first time. The door to the apartment was right in front of him, behind the sofa, and there was a large window to his left. It dawned on him that it must have been the apartment whose window he had tried to duck under, and that window must have been in the kitchen behind him.

When he turned to sit down, he noticed the photographs on a shelf above an old fireplace. The photos were of different people and some even had the man in them. Some of them showed a young boy, smiling and happy. One of them was a football team photo, and in another, were some people at a funfair. There was another photo with the man and the same boy, and a snowman between them. The boy was wearing a woollen hat and a thick coat. Just inside the coat he could make out the faint image of a jumper...

The sound of a plate being put down on the table made the boy jump round. The man had put the bowl on a plate and surrounded it with big chunks of bread. He stood with a mild smile, as if he were proud of presenting to his guest a meal that had taken some effort. He waited a moment before he turned and walked back to the kitchen to get his own helping.

The boy looked without moving at first, until the smell of the soup woke up his aching stomach. It was as if the boy's body was telling him that, all fears aside, it needed food. The soup looked creamy and smooth, and the steam coming off it looked so welcoming. The boy knew all too well that he'd be breaking so many rules he had been taught about not taking food from strangers, but his body seemed to be taking over his mind and was already moving towards the sofa, sitting down and picking up the spoon.

The man returned to his seat, placing his own bowl and plate on the table, and lowering himself carefully to the chair.

They both ate in silence for a few moments.

The boy was surprised by how good the soup tasted. He wasn't sure if that was the hunger talking, or if it genuinely was a really good soup. He worked his way through it somewhat quicker than he'd intended. The extra-thick pieces of bread seemed to taste different to normal bread bought from the shop, and certainly soaked up a lot of soup.

The boy glanced up at the man, whose kind eyes glanced and smiled back. He nodded again as if to tell the boy to eat up.

The boy nodded back…and smiled.

When they had both finished, the old man picked up the two plates and took them back to the kitchen, placing them in the sink and turning the tap on. As the sink filled, he turned his attention to the dirty clothes, pulling out the boy's t-shirt and holding it up. The man turned the tap off and walked back into the living room with the t-shirt. He held it up so the boy could see it.

'That's an awful lot of blood to be on a t-shirt for such a little man.' He didn't pitch it as a question, but the boy knew it was one. There was something about the way he asked that surprised the boy, though. It hadn't been an accusation, and he didn't feel like he was in trouble. If anything, the boy thought it sounded more like the man was concerned.

'I saw the grazes on your arms an' legs,' said the man, 'and there was the...' he touched the back of his own head. 'But I reckon *you* ain't hurt that bad.' Again, he managed to say it as if he was inviting more explanation, without actually asking. The man sat down on the sofa next to the boy, whose eyes had dropped like lead weights to the grubby carpet between his two feet.

The boy looked at his hands, realising how clean they now were, and he saw them slowly begin to tremble. Then his whole body started to shake, but the boy couldn't tell whether it was through cold – he didn't feel cold – or something else.

His eyes squeezed tightly shut without being asked to.

He felt the man move next to him, followed by a feeling of warmth wrapping heavily round his shoulders, holding tightly, gripping him, soaking up the trembles.

The feeling of the heavy blanket was reassuring and comforting, and the boy pulled it gently up over the top of his head, creating a small, private hiding place as his tears began to gently trickle down his face.

His mind took him back to the canal, under the bridge. It took him back to the chase. It took him back further, to the place he'd been running from. No matter how tightly he squeezed them shut, he couldn't stop his eyes seeing what they had seen. He pulled the blanket over his head completely and lay down on the sofa, hiding from the world. The man just sat there and let the boy hide.

That's when the boy heard the tune again and the words he knew slowly came back to him.

'It's raining, it's pouring,
The old man is snoring...'

An ugly screech suddenly broke through the tune. It sounded to the boy like some poor animal was being squeezed tightly by vicious hands. The man got up and walked round the back of the sofa to the front door of the apartment, where he answered a strange, plain telephone on the wall.

The boy listened.

'Yes?' the man snarled, as though he'd been disturbed from something. Then he put down the phone. Moments later the man opened the door, but only slightly.

The boy couldn't make out what the murmured voices were saying, but the conversation was short and then the door was closed. For about a minute the boy heard no movement at all from inside the flat and he began to wonder if the man had gone outside. He didn't dare come out of hiding, so he just listened as hard as he could, holding his breath to ensure total silence.

When he finally heard the sound of the man walking back to the sofa, the boy let out a breath and felt himself relax. The man sat down on the sofa next to the boy's feet and lightly patted him on the ankle.

His voice was soft as he spoke.

'I think you'd better tell me why the police are looking for you.'

Chapter 37

The incident room exploded into action, and everyone known for their ability to decode anything from sudoku to crossword puzzles was dragged in to work out the riddle. The energy was starting to feel positive as they finally had a lead to follow. Stone remained wholly cynical, however, knowing that the killer had pictured the incident room just like this. Something told him that he'd already killed the woman and was probably sitting watching the incident room at that very moment.

Probably through binoculars.

Stone called Carter into his office with a wave of urgency. Shutting the door behind him, he blurted it out. 'Ma'am, I think we have a serious problem with Sharp.'

'Not this again, Mike, this is getting ridiculous.'

'He's gone AWOL.'

'When?'

'During the briefing, earlier. He mouthed off at me, then had Harry up against the wall in the gents. He walked out of the station without telling anyone where he was going. Harry followed him to his car, and when he nearly got run over by Sharp, he noticed the long-lens camera and high-grade binoculars on the passenger seat.'

She was understandably annoyed by this development, especially since Stone had not mentioned it earlier.

'You think he is a genuine suspect? Mike? Seriously?' she said, pacing his office.

'You know I don't like coincidences. I have Bolton and Khan…' he started.

'If you say tracking him, I am going to cut your balls off right now.'

Stone quickly changed what he'd been going to say.

'No, ma'am. I have them…chasing up some leads, checking locations. But they did try to call him, and it appears his phone has been switched off.'

A silence hung between them.

'Well,' Carter said, 'under the circumstances I think we'd better at least find out where he is. Get those two to check out his address, and we'll have his number plate flagged up on ANPR. But I am not sending out a full search warrant for him based on your bloody hunch, Mike. Hunch or grudge.'

A knock at his door cut through the palpable tension.

'Sorry, ma'am, sir, but I've had a thought,' said DC Sarah King.

'Never apologise for having a thought, constable – it's a refreshing rarity in this sodding place. What is it?' Carter said, shooting an accusatory sideways glance at the Stone.

'The road to Damascus, ma'am,' she replied.

'What about it?' Stone snapped, receiving another glare from Carter for doing so, too.

'That's the road, the long journey on which St Paul was converted. *St Paul*, sir. If you look at the concentration of murders, St Paul's square, and church, is pretty central to them all.'

Stone rushed past her out of his office and into the incident room. He found St Paul's on the map, and leaving his fingers on it, turned to the room. 'That's it! That's bloody it! St Paul on the road to Damascus. St Paul's church, people.'

A lot of blank looks came back his way.

'Come on – the nails – Jesus crucified – through his wrists,' he continued.

'And the third nail, sir?' came another voice. The room was on fire.

Stone's over-shoulder voice whispered to him: 'Through his feet to hold him still – just like the nails he has used so far.'

'The rope?' another voice came.

Pete Barry stood up: 'The nails went through the hand, sir, not the wrist, to prevent the man bleeding out too quickly. They would tie the wrist with rope to stop the hand from...well, the rope would take the weight.' Everyone looked at Barry as if he'd just stamped on a kitten.

'The clothes hanger?' Carter asked... but almost answered it herself when she remembered that the victim they were trying to find was pregnant.

'Right, listen up,' Stone announced. 'She's alive until we *know* she's dead.'

With that, he gathered a team, got the Armed Response officers to get moving, and made a hasty exit from the incident room, stopping only to kiss DC King on the head for her inspired contribution.

Chapter 38

As a whole team of detectives and uniformed offices sprinted to their cars, Stone made a quick call to Bolton.

'Where are you?' he asked.

'Doing as you said, trying to track down...'

'Stop!' He cut her off. 'We're heading to St Paul's church – we think that's where he's taking her. Meet me there.'

'But, sir, we're headed out towards south Birmingham, following the rail track. We figured if we follow that pattern, he could be somewhere down here. Then we are headed to Sharp's address,' Bolton replied.

Weighing up the odds of finding the victim alive, Stone decided it was better if they continued their own informal search. Something else was bothering Stone as well, about how easily the team seemed to have made this connection, and how much risk the killer was taking by making his moves so close together.

Especially if it was who he thought it was.

Something wasn't quite sitting right with the inspector, and the voice over his shoulder was moaning with doubt. He knew that true serial killers spread outwards from an epicentre the more confident they get, not back in on themselves. And they rarely kill with such ferocious speed.

'Okay, Sands, you and Harry keep on that. I am going to send you copies of the texts he sent me – see if you can make any sense of them just in case we are… well, just in case you need them.'

He hung up just as he got to his car. As he started the engine he got another text.

'I'm waiting for you, Mike. Let's hope you don't get this one wrong, otherwise the next one really will look like the end of the line.'

He knew it was another cryptic clue and he put the phone down with great reluctance as he pulled out of the station to make his way to St Paul's church. It was only a ten-minute drive at most if you stuck to speed limits and in behind traffic, but with lights and sirens on, it really was close.

Too close.

By the time he got there, the ARU were already setting up to enter and cars were being parked up all round the square.

St Paul's Square in Birmingham is a small, peaceful hideaway on the edge of the Jewellery Quarter, just outside the central ring road. The four sides of the square are adorned with good-quality bars, restaurants and buildings that have a naturally quiet effect on the setting. It certainly wasn't a regular centre of such police attention.

A cold shiver down his spine warned him of a grave error being made. He couldn't shake the feeling that it had been too easy, and that the location provided no panoramic image. Nor was it close to a train station, other than one the killer had already used.

Something didn't feel right.

He took out the phone again and looked at the message.

'*I found three nails, two pieces of rope, and a clothes hanger on the road to Damascus. Meet me there in time and I promise to confess!*'

What were they missing?

He phoned Bolton again to ask her. 'What am I missing, Sands? He's not here. I just know it.'

'You've already searched the place, sir?' she asked, sounding a little shocked.

'Not yet, but my gut just tells me this is too close. I've missed something. He's playing with us, yes, but he's not stupid – we know that.'

Stone took a few deep breaths as he sat in his car for a few more moments, hoping that something could come of this. But he just couldn't see it – he couldn't see the killer getting to this location unnoticed. There were too many people around, too much traffic to risk it.

That's when the thought hit him. St Paul's church.

'Is there more than one St. Paul's in Birmingham?' he said in perfect unison with DS 'Jedi' Bolton on the other end of the phone.

'Where's the other one, Sands?!'

A silence. Something was clearer now. 'You're not going to believe this, sir.'

'Where the hell is it, Bolton?' he shouted down his phone, not at her, more in anger with himself.

'The other St Pauls, sir, is further down the train line from the last body, close to Kings Norton station. And it's also a *Catholic* church,' the sergeant said.

Stone thought for a moment, and then it snapped into place: '...I promise to confess.'

It's a fucking Catholic thing.

And the St Paul's they were all gathered around was Church of England.

They had gone to the wrong church.

He knew I'd screw up like that.

Stone slammed his steering wheel and let out a guttural groan loud enough for nearby officers to hear. It would have taken them longer to get to Kings Norton than to the Jewellery Quarter from the Aston station. He still doubted that the killer would leave it close enough to chance getting caught, and might well be staging all of this for his own entertainment.

Stone started his engine, slammed the car into gear as hard as he could, and took off with a screech of his tyres, swinging the car round the square to make his way to the south side of the city.

* * *

This was not one of those times where Stone was glad to have been right. He'd felt that they would be too late

342

no matter what time they turned up. He knew that the killer wouldn't risk missing out on telling the next part of the story. What was really bearing heavy on Stone's shoulders was how the last text had already made the threat that *this* was not the end of the line.

The scene was so packed with images, metaphors and symbols that Stone couldn't decide what was more horrific: the act of violence itself, or the callousness and coldness with which the killer treated these acts, as if they were some kind of personal art project. Bolton and Khan had arrived at the scene before Stone, and it was the sight of Harry Khan, doubled over with his head in his hands outside the small church, that filled Stone with dread before he'd even gone inside. Bolton's face was as grey as stone, and it was all he could do to just lightly touch her on the arm as he walked past, trying his best to steel himself.

He passed a young PC who was gently rubbing a cross on her necklace as small group of uniform parted without the need for Stone to show his ID. It was a mournful, not a ceremonial parting.

The small church had been broken into and it was clear from the drops of blood all the way up the aisle that the killer had inflicted some of the wounds before getting his victim to the church. He'd taken the woman up onto the altar, and from the pooling of blood, it appeared they had stood there a while. Perhaps long enough to say a prayer.

Stone then followed the trail of blood, which was also marked out by a line of officers all looking more sombre than darkest of funeral-goers. The trail led round to the private area that housed the boxes so cruelly encapsulated with irony, and framed with tragedy. He'd never been a religious man, but he did understand the importance and reverence that the confessional held. In fact, he had great respect for priests, appreciating how hard it must be to hear some confessions and be unable to share them with anyone.

He saw depravity almost every day in his job, but he knew he could go and discuss it with colleagues, and purge his mind of it with the aid of alcohol. But to listen to someone confess such sins and allow them to merely mutter a few words in confession: he couldn't bring himself to shake a hatred of what he saw as a poor cover for condoning such acts. It was that disgusting thought that gave him at least a professional appreciation of the priesthood.

Then he saw the victim.

The woman was sitting in the confession box with her head leaning on her left shoulder, looking down to her lap where her arms held what looked like an infant wrapped in a white blanket. The infant was suckling on its mother's breast, but the face was drenched in blood and its complexion gave away the plastic it was made from.

A nail had been driven through each of her palms, and a rope loosely tied around her wrists. A third nail was driven through her overlapping feet into the ground below. It was as if she had been crucified without a cross.

The most disturbing part was the clothes hanger protruding from between the woman's legs and the pool of blood collecting on her thighs and on the floor.

Something caught in his throat. Something else rolled in his stomach. Something else filled his eyes. Of all the depravity he had seen over the past week, what he stood looking at in those few moments was burning a place in his memory that he knew would never heal.

'Who is the on-call pathologist?' he finally managed to stammer out.

'I am,' Reg Walters said with a coldness that shook Stone to annoyance.

'Does this not move you or affect you in any way, Reg?' Stone said as he turned to stare the man in the eyes.

'Mike, please. This is hard enough. Don't try to switch my emotions on right now. It's taking enough energy to keep them locked away. I'll deal with them later with a glass…or a bottle of the finest Shiraz I can find.' He then went about his business with a cool professionalism, but not before privately making the sign of the cross and kissing a small crucifix on a necklace that Stone had never noticed before.

Stone had had no idea that Reg Walters was a religious man, and indeed there had never been a need for it to come up in conversation. But he decided to store that line of questioning for another time as he made his way out to the front of the church, joining the rest of the team of speechless officers.

'Was she already dead? Could we have got here on time?' Carter asked, pleading for some kind of empty reassurance.

'We don't have time of death yet, but judging from how wet all that blood is, I doubt she has been here that long. I still don't think there's any way he would have let us save her,' Stone replied.

He moved aside to speak to Bolton and Khan, who had managed to regain his composure.

'Sir, I'm really sorry…' Khan began, until he was stopped by Stone. The apology wasn't necessary, and Stone's pragmatic mind was kicking in.

That's when his mobile began to ring. He picked it up and answered it in one go, making it clear that he really was too busy to talk.

'Do you think she confessed all her sins before she died, Mike?'

His face dropped. His eyes darted to the screen of his phone. The number was unknown. The voice was muffled, but the identity was clear.

'You didn't make it in time, Mike, so I am afraid I cannot confess right now,' the voice continued, with a mocking tone.

The others gathered round as Stone put the phone on loudspeaker.

'Yes, that's right, all gather round.'

He's bloody watching us now.

Stone felt his blood begin to boil.

'You sick, twisted bastard,' Stone spat at the phone. 'Show yourself! Come on!'

Grabbing Stone's wrist to hold the phone still, Carter stepped in. 'What is it you want?' It was such a futile thing to ask, but without the time to plan a strategy, Carter was falling back on standard phrases in order to keep him talking, knowing that the longer they could keep him in one place, the easier it would be to trace the location of the call.

'What do I want? What do you think this is, some kind of Hollywood hostage negotiation?' he replied.

'When I find you...' Stone began, only to have his voice sliced in half by the shrill laughter on the line.

'That's a funny joke, Detective Inspector Stone! You've never needed to *find* me. I've been here all along.'

Standing outside the church, the four people poised over the one phone looked more like a group of teenagers gawping at an internet video than four officers talking to a psychotic killer.

'What makes this so sweet,' the voice continued 'is that I am sitting here now, from as near or far as you might be able to imagine, watching a quartet of misfits all in rank order – a constable, a sergeant, an inspector and a chief superintendent – and not one of you can see what is right in front of you.' The laughter trickled in.

'You like to make a show; you like to play chase. This is just a game to you. But if you fix this game too much then you aren't really the winner, are you? That makes you the coward!' Stone shouted into the phone. 'It makes you weak...'

'Enough!' the voice growled back in anger, making the phone's small speaker crackle. 'The question now is: how can you follow a path you haven't even found yet? I told you, Stone. I warned you. The next one could be the end of the line.'

The line went dead. It took the all his inner strength not to throw the phone as far as he could.

Carter was the first to speak. 'So, he's watching us. That is for certain. It was clear he could see us from wherever he is now. That means he has to be extremely close.'

'Or it means he has high-powered binoculars, ma'am,' Khan said.

'Well, let's bloody find out then,' Stone barked. His frustration echoed what other felt. 'Get someone to trace than damn call – tell us where it was made, and see if the phone is still live.'

There was a sudden rush of activity. An order to arrest Sharp was put out immediately and communicated across all channels, together with a description of his car. Bolton and Khan were officially dispatched to his home in case he returned to retrieve any evidence. They weren't certain that he would be there, but it was highly likely that evidence could be.

Carter began making phone calls for warrants to search Sharp's property, now that she felt she had enough to convince the powers-that-be to grant one.

Stone was scratching roughly at his neck as if he knew something was seriously out of joint in the atmosphere. The voice over his shoulder was shouting at him to call Claire.

She's fine. Jack's fine. Get the job done; get everyone safe.

His attention was snapped back into focus when he saw Reg Walters leaving the church and hurrying morosely towards his car. It took two calls of his name for the inspector to get his attention.

'What's the score, Reg?'

Reg sighed, taking a moment.

'Judging b–' He cleared his throat. 'Judging by the lack of coagulation of the blood, and the liver temperature, I'd say she has only been dead for an hour, maybe two at most. I can't tell yet the exact cause of death, but it appears to be the same: heart failure due to loss of blood.' That was all he could usefully add before he confirmed the body could be moved as soon as the SOCO team had all the photographs. He then went back to his car, which was parked awkwardly on the path in the only space left between the cars, ambulances and various SOCO equipment being set up.

Stone saw Reg get back into his car, take a deep breath, and then rest his head on the steering wheel. As he sat up, he wiped his eyes before starting the engine.

Carter was ordering officers to man stations all along the train line that appeared to be linking these locations together. Others were being sent on a door-to-door search of the surrounding area.

'If anyone won't let you in, arrest them,' she snapped. She also dispatched officers to the school right next to the church, taking note of Stone's point about the escalation of the killer's intent.

And then she stopped for a moment. She appeared to be taking in her surroundings, as if she knew the area well. Her mood regarding the case had changed somehow since she'd seen the photograph in Stone's apartment, and the inspector couldn't quite put his finger on why.

Something's nibbling at that mind; something you aren't telling me.

'Where's the priest?' Stone suddenly asked, snapping Carter from her moment of thought.

'No one knows,' replied a constable in uniform. 'We've checked at his address and all around the church, but he's nowhere to be found.'

Stone looked at Carter. 'He needs to be found, ma'am.'

'I'm heading back to Aston to co-ordinate from there. Let's meet in my office before a full briefing in the incident room.' Carter took a deep breath before marching back to her marked police car in the gathering dusk, ordering the driver to get her back 'pronto.'

'Ma'am, with all due respect…' Stone began.

'You usually say that just before you piss me off.'

'We're hot on this bastard's tail here – we can't go sitting on our asses in offices.'

A flare of anger seemed to flash across her face momentarily. 'We have people on the ground here, Mike. I want you back in Aston. My office. Now.' She slammed the door of her car. Stone couldn't decide if she also needed a moment alone in her own space to reflect.

But there's something you still aren't telling me.

Stone knew there was nothing else useful he could do at the scene. He made his way back to his car half in a daze. His head was buzzing with the fear that something bigger was about to happen. The pit of his stomach ached with a feeling of dread.

We're too close not to have caught him.

He expected another call to come very soon.

And it did…

Chapter 39

The Boy

The old man gently rested a hand on the boy's shoulder, giving it a reassuring squeeze that was enough to send a secret, coded message to the boy that there was no danger. It was as if he'd already known the pain he had seen in the boy's eyes, like he had read his mind. The boy felt the sofa lift slightly as the old man stood up, and he watched him through a tiny slit in the blanket as he walked awkwardly over to the shelf above the fireplace. The man picked up a photo and dusted it off with one hand, letting his fingers rest a little longer on the front as he turned back and returned to sit on the table in front of the boy.

He held out the photo for the boy to see. 'This is…was my son. He was around the same age as you are now.' The old man's voice had softened to a weary croak and his

351

hand trembled just slightly as if it was trying to find the courage to hold still. The boy gently opened up the slit in the blanket to he could see the picture. It was the same one that he had looked at earlier, with the boy wearing the same jumper he was wearing. The boy in the photo was smiling and happy, his face beaming like sunlight next to the old man. It was the same old man indeed, only he seemed to have more colour in his face in the photograph than in real life.

The boy sat up and glanced in the old man's eyes. They no longer held kindness, only sorrow.

'What happened to him?' asked the boy.

'I no longer see him. He was taken from me.'

'Who took him?' the boy asked, innocently, quietly. And when the old man did not answer, the boy dared the next part of the question. 'Did he die?'

'Oh, no, he didn't die,' said the old man, with the faintest of reassuring smiles. 'I died, for him: in here.' He touched his chest where his heart would be, but the boy wondered if this grey man had a heart any more.

'What happened?'

'He was told a very bad thing. About me. And he couldn't shake it away. So, I had to leave him.'

The boy frowned as he held the photo, trying to work out what a boy could learn about his father that could be so bad. He looked at the old man. He looked into his eyes, which continued to drip sorrow more than eyes could ever shed tears. They seemed to hang lower than before. It was only when the boy tried to speak again that he felt the lump filling his throat, and he had to squeeze his voice past it. 'What did he learn?'

'He learnt how to hate me.'

The boy understood what the old man meant. He knew the feeling, but he asked nonetheless: 'How did he learn that?'

The man stood up and went into the kitchen to make a cup of tea. He got two mugs out of the cupboard and held one up with a little wave to the boy as an offer. 'You can have a hot chocolate if you like. I'm sorry, I don't have much else – well, that you're allowed to drink, anyway.' He smiled. But he'd watched the boy's reactions carefully and knew that hot chocolate had won the vote. 'What is it with boys and chocolate? Boys always say yes to a bit of chocolate.'

The boy looked at the photo again and then placed the picture frame carefully on the table. He had a lot more questions about the boy and what had happened to him, and why he'd somehow learnt to hate this old man who seemed too kind to dislike. But the silence in the room was hard to break, and the sounds of metal spoons clinking on mugs was strangely reassuring.

The man came back over to the sofa and the two of them sat side by side, sipping carefully.

'Enough about him,' said the old man. 'You still haven't told me why the police are looking for you.' The boy's head went down. The old man pursued carefully. 'I don't think they looked angry. They looked worried. I don't think you're in trouble.'

The boy said nothing. He squeezed his eyes tight shut, as if to try to banish a bad thought.

'Did something happen?' asked the old man.

After several seconds, the boy nodded, reluctantly.

'Did someone get hurt?'

He nodded again.

'Badly?'

The boy's hands began to tremble and sweat, so he put his mug on the table, fearing that he'd drop it and get the nice jumper dirty.

'Well, not to worry,' said the old man, getting up and walking over to the bathroom. 'I'm sure it'll be okay when we get you home,' he said as he closed the door behind him.

Home.

And that was it. The boy's instincts kicked in, and he knew he had to get out. He threw off the blanket and launched himself over the back of the sofa. It was only when he landed that he remembered he had no shoes on. His eyes darted around the apartment, searching for his trainers. He knew he had only a few moments left to get out, so he made the snap decision to leave the shoes...

The toilet flushed.

... and the boy ran to the door and snatched at the lock...

The taps in the bathroom splashed on.

... but the lock defied the boy's numb fingers...

The taps stopped: the man must have been drying his hands.

... until it clicked open just as the bathroom door opened...

The old man's face dropped in shock.

... and the boy felt the door slam hard against the chain.

'Where are you going?' shouted the old man, as he began his chase like a steam locomotive: slowly at first, but so clearly powerful.

The boy scrabbled at the chain, slipping it off just in time to grab at the door to pull it open. He felt a hand grip his shoulder, but he swung the door with all the strength he could muster. There was a loud smack, and the hand disappeared. Taking the opportunity for what it was, his small legs instinctively kicked into high gear and sprang him to escape through the door.

Turning immediately left, he found himself at the external door, which had another one of those fiddly locks. He battled with it as he checked over his shoulder. The man appeared at the door, clutching his head.

'Stop!'

The lock came undone and the boy launched out of the building onto the soaking, ice-cold concrete. Turning instinctively to his right, he headed back towards the canal. Heavy, freezing rain pounded his shoulders again as he slipped and scrambled across the muddy grass.

The chase was on again…

Chapter 40

Stone took the call through his car's hands-free as soon as he was clear of the crime scene.

'How are you holding up, Mike?' the voice said.

'What do you want?' replied the detective.

'I want you to pay attention – very close attention.'

'We know who you are!' said Stone, trying as hard as he could to make it sound like a threat. The only response he got was laughter, which only tightened the grip that Stone had on his steering wheel.

Stone began to picture his hands around the man's throat. 'Why me? Why so obsessed with me? Have I wronged you in some way?'

'You have wronged many people, Mike, and you know it.'

'Then meet me, you fucking coward!' he bellowed as he hit his steering wheel so hard the car swerved, causing other drivers to bellow back with their horns.

'I will, Mike, I will. All in good time.'

'Name a place and time, and I will be there.'

'Okay, Mike. Have it your way, just this once. Meet me at home.'

A heavy, black cloud descended upon Mike Stone's world. He knew what that meant. Another time when he hoped so dearly to be wrong...

'Meet me, Claire...and Jack...at home.'

The line went dead.

* * *

Bolton and Khan arrived at Sharp's address. The ARU officers took the lead, going straight at the door to the terraced house with an enforcer. It took three cracking blows to get the door open, followed by a rush of officers, all shouting and brandishing MP5 submachine guns. They swiftly checked each downstairs room and then moved upstairs in strict formation. Bolton and Khan stayed outside the house until it had been cleared. They then entered and slowly made their way down the hall.

The house was dark and musty, and although not messy or dirty, it had a decidedly tired look about it. It was not a family home in any way. The living room had only one sofa, pointing straight at the TV stand, with various other consoles, speakers and technology all fed by an array of cables. The shelves were filled with DVDs and disturbed dust, and the walls were adorned with a wide range of photography. They appeared to be of a good quality and well framed, suggesting the level of a semi-pro, or a serious enthusiast. The black and white photos in thin black frames showed a personality that appreciated the art of the human eye.

'DS Bolton, I think you'd better come and see this,' an ARU officer called from upstairs. Bolton and Khan followed the voice, anxious about its tone, which suggested something significant had been found.

Bolton had her phone out and ready to get Stone on the line for a live update. As far as she knew, this was now a manhunt.

The upstairs was dark, lit only by the torches on the MP5s. The two detectives were walking in the opposite direction to a steady flow of officers, who seemed almost disappointed that their hunt had scored no kill.

They reached the door at the end of the landing, which appeared to be the small third bedroom. The lights in the property had just been switched on after a full check that it was safe to do so. Bolton's eyes were dazzled by the glare at first, but it quickly faded, as if the old, dark walls had soaked it up. The house upstairs looked like it had barely been decorated in decades.

It was not what Bolton had imagined Sharp would live in.

As Bolton and Khan entered the room, their eyes were immediately drawn to the back wall. It was a different world. Photographs of all styles, colour and black and white; long-focus shots. Clearly these were photographs taken for a purpose other than art.

Khan's mobile phone began to ring.

Besides the copies of the case photographs up on the wall, there were a range of shots that could only be described as surveillance. This was the room of someone quite clearly obsessed with their target.

Khan took the call.

The notes, maps, plans and many other details showed all the trappings of a detailed private investigation. It was clear to the two detectives what they were looking at, but both were at a loss to explain it.

'How the hell did we miss this, Harry?' she said, scanning over the mass of collected information, photos and notes.

Khan was ending his call. 'Right, thanks: send me the image.' His face bore the look of death.

'Hidden in full view, Harry.'

'CCTV footage from the pub in town that recorded Mike and Steve Simpson has been found. They're sending me one particular enlarged image right now.' His phone received a picture message which he opened. His expression soke volumes.

Bolton snatched the phone from Khan. An image of Steve Simpson being handed Mike's ID Card and walking away from the pub with the man who would kill him hours later.

They looked at each other for a moment. Then Bolton dialled Stone's number and Khan took out his phone to call Carter.

The answers to so many questions about the case were beginning to become clear. But, more urgently, the threat to Mike Stone and his family was now in full focus.

Chapter 41

The Boy

The boy sprinted as fast as his wet, shoeless feet would allow him, but his borrowed clothes weighing him down as the torrential rain soaked them with water. Surrounded by darkness, he looked over his shoulder to see the large shadow bounding after him. He could just about make out the calls of the old man as he tried to gain some distance and get away from the threat of being taken home.

He crossed the path and felt the stinging pain of its rough surface on his freezing cold feet, but kept flying into the thicket of bushes. He tore through and immediately lost his feet from beneath him, tumbling down the slope, cursing himself for forgetting how last time he'd done the same thing. He crashed from branch to branch, trunk to trunk, desperately trying to beat a route through.

The boy heard the cries of the old man at the top of the slope, and the curse as he finally decided to follow the same route. The boy tripped and rolled onto the tow-path, scraping his elbows and adding further layers of wounds. Scrambling back to his feet, he looked around before turning left and trying to break out into his fastest run. But his legs felt like lead, and running became a battle through thick tar, just like so many of the nightmares he'd had his whole life.

His chest was seizing, and he couldn't breathe. The rain had become so heavy it was like trying to breathe through a wall of water.

The heavy footfall of the old man was getting closer and closer; the shouts, louder and louder.

And then the boy's nightmare darkened.

The path was coming to a terrifying end where it was swallowed up by the pitch-black mouth of a tunnel ahead of him. But the tunnel wasn't like the bridge in the other direction: swallowed up the light and had no end to it.

The sound of the old man was getting closer and the boy could feel his presence behind him. He stopped at the opening to the tunnel. Trapped. He turned around and put his back to the wall, his hands clawing at the brickwork. The canal was to his left; the slope of bushes and trees to his right; and the old man appeared in front of him, getting ever closer. As dark and terrifying as it was, the tunnel behind him was his only escape.

The boy turned and allowed the blackness of the tunnel to swallow him up. It was his only chance.

Chapter 42

Sharp parked his red saloon outside the house, turned the lights off, and then the engine. He took a moment to look in the mirror and practise his most charming, trustworthy smile in the glow of the streetlamps. He adjusted his tie and checked the time.

Picking up his camera, he got out of the car.

He walked up the driveway, turning to check around him to see if anyone else was there or if he had been followed. He knew that time was in short supply, but he also knew the importance of making sure that Claire Stone remained calm. His first priorities were to gain entry, check that Mike Stone's son was there in the house, and keep them both calm.

Getting his ID card at the ready, he approached the front door and rang the bell, taking a step back so as not to cause unnecessary alarm.

He waited.

A light came on in the hallway.

A pause.

Sharp assumed that Claire Stone was checking through the spy hole to see who it was. The door opened just slightly, evidently restricted by the chain. *Sensible woman,* Sharp thought.

'Can I help you?' Claire asked.

'Hello, are you Mrs Claire Stone?' Sharp asked in his softest tone.

'Yes, why? Who are you?'

Sharp assumed that the woman must still be shaken by the death of her boyfriend, which was wholly understandable. 'I am Detective Sergeant Sharp – I work with Mike.' He showed his ID, holding it close so that she could see its validity. 'Mike is on his way, but he asked me to stop by because he knew that I was closer. He said he would call ahead.'

'Well, no, he didn't call me. What's going on?'

Sharp knew he had precious few moments to gain the woman's trust so she would let him inside. 'Let me call him and check where he is.'

'What's this about?' Claire asked.

'There's nothing to worry about, Mrs Stone. We're just looking into a development in the case Mike and I are working on, as we think we've made good progress. I need a little help from you on some details, that's all.' Sharp could see her wavering.

'I don't see how I could help you.'

'I could wait in my car if you like…' Sharp knew that time was of the essence.

'… No, you'd better come in.'

'Thank you, I appreciate it,' Sharp said, waiting for Claire to slightly shut the door to take the chain off. As she cautiously opened the door fully, Sharp offered to show his ID card again, but she declined.

He was in.

'How are you doing?' asked Sharp. 'I mean…well, with everything that has happened.'

Claire closed the door behind Sharp and then walked past him, guiding him into the living room. 'I don't know how I'm doing, to be honest. My main concern is looking after our son.'

'Oh yes, of course. How's is your son? Jack, isn't it?'

'He's fine. Asleep.' Claire's maternal instinct was beginning to tickle the back of her neck. Something wasn't right. Something about this Sharp she sensed was wrong. Why was he on his own? Why hadn't Mike phoned ahead? 'What's the camera for?' Claire asked, only realising by his reaction that she'd let that thought slip out.

'What, this? Oh, er – it just has a few shots on it that I want to run past Mike.' He paused. 'When he gets here.'

Sharp looked around the room, and slowly walked over to the patio doors and checked to see if they were locked.

They weren't.

Sharp turned and looked at Claire with a dry smile. 'You really should make sure you lock all your doors, Mrs Stone.'

That's when Claire saw the knife.

* * *

Stone turned into the street he used to call home just in time to see the red saloon driving away at speed. He was about to put the pedal to the metal when he glanced across at the house and slammed the brakes on.

The front door was open.

Leaving his car in the middle of the road, he scrambled out and sprinted towards the house. He could see the living room light was the only light left on.

Don't let that be a fucking sign, please.

He shouted Claire's name from the bottom of the path, feeling the burning, tearing at his throat. His heart pounded, threatening to explode from his chest as he leapt into the house and swung round into the living room, nearly losing his footing.

Mike's heart stopped and his mind filled with a thick fog. All sense of the world around him vanished as he fell to his knees at the body before him. He knew the answer before he checked for a pulse.

There was too much blood.

His mind was a blur, misfiring thoughts trying to find a connection, trying to explain. Desperate to understand.

The car: he'd seen the car speeding away.

Where's Jack? If he's touched...find Jack!

He slipped in the growing pool of blood as he scrambled to his feet. His legs felt like lead and refused to obey his call to action. Grabbing the corner of a wall, he pulled himself up and swung his body round the corner to head for the stairs.

The chiming noise of a phone barely cut through the fog in his mind as he desperately climbed the stairs, unable to shout out, his voice severed by shock. His hands numbly grappled with the pocket to reach inside, gripping the phone but getting trapped. Finally, he tore the pocket to release his personal phone.

Hands shaking, he staggered drunkenly to his son's bedroom door, which he pushed open as he answered the phone.

'Mike!' a voice shouted. 'MIKE! Where the fuck are you?'

He recognised the voice – he knew he did – but he couldn't remember. His mind was far too buried by the image before him.

'Answer me, Mike!' Bolton screamed down the line.

'Claire?' Mike said.

'Mike, listen to me!'

Mike Stone stood at the doorway, staring at the body of his wife on the floor next to his son's bed.

His son's *empty* bed.

'Mike! Can you hear me?' his phone shouted.

Mike rushed to Claire, her clothes smeared and splattered with blood. He felt her body, searching for the wound, whispering her name over and over, still holding the phone in his numb hand. He couldn't find any wound other than a cut to her head and a fast-developing bruise around her eye.

The phone kept shouting the same thing.

Mike crouched right over Claire, their faces almost touching. He kept whispering her name as he caressed her face until he saw her slowly move her head, squint her eyes and gasp for breath.

The phone shouted again. 'Mike…!'

Claire's eyes shot open.

'It's *not* Sharp!' Bolton shouted.

… as Claire screamed her son's name.

Mike put the phone to his ear: 'Sharp's dead.' The sergeant's blood-soaked body lay slumped on the floor in the living room. Several stab-wounds and a cut to the throat had spilled and sprayed blood everywhere.

'It's Malcolm Glenn, sir. *Malcolm Glenn.*'

Claire's whole face shattered into the very picture of hell as she choked out the words: 'He's taken Jack!'

* * *

Malcolm Glenn smiled to himself as he looked at the unconscious boy lying on the back seat of the red saloon. Killing the other detective had been merely a necessary, if slightly surprising, extra bonus to his plan. But leaving the mother alive had been a master-stroke.

He could easily have killed her too, but he needed her alive. He wanted her hatred and her blame to fuel Mike Stone's fury even more. The other women had suffered death, but that woman would have to suffer life.

And the doors of hell were only beginning to open for Mike Stone.

Chapter 43

The Boy

As the boy frantically tried to scramble along the tow-path in pitch-black tunnel, he kept one hand on the wall on his left and kept himself hunched instinctively, even though at his small height he didn't really need to. The pain on the back of his head was returning with the throb of his heart.

He had no idea where he was going, although the increasing echoes of his feet told him he was getting deeper and deeper into the long, dark throat of the earth. He imagined that he had run into a terrifying snake, and at some point he was going to find himself trapped at the end of its body.

The constant dripping sounds were the only indication of the water to his right – that still canal water, undisturbed by the waves or currents. The smell was thick with damp and dirt. It wasn't quite as bad as sewage waste, but that was the only comparison he could think of.

But worse still was the temperature. Cold. So cold. He was soaking wet from the rain, but this tunnel, for all the shelter it provided, gave no warmth either to his skin or to his mind.

He could still hear the old man trying to pursue him, but imagined that he must be gaining distance, since the man was surely too tall to be standing upright in this low, low tunnel.

The path was uneven and his shoeless feet were almost too numb to hurt, but they kept catching shards of gravel, and he could feel them getting cut and grazed. But he had to keep running. There was no way he could go back. No way he could go home after what had happened. He might well have washed the blood off his hands, but he could feel it in his memory. He could see it, dripping from his fingers. Deep, crimson, thick and sticky. He could remember the smell of it, sickly sweet. It was a syrup like no other.

Occasionally he heard the old man shout to him to stop, that it was so unsafe. But there was no way he could stop. He had to keep running as far as he could, hoping that the old man would give up.

Suddenly the wall gave way to broken brick and his knuckles scraped deep into a crack, causing him to suddenly clutch his hand in pain. Forced into a sudden swerve, he tripped over his own feet. He fell hard on his right shoulder and rolled until the ground quickly vanished and he once again felt the searing pain of the ice-cold water in the pitch black. He squeezed his eyes and mouth shut, but the water flooded up into his nose as he twisted and writhed under water.

The old man heard the splash and screamed out as he tried to increase his speed. He knew he was at least a hundred yards behind the boy when he decided there was only one thing he could do. The faster pursuit would be from in the water. He knew it was a bad idea, but his instincts to save the boy had kicked in.

Keeping to a shallow dive, he plunged into the water.

The shock of the cold initially stunned him, but the rushing adrenaline powered his arms and legs. It had been a long time since he'd been swimming but the old instincts of a strong swimmer took over and he powered on.

After having swum what he thought was about the same distance from the splashes he'd heard, he stopped and found the uneven floor with his feet.

He held his breath so he could listen out for any noise from the boy. Struggling to hear above the sound of his pounding heart, he could make out no signs of life.

Panic set in.

Chapter 44

'He's taken Jack! You bastard, this is all your fault. He's taken our boy!' Claire grabbed at Mike's jacket as she screamed at him through her sobs.

Bolton had just arrived outside the house and leapt from her car, sprinting up to the door and into the house. She shouted as she searched from room to room downstairs.

Her voice snapped Mike out of his dazed shock and his mind suddenly kicked into gear. For what it was worth, the gear was that of a police officer. It rang true to what Reg Walters had said to him earlier that day about switching off the emotions. His were not switched off, but he knew what had to be done.

'Claire, listen to me,' he said, shaking the mother of his son. 'I'm going to find him. I'll find him, I promise you.

I'll bring him home.' He stood up and went to Jack's bedside table. 'Where's Jack's phone?'

'On the side.'

'No, it's gone.' Stone turned in time to see Bolton appear at the door. 'He's taken Jack.'

'And he must have taken Sharp's car,' she replied.

Khan burst into the room to find Stone with both hands grasping at the hair on the back of his head.

'Harry, I want full tracking on a phone number, and I want it now.'

Khan took a moment too long to follow the command.

'He has taken my son, Harry: I have sent you the number – get it tracked!'

Khan's inexperience was causing him to falter as he fumbled through his phone to get to his contacts. At the same time, Bolton radioed the full alert on all channels for a kidnapped child.

No one wanted to mention the elephant in the room, but after having seen the escalations in Malcolm Glenn's actions, everyone was thinking the same thing…

He has minutes left – not days, or hours. He has minutes.

Stone called his son's number.

It was answered almost immediately.

'That took you longer than I thought it would, Mike,' Malcolm Glenn answered with a chilling sneer to his voice.

'Where is my son?'

'Aren't you going to say hello properly, Mike?'

'Cut out this shit, Malcolm. Where is my son?'

'He's fine, he's fine. Just having a bit of a snooze at the moment. He's a noisy one, I must say. He must get that from someone.'

Stone turned away from everyone else in the room and couldn't help but spit the words down the phone line: 'I am going to hunt you down and rip you limb from fucking limb. Do you hear me?'

'That's not a nice thing to say to the man who decides the fate of your son, Mike.'

He took a deep breath. 'Whatever you want, you want it from me. Leave the boy out of it.'

Silence.

Mike Stone's red mist took over. With a searing growl that came from somewhere very dark, he rasped: 'Where. Are. You. Taking. My. Son?'

'I know you are tracking this phone, Mike. Don't treat me like I'm stupid.'

'This will not end the way *you* want it to.'

Another silence. He couldn't tell if this was a sign he was getting through to the man. He didn't even know if Glenn had planned to kill Sharp. Gut instinct told him none of this was by chance. But he still didn't know *why* this psychopath was so obsessed with him.

'I am taking him *home*, Mike. To the end of the line. Or so it may seem.'

'Fuck you and your riddles!' Stone growled. 'It's me you want. Come and get *me!* You coward.'

'No, Mike. *You* come and get *him*.' The line went dead.

Stone immediately turned to Khan. 'Do you have a GPS fix yet?'

'Nearly, sir, hold on.'

Stone started barking out orders, spreading his team far and wide. The police helicopter was already overhead, but without a direction to go in, they were struggling to know what to do other than to stand by for a sighting of the red saloon.

Stone made his way downstairs and out of the house, heading for his own car. There was no way he could be stationary at this time – he had to be moving, to be *doing* something. It wasn't in his nature to wait. Not when it mattered.

To the end of the line. Or so it may seem. What the hell does it mean?

The riddle went round and round in his head. What line? The only line he could think of was the link to the train line for the murder locations so far. Every murder except Sharp's, of course.

His mind wanted to mull over Sharp's involvement, but that was something for later. 'I need a map, I need a map of the city,' he suddenly shouted out. Several people reached for their pockets and got out smartphones – one even took out a tablet – but Stone knew he wanted paper, hard paper.

As if from nowhere, a large, folded map was thrust under his nose. Someone had read his mind. Bolton.

Stone took the map from her as he walked to his car, unfolding it in a frenzy and slamming it onto the bonnet. A torch appeared over his shoulder – he didn't need to think who had provided it. He kept repeating the riddle as he patted himself down for a pen.

Bolton provided that, too. She was cool, she was calm, she was everything he needed her to be right then, short of a magician who could conjure his son from thin air.

They both began to circle each of the locations for the murders, from the first woman found in her home – Malcolm Glenn's ex-wife – right up to the horrific scene in the church earlier that day. Sure enough, there was a best fit to the train network, and Stone could remember being close to the train line on every location.

At that moment, Khan came running up to Stone's car. 'We have a GPS signal from your son's phone. It is still on and it is still transmitting.'

'Where's he going, Harry?'

'Sir, it looks like he's headed in the direction of St Paul's church, where we were earlier.'

'Get the chopper in that direction; get cars coming from all directions; transport police at Kings Norton train station and at every station along that line; put the alert out.' Stone blurted this list out at tremendous speed.

Bolton also told Khan to get recent photos of Jack and Malcolm Glenn and put them on to social media with non-stop repeats. She also told Khan to alert all newspapers and journalists he knew. She had been in the job long enough to know that even that slime had its uses, and, as infuriating as the media could be, when it came to a missing or abducted child, even the most vile of journalists would join the search. And she didn't care whether it was for their own glory.

'Why is he going back that way, Sands?' Stone asked.

They both looked at the map again and followed the line of the killings.

Then it hit them.

Stone traced his finger along the map again, but not along the train line.

Along the canal.

The route was clear. All the murder locations were a short walk from the canal. The last two bodies – not including that of DS Sharp – were left at locations close to the Birmingham and Worcester canal, which Stone knew very well, having developed his affinity with them from a young age. He felt a personal connection, but it wasn't all happy memories.

The third body had been discovered right next to the canal, and Stone wondered if that had been Malcolm Glenn's early nod to the clue…which the and everyone else had missed.

'Harry! Find out if Malcolm Glenn has a boating licence or is in any way registered with the waterways. He might have a barge of his own.' Stone turned back to the map, talking aloud as much to himself as to anyone else.

The fucking canals. You clever bastard.

'What's the next move, Mike?' Bolton ask, energised.

'If he has a barge, that could be where he took the victims to *prepare* them. It could also explain how the third victim's semen was found inside the second victim and the confusion with the times of death. But how do we use this to work out where he's taking Jack?' His voice cracked, and he squeezed his eyes shut for moment, as if to dismiss a thought he didn't want.

'What was Glenn's riddle?' she replied.

At that moment, Khan came back with an update. His eyes were dark and he seemed to have aged several years that day. 'Sir: they've lost the GPS signal.'

Stone hammered the bonnet of his car so hard the others were sure it would have a dent.

'They tracked it to a location close to the Kings Norton train station. Very close to the church, in fact. There are four tower blocks there, so it could be that he is in one of them but lost the signal.'

'No! No, he's on a barge, I know it, I can feel it,' Stone said.

'There's something else, sir. Another body has been found.' Khan said, hesitantly. The snappish look from Stone was enough. 'The chopper picked it up purely by chance. It's on the roof of *this* tower block.'

Khan circled one of four blocks of flats close to the canals, and somewhat close to St Paul's church.

Stone instantly recognised the building. A chill ran down his spine that confirmed the uneasiness he had felt all evening, being in that southern area of the city. Dark shadows from his past were beginning to come into a sharper focus and his mind began to spin a web of connections.

What makes you the spider, though? Who are you? Who are you to me?

The whole case was beginning to seem a very personal attack.

'He was watching us, remember,' Stone said. 'He must have had a height advantage. We should all know whose body it is, Harry.'

'The body was left in the centre of the roof, posed as if on a crucifix, and is wearing all black.'

Stone bowed his head in resignation.

'Mike, look at the canal,' Bolton said. 'It stops.'

Stone didn't need to look at the map. 'No, Sands. It doesn't stop.' Stone got into his car and started the engine. 'It goes into a bloody long tunnel. And that is where he's taken Jack. He's in *that* tunnel.'

'That would kill the GPS lock,' Khan added.

Bolton to got into the car as Stone told Khan to update the police helicopter and Carter.

'What's the plan, sir?' Bolton asked.

The DI's face betrayed his unspoken reply.

Plan?

* * *

The tunnel was dark, damp, unwelcoming and foreboding. There was barely any light at all behind the barge; the evening glow outside had given way to the pitch black of a deep, two-kilometre tunnel. The canal ahead of the barge was muddily lit with a mild front floodlight, pitched at an angle so as not to spread too wide, but still casting enough light so the roof of the tunnel could just be seen.

Malcolm Glenn switched off the engine and let the boat come to a slow stop. Down below, Mike Stone's son was still out cold from the chloroform, but Malcolm knew that wouldn't last much longer. It didn't need to. He wanted him awake for the next part of the whole plan. He wanted the boy to know true terror: he wanted him to stare it right in the eyes.

Especially if those belonged to his father.

Chapter 45

The Boy

Through the darkness and the silence, when he halted his frantic swimming to listen, the old man finally felt his arm brush against something under water. His heart jumped as he desperately tried to find the child. It felt as though he had been searching for ever in the freezing water.

Then he felt something again.

He grabbed at a dead weight. An arm, a hand, a shoulder, a head. He dragged it to the surface and stood up in the water. The body weighed more than the old man had ever lifted as he desperately listened for sounds of life.

Holding the body as high as he could, the old man waded to the side and heaved it up onto the narrow towpath. Clambering out himself, he rolled the body onto its back and listened to its chest. No breathing, but a faint heartbeat. Trying desperately to recall basic training in CPR he'd had many years before, he tipped the boy's head back, opened his mouth, fished out the detritus that could be blocking his airway, gave two sharp puffs of air into his lungs, and waited.

Nothing.

He gave another two sharp breaths.

Still nothing.

He shouted at the boy, and gave two more breaths.

On the second breath, he felt the convulsion, followed by the most horrific bout of choking he had ever heard. Had it not been that he was holding the body, he would have sworn the sound could only have come from a dying animal, and not that of a small boy.

The boy coughed and spluttered: water, mucus and bile all stung his throat and nostrils again. His whole body contorted with the power of the desperate attempts to empty itself, until finally it switched direction and attempting a heaving inward breath. As if he was waking from a nightmare, the boy's eyes exploded open and his head shot from side to side, but he couldn't see or hear anything.

The old man could feel a heavy, dreadful shiver began to envelop the boy's whole frame. And he knew what it was. The boy had been under the water for well over a minute and hypothermia was beginning to take its boa-constrictor hold, squeezing the life from the boy.

The old man knew there was very little time to free the boy from the venomous grip of cold, but there was no way he could carry his lead weight. Even if he could stand up straight, his own aging muscles were beginning to give in.

He took off his jumper and shirt, laid them on the floor, and laid the boy on top of them. Keeping his head low and gripping the clothes together with the boy's collar, he started to drag the boy down the tow-path, hoping that he wasn't tearing into his skin.

The only sound was the crunching and scraping of the thin gravel of the tow-path, framed against the heavy rain throbbing down on the surface of the water at the end of the tunnel.

Lactic acid was filling the old man's muscles with stiffness and fatigue. The mixture of chilled numbness and the burning pain of exertion was threatening to make him collapse at any moment. His reserves of adrenaline were fast running out.

The old man didn't dare look back to see how far the end of the tunnel was.

He just kept pulling.

Chapter 46

Stone's car pulled up on the road overlooking the entrance to the canal tunnel, and he got out without closing the door. Uniformed officers had already arrived and the helicopter was already overhead after discovering the body on top of the nearby high-rise flats

Carter's car screeched to a halt seconds later as she's been diverted to the location.

'Get that bloody chopper's searchlight down there,' Stone screamed as he began to make his way to the slope.

'Where the hell do you think you're going?' Carter bellowed, grabbing Stone's arm. A light misty rain had begun to fall, and it was clinging to both their faces. There was a coldness, almost a glare in her eye.

'I'm not waiting,' Stone said, snatching his arm from the stand-off.

'You're no use down there, Mike. Let the search and rescue team go in first.'

'That's my son. You wait; I'm going down there.'

'Inspector – you will wait: that's an order!'

'Consider this my resignation.' Stone had already turned away.

He clambered down the slope, battling through trees and bushes, scraping and scratching at his face in the darkness, and nearly losing his footing. A sudden shock of cold air hit him as he came out onto the tow-path just a few paces from the tunnel opening. He took out the torch Bolton had given him but it did little to stretch the helicopter searchlight further into the tunnel.

How far had Malcolm taken the barge? How deep into the chasm had he gone? What would he find when he got there?

Is Jack still alive?

Mike shook off the last thought, knowing that he had to believe his son was still alive to drive himself on.

He entered the tunnel and picked up the pace as much as he could, given the low ceiling. His eyes were struggling to find anything to focus on. After a hundred yards or so, he could just about make out a very faint glow of light in the tunnel. Not bright, not definite, just a presence at first.

He closed in on it until he could see the faint outline of a dark shadow obstructing the light. Shining the torch downwards, he could see that the water was still moving from a recent disturbance.

Torch raised to the path, he picked up the pace, scraping and tearing his sleeve along the wall, ripping at the leather. The claustrophobia of the tunnel was closing in on him, squeezing tighter and tighter the deeper he went. He knew that time was against him, every second mattered, and he didn't care that his chest and legs were throbbing in protest.

Now he could see the barge more clearly, but he didn't slow his pace until he was only ten feet away. Slowing down and focusing the torch, he could now see all the detail he needed.

Mike approached slowly, knowing that his arrival was expected, and that Malcolm would have prepared for the whole event. He knew that he was *not* in control of this situation and he had no cards to play. He had no weapon, and no back-up with him inside the tunnel.

But he also had no choice.

He stepped onto the boat quietly and carefully, putting the small torch between his teeth so he could grip with both hands. He felt the boat rock gently on the water and cursed himself for what was undoubtedly a give-away move.

The small doors to the boat opened with a gentle creak, and the first thing that hit him was the strong, unpleasant odour of propane. The voice over Mike's shoulder told him to assume this was all part of the plan, and to keep going.

As he entered what looked like the living area of the boat, he stopped to shine the torch around. A table and a seating area to the right led were separated from the next part of the boat by a narrow doorway. On the table sat a camera and a laptop, which had been left switched on. As he leaned round to look, Mike could see the screensaver bouncing text around.

'Take a look, Mike.'

Mike tapped the keyboard space bar and was immediately greeted with a scrolling slideshow. Image flicked to image quickly. A collection of photographs. The trophy cabinet of a serial killer: photos from each of the crime scenes, mixed with photos of Stone. There was an image of Jack, smiling. Then another picture of him asleep in his bed.

When the hell did you take that?

He composed himself and refocused, refusing to be party to Glenn's indulgent need to twist his mind into knots.

There was an acrid, thick smell hanging in the air. It was the smell of death: congealed blood and the early stages of decomposition. Large plastic sheets were crumbled together in the corner of the seat. The windowsill behind them was filled with tubes, pipes and needles: medical supplies.

He made his way round to the doorway that led to the galley kitchen. The smell of propane was even stronger. Mike looked at the hob and noticed each control was turned to maximum. The gas was almost choking, but turning the dials made no difference, and there was no luxury of time to try to clear the build-up.

The barge was a ticking time bomb.

'Malcolm!' he called out. 'Time to stop messing around. I'm here now.'

Silence. He walked through the kitchen area and came to a doorway. He could hear a familiar tune being hummed in the trembling, muffled voice of his son.

'It's raining, it's pouring,
The old man is snoring…'

'Come in, Mike,' Malcolm Glenn said with an eerie softness.

Mike Stone pushed the door open slowly.

Malcolm was standing in the narrow walkway between bunk-beds on either side. He held Jack in front of him; his left hand was over the boy's mouth, and his right held a short-bladed knife to the boy's throat. Jack's eyes were wide with terror and confusion, and streaming with tears.

'Hi, Daddy. Little Jack and I were just singing a song together. Do you want to join us? Come on, Jack…'

Malcolm tightened his grip on the boy – who carried on trying to hum the tune through the fear – and accompanied him with the words.

'He went to bed, and bumped his head,

and couldn't get up in the morning.'

Jack was still wearing his pyjamas, which were soaked wet at the front. Malcolm Glenn saw Mike's glance.

'Little Jack here has had a bit of an accident, Mike. Do you want to shout at him, or shall I, Mike?'

Mike didn't reply. He just stared into his son's eyes, trying desperately to give him some sort of reassurance. If ever he needed to think his dad was his hero, now was that time.

Then he noticed what Jack was wearing. A jumper. It was familiar. He'd never seen Jack wearing it before, but he recognised it. He tried to dig deep into his memory. It had a distinctive pattern knitted into the front that looked a little like a big yellow face with its mouth open wide, just like the well-known arcade computer game character.

His eyes darted up to Malcolm, who was smiling and seeming pleased with himself.

'Let him go, Malcolm. You have me here. You've got my attention. Now let him go.'

'Don't you recognise it, Mike? The jumper. Don't you remember it?' Malcolm lowered his head to Jack's ear and whispered menacingly; loud enough that Mike could make out the chillingly calm tone, but soft enough that the words were a dark secret. He then turned his attention back to the detective as Jack revealed what he was holding in his hands.

'I take it you smelt the propane when you came in, Mike?' Malcolm said. 'Well, that's to help you understand that the choice I am giving you now is a real choice. I am going to let you decide this one.'

Malcolm nodded to the bunk bed beside Stone, who reluctantly took his eyes off his son to see the knife lying there. Confusion flashed through his mind. Why was he being given a weapon? What part of the plan was this? A kidnapper arming a police officer with a weapon made no sense, unless…

'It's your choice, Mike. How much do you love your son? How far will you go to protect him?' He nudged the boy to cue him, and Jack showed what he was holding. A box of matches in one hand, and a match in the other.

'Tell me — no, tell Jack, Mike. Do you love him enough?'

Mike looked at the knife, the matches, his son, and then Malcolm.

'Take that knife and finish yourself and I will walk away. Or I make your son strike that match, and we all live just long enough for you to see him go up in flames…'

Mike Stone looked into his son's terrified eyes and then at Malcolm.

'So, Mike. Do you love your son enough to die for him?'

Chapter 47

The Boy

The old man collapsed to the floor as he emerged from the tunnel, having pulled the boy for what seemed like an eternity. He was gasping for breath, and his whole body was burning from effort. He looked at the boy's face and even in the cold moonlight he could see the boy was the wrong colour.

The boy was still breathing, and his heart still beating, but he was barely conscious. Soaked through with rancid water, he wouldn't have long before he lost the battle with hypothermia. The old man knew he had to move as fast as he could, and get the boy warm. He stood, picked up the dead weight of the boy's body, and carried him over his shoulder. He powered up the slope, driven by an anger and a hatred from deep down; battling through the bushes; breaking out the other side and onto the path.

The rain was lighter, but the chill wind still thickened the air, so it was a struggle to reach the door to the flats.

Thankful that he had left in a hurry and not locked up after himself, the old man pushed his way into his apartment and dropped the boy back on the sofa. He then rushed to turn the electric fire-heater on to maximum to begin heating the room. Collecting some blankets and towels from a cupboard, he set them down on the floor.

The man took the soaked jumper, t-shirt and trousers off the boy, desperately trying to remember how to treat hypothermia. He had vague memories of how to treat it from basic first aid courses he had been on. There wasn't time to prepare a hot water bottle, so he knew the next best thing was skin-to-skin contact. He held the boy tight to his chest and wrapped them both in a blanket. He turned the boy's back to the heater to give him the most of its warmth.

The man hadn't held a boy so close since the last time he had held his own distraught son. Squeezing the boy, he dried his hair gently with a small towel.

Rocking back and forth, he sang the song whisper-quiet:

'It's raining, it's pouring,
the old man is snoring.
He went to bed and bumped his head
and couldn't get up in the morning.'

Squeezing his eyes tightly shut, the old man kept rocking back and forth, repeating himself.

'It's okay, Mike. It's okay. You're going to be just fine.'

Chapter 48

The choice was there. His son held a box of matches and Malcolm held a knife to his throat. Mike's mind was trying to calculate a plan, but nothing came up that didn't result in his son getting hurt. He couldn't do what Malcolm asked; that would scar his son for life…if Malcolm even let him live. He couldn't make a move, since it would take just a split second for Malcolm to plunge his knife into Jack's throat.

Malcolm sneered into Jack's ear: 'It's okay, Jack: Daddy's here.'

Mike Stone's mind had to move faster than ever before.

'Is this how it happened for you, Malcolm? A boy who watched his father die?'

Malcolm smiled with his mouth, but his eyes betrayed the smile and flashed with anger. 'You know nothing.'

'You watched your father bleed to death.'

Malcolm laughed.

'Right after he'd killed your mother.'

'Stop!' Malcolm shouted. Jack was beginning to shake, barely able to keep hold of the box of matches. Malcolm squeezed his eyes tight shut as if to try to banish images from his mind.

'What did it look like, Malcolm: all the blood, draining from her body?'

Malcolm's face turned red with rage. 'Don't try and stir me, Mike.'

'Is that why you drained their blood, Malcolm? All those women?'

'I swear I'll cut your boy's throat!'

Mike knew the risks of antagonising a hostage-taker in a volatile situation. But he also knew he was looking for one split-second moment to move. He just needed that moment. Malcolm squeezed his eyes closed again, shaking his head, trying to drive out a memory.

Mike picked up the knife, looked his son in the eyes, and gave him the slightest, almost imperceptible nod of the head. It was all he could do to send the message that he remembered from somewhere in the depths of his mind: *'It's okay, Jack, it's okay. You're going to be just fine.'* All communicated in one nod.

And that's when it came. Jack nodded back.

So, Mike pushed: 'Is that it, Malcolm? Did daddy kill mummy because she made you hate him?'

'Stop!'

'Then he turned the knife on himself! You watched the blood drain. You tried to stop it, but you couldn't.'

'No!'

'You killed him! Malcolm – you let him die.'

'NO!' His breathing was getting heavier…

Mike held the knife out, pointed at Malcolm.

'You ran, didn't you, Malcolm? To the canals. You pissed your pants and you ran.'

With a guttural growl, he said: 'I will slice your son's throat…'

'What's the matter, Malcolm, can't say his name?'

Malcolm glared: 'I will kill the boy!'

'Say his name, Malcolm. *Say it!*'

* * *

The Boy

The boy's eyes opened and he looked up at the old man, whose face appeared even more grey than before. He could see the tears rolling down the old man's cheeks as he whispered, over and over: *'It's okay, Mike. It's okay. You're going to be just fine.'*

The boy felt that same supporting hand hold him between the shoulder-blades through the blanket. His whole body was shaking, but he felt warmth very slowly start to come back. He opened his mouth, and, with a trembling jaw, teeth rattling, he forced out his words.

'My name is Malcolm.'

* * *

'You aren't in control here, Malcolm,' Mike said. 'You don't get to choose.'

'No, *YOU choose.* Do you love your son enough to die for him?'

'No,' Mike said. Dropping the knife to the floor.

A stunned silence.

'What?' Malcolm said, his eyes and face betraying the blow to his confidence.

'Strike the match, Jack,' Mike said, coldly.

Malcolm took his knife from the boy's throat and pointed it at Mike. 'No! No way! You don't get to choose like that…'

That was the moment.

Mike shouted at Jack with such force he knew the shock would make him drop the matches he could barely hold. At the same time, he launched himself at Malcolm, grabbing the wrist that held the knife, and smashing his own head into the bridge of Malcolm's nose. He felt and heard the bone shatter.

Malcolm's left hand instinctively shot to his face as blood poured out, releasing Jack from his grip. Mike delivered the second blow to his chin as he pushed the killer back through the alleyway of beds, landing in a heap on top of him. He screamed out to his son.

'Run, Jack, get off the boat.'

The boy did as he was told and ran out into the kitchen area, through into the living room and up onto the outside steps, where he froze, terrified by the darkness, the cold…and the fact he'd left his dad behind.

Mike and Malcolm grappled on the floor, slamming each other from side to side, neither able to gain enough space to swing a punch. Malcolm tried to return a blow with his own head, but missed Mike's nose and caught his chin.

And he was still holding the knife.

Being on top of the clamouring mess, Mike pushed himself up, gave two sharp jabs to Malcolm's wrist to free the knife, and then drove down with an elbow right into the other man's stomach.

Malcolm's eyes shot wide open, and then tight shut, as every ounce of air rushed from his lungs. With the same force, Mike threw himself backwards, away from the killer. He rolled over and began trying to drag himself to his feet, but a sharp, searing pain suddenly engulfed the calf of his right leg. He could feel the burn of the knife rip through flesh and muscle. He kicked back with his left leg, his heel catching something solid – a shoulder, an arm, the killer's head – he couldn't tell. But it gave him the momentum to pull himself half up.

He took a moment to look back where Malcolm was still struggling to breathe through the blood pouring down his face. The killer rolled over and reached for the matchbox.

Mike knew he had to move.

Leaving the knife embedded in his right calf, and feeling the throb in his head, he dragged himself through the kitchen and into the living area, powered only by adrenaline. The detective instinct kicked in and he reached for the laptop on the table, slamming the lid shut and picking it up as he passed.

Then he saw Jack still standing at the rear edge of the boat.

His heart stopped.

'Mike!' bellowed a voice from somewhere in the belly of the boat behind him.

With his mind focused clearly on the imminent explosion, Mike shouted his son's name. Jack turned and reached his arms out. Ignoring the pain, Mike pulled himself up the steps to the small deck in one movement.

The whole atmosphere changed: he heard the noise of the helicopter and saw the dancing lightsabres of torchlights. There was a battery of noise coming from the end of the tunnel: engines, shouting, chaos.

A split-second decision.

Throwing the laptop to his right and hoping it landed on the tow-path, he grabbed his son with both arms, lifted him to his chest. And jumped.

The explosion filled the tunnel with heat, light and an ear-shattering wall of sound.

With Jack in his arms, Mike plunged into the freezing water, numbing the blast, and blinding the senses.

Mike Stone blacked out.

Chapter 49

The first thing that Mike Stone sensed was a familiar smell that he would struggle to describe with words. He recognised it, though, and as the grogginess began to subside, he connected it with the gentle weight at his side that seemed to rise and fall with his own breathing, but in its own slightly faster, more delicate rhythm.

As his eyes opened and fought for focus, he looked down and was filled with an overwhelming relief as he saw his son lying next to him, his small head pressed up against his father's cheek, and his tiny arm trying to wrap round his father's broad chest. He seemed so much younger than his ten years.

Mike's senses slowly returned, and various parts of his body seemed to gain their own heartbeat: his head, his elbows, and, more than anything else, his right calf. For some unknown reason, he suddenly felt quite amused by the way his right leg was raised, almost as if to display its superior throb to the rest of the world – an amusement he assumed he could thank 'mother morphine' for.

The squeeze to his hand came as more of a surprise, and as he rolled his eyes to his left, over his sleeping son, he saw Claire.

'I haven't been able to take him from your side,' she said, placing her other hand on their son's shoulder.

'Is he...?' Mike struggled to get the words out, owing to a dry mouth and a distinctively large lump growing in his throat.

'He's fine,' Claire finished for him.

'And you?'

She smiled at him, weakly. 'Mike, I'm so glad you're okay, and I'm...'

'Don't,' said Mike, with a smile and a roll of the eyes.

He tried to shake his head. He didn't want to dwell on emotional outbursts that had been shouted out in extreme circumstances. He also pretty much thought she'd been spot on, anyway.

He *was* a bastard. And it had been his fault.

'We'll talk. Soon. Okay?' Claire said.

And it was enough for Mike. He didn't want to get into long, life-changing conversations whilst lying on a hospital bed, doped up on morphine – which he decided he could do with a little more of.

Jack slowly woke up, took one look at his dad awake, and squeezed him a little harder. He didn't say anything, and it seemed that just lying there with his father was all he needed.

And was long overdue.

A very quiet knock at the door brought in two more familiar faces. There was a wry smile from Bolton, and a jolly little wave from an overly apologetic Khan.

Claire stood up and gathered up their son. After assuring Mike she would come back later, she leaned over to lay a light kiss on his cheek. Light, but lasting a bit longer than just a friendly gesture.

A silent moment that spoke at great volume.

As she walked Jack slowly out of the room, the boy looked back, smiled, and nodded to his father.

Mike nodded back, just managing to keep his filling eyes from letting a tear slip.

Once they had gone, Bolton and Khan came right into the room.

'Sorry if we're disturbing you, sir,' Bolton began.

'No, no it's fine,' he croaked. He looked at Khan and smiled. 'Harry? You look like shit!'

'To be honest,' he replied, 'I'm pretty disappointed. I expected far more dramatic injuries.'

The awkward hospital-visit silence threatened to creep in, so Bolton decided to rescue the situation by delving into work-speak.

'Malcolm Glenn all along, then. How the hell did you miss that?' she said with a rueful smile.

Stone didn't know. 'Hidden in plain view the whole time. Let's face it – he had us running around like headless chickens, and he stood in the middle of the field running birdseed through his fingers.' Stone sounded almost defeated. 'What about Sharp?'

Bolton took a moment. 'It seems that Sharp had taken to doing a little moonlighting. Word has it he fancied himself as a bit of a PI and was planning on leaving the Force.' All three of them avoided eye contact as they shared the thought that Sharp had always seemed partial to some mercenary action, most probably to compensate for not being much good at his *real* detective job.

She continued: 'It looks like Malcolm Glenn had hired him to investigate you, Mike. We're not even sure if Sharp had made the connection between Glenn and the murders before...'

'He'd worked it out, Sands. That's why he was at my house – to warn Claire, and show me some proof.'

The thought trailed off and silence threatened again.

'When did the penny drop, Sand's?' Stone asked.

'CCTV from moments after you left Steve Simpson showed Malcolm Glenn emerge from the same pub. He handed Simpson what we now believe to be your ID, and then the two walked off together.'

'We have more info on Glenn's history, too,' Khan said. 'But I don't think you're going to want to hear this just yet...'

'Harry: spill.'

Reluctantly, Khan gave a brief outline of how Malcolm Glenn's father had murdered his mother in a moment of rage over custody and visitation arrangements – and the fact that she was pregnant with another man's child. At the time, he couldn't get close to Malcolm because the boy had been brainwashed into hating and fearing his father. With a new father, and a new baby on the way, it had all become too much.

'Hence the obsession with pregnancy tests and childbirth.' Stone commented. 'So, Parental Alienation was all too real for him: as a child and as a father.'

'Indeed, Sir. But it would have been even less heard of, let alone understood, all those years ago,' Khan replied. 'Malcolm's father hadn't realised that his son was standing right behind him when he'd killed his wife. The boy had watched him hold her as the blood sprayed and poured from a neck wound. The official coroner's report concluded that his father turned the knife on himself, cutting his own throat just before the police and ambulance arrived.'

Stone spotted a quick glance between the two detectives. 'Sands?'

'The original pathologist's report also cited a blunt-force trauma to the back of Mr. Glenn Senior's head. Small shards of dark green glass were embedded in the wound.' She paused for a moment. 'That part of the pathologist's report wasn't included in the coroner's inquest.'

Khan continued. 'The boy…'

'Don't call him that, Harry,' Stone croaked.

'… Malcolm had run away from them scene, and was finally discovered the following day when he fell into the canal right where we were yesterday.'

Another pause. Another uncertain look.

Bolton took over.

'The man who saved him from the canal, and contacted the police, was a Mr. Arnold Stone. He lived in the block where we found the priest.' She waited. 'Suffice to say, sir, it hadn't looked good when the police arrived to a find a near-naked man embracing a virtually naked boy.'

There was a new elephant in the room. Mike Stone had grown up under a dark rumour-cloud about his father.

Khan broke the heavy silence. 'Malcolm Glenn spent the rest of his childhood in care, and was subject to a range of therapy and psych interventions, but managed to avoid bringing himself to the attention of the police. That's why nothing prevented him from training and working as a care worker…'

'…where would have had access to an array of drugs and medical resources to slowly develop his skills over the years.' Stone finished the last pieces of that jigsaw.

Bolton added: 'Mr Stone kept in contact with Malcolm throughout that time…until his death…'

'Last year,' Stone finished. It was as if he was completing a checklist.

Khan dared to break a lingering silence. 'Sir, I still don't understand why Glenn made this so…personal.'

'I never went to the funeral, Harry. And the anniversary of his death was last Saturday.' Mike Stone was aware of the likelihood that all the details would come out in the inevitable inquest, but the significance of the link was clear to him.

Arnold Stone had been stopped from seeing the young Mike Stone by around his tenth birthday. There had been problems with custody from the first day his parents had separated. Mike had grown up believing that his father never cared.

Or so he had been told. Over and over again.

There had been rumours of child abuse investigations, and the young Mike was interviewed by the police. He couldn't remember anything having happened, but he was told not to worry; told that no matter what had happened, he wasn't to blame.

Told over and over again.

Told enough times that hatred became easier.

The last time he had spent any real quality time with his father had been on a weekend visit one winter when it had been colder than usual. Arnold Stone had bought his son a new jumper with a distinctive yellow character on the front. They had asked a shopkeeper to take a photo of them both. Mike could remember forcing a smile. It was as if the jumper marked the end of their relationship. He'd left it at his father's flat.

Arnold Stone's death had been officially recorded as unexplained. He had fallen from the roof of the flats he lived in, and although it seemed an obvious suicide, there were unofficial suspicions surrounding the circumstances. An early report had included blunt-force trauma to the back of the head, with glass fragments embedded in the injury. But that had been redacted from later reports, and the case was closed.

The police had plenty of other directions to invest their resources than into the apparent suicide of a suspected paedophile.

Khan and Bolton made their excuses to leave as it was clear Mike Stone needed rest, and needed some time to soak up what had been discussed.

Just before leaving the room, Bolton turned back and looked at the inspector. A dark, worried complexion greyed her faced.

'Sir, just one more thing. I don't know if you're aware but...the original Glenn murder case had a large team that included a WPC Simmons. That was the maiden name for a copper who later trained as a detective Carter.' She paused. 'Detective Carter worked the Arnold Stone case.'

Stone didn't respond, and Bolton gave it only a couple of moments before taking her cue to leave.

It was a history Stone knew he'd need to unpack.

But all in good time.

Refusing to submit to melodramatic melancholy, Mike resisted the temptation to dwell on the distant past.

Despite Malcolm Glenn's attempts to break him, he was sure of one thing: the real test was not to see whether he had a son he was willing to die for.

It was whether his son knew his father was dedicated enough to live for.

Epilogue

The Boy

Malcolm refused to let anyone stand with him at the funerals of his mother and father, which were held on separate days due to the wishes of the two families. Some questioned the impact that would have on young Malcolm, whereas others simply didn't care.

Malcolm just wanted to be left alone.

He stood at the foot of his father's grave and squeezed his eyes tight shut. What he had witnessed was truly horrific and his young mind was torn in all directions, unable to make any sense of it.

Malcolm thought back to the fateful moment when his eyes met his mother's. She knew she was dying as she lay on her bed with blood gushing from her throat, draining her body dry.

His father had turned to him with a look of shock and terror in his eyes, dropping the knife as he looked at his hands like they weren't his own. Malcolm's father had said it was all going to be okay – that he'd been freed from the hatred his mother had poisoned his mind with. He'd said that the boy could finally go home with him, as the sobbing had slowly softened into a smile.

A chilling smile.

Malcolm squeezed his eyes closed even tighter. He was trying to banish the memory of his father telling him that his mother had to die for him so that father and son could love each other again.

That was just moments before the boy had bludgeoned his father with a bottle, and then cut his throat with the knife.

Acknowledgements

I could never have finally achieved the finished copy of this book without the excellent work of *Carrie O'Grady*, whose amazing professional editing brought a breath of fresh air, and a much-needed polishing to the book. Special thanks also to *Fluid Arts*, *Gary S. Crutchley*, and *Daniel Sturley* for permission to use their stunning photography on the cover of the book.

It was always going to be a huge learning curve to write and self-publish my debut novel. The journey has been made far more manageable and enjoyable thanks to Amanda, Patricia, Michelle, Berenice, and many more from *The Writing Tree* on Facebook. I have been inspired by their invaluable support, advice and fellowship, as both writers and publishers.